IF THE

SHARE YOUR THOUGHTS

Want to help make *If the Light Escapes* a bestselling novel? Consider leaving an honest review of this book on Goodreads, on your personal author website or blog, and anywhere else readers go for recommendations. It's our priority at SFK Press to publish books for readers to enjoy, and our authors appreciate and value your feedback.

OUR SOUTHERN FRIED GUARANTEE

If you wouldn't enthusiastically recommend one of our books with a 4- or 5-star rating to a friend, then the next story is on us. We believe that much in the stories we're telling. Simply email us at pr@sfkmultimedia.com.

SFK
PRESS

IF THE LIGHT ESCAPES

A BRAVING THE LIGHT NOVEL

BRENDA MARIE SMITH

SFK
PRESS

Southern Fried Karma, LLC
Atlanta, GA
sfkpress.com

Books are available in quantity for promotional or premium use.
For information, email southernfriedkarma@gmail.com.

ISBN: 978-1-970137-22-4
eISBN: 978-1-970137-23-1
Library of Congress Control Number available upon request

Cover & interior design by Olivia Hammerman

Printed in the United States of America

To the boys in my life whom I have loved and ached for through the hardships and wonders of their coming of age:

*My brothers Les, Steve, and David
My sons and stepsons Ron, Jeremy, Matt, Aaron, and J.D.
And my stellar grandson Miles*

What do you do when the rivers all run dry?
What do you do when your baby starts to cry?
Where do you run when the flames have filled the sky?

Blown away...
By the situation today.

—From the song "Blown Away"
As performed by Douglas Goebel

PART I

CHAPTER 1

Bright green lights stream and pulse across the northern sky all night now, growing from thin and wispy to bold and fat, expanding, contracting, sending out bands of yellow streamers like they're partying on ecstasy at some cosmic rave. The lights are pretty, and they're hypnotic, and they creep me out to the core.

Northern lights every night for two solid weeks in Texas. Halfway to the equator from where they belong. They're supposed to be a phenomenon tied to the magnetic poles—it's a scientific fact.

Nothing is right about this. The only explanation I can think of is that the north and south poles are shifting. I don't know what that means for the planet and the future of its creatures. We don't have TVs or talking-head scientists to tell us—if any of them would even know.

The universe just won't stop fucking with us.

TODAY, I'M HOEING CORN IN our front yard, sweat stinging my eyes. It's blistering hot out here—early December in what used to be high-tech Austin, until the fucking sun zapped us with an electromagnetic pulse and took our power, our cars, the damned running water. It stopped pretty much everything—everything modern, that is.

It's been fourteen months, and all the front yards in our subdivision are mini-cornfields now. We grow beans and veggies in the backyards. It's a desperate attempt to keep us alive when our food stockpiles run out. Don't know if it will work, but I'm doing my damnedest to make sure it does.

Nana thinks God smacked us with a solar pulse to make us stop wrecking the planet, but I can't believe in a God who would be so cruel. This shit is killing people, and it's so wrong I can't see straight.

I don't know how my heart is still beating after I watched my sister Tasha bleed to death last winter—no ambulances or doctors to save her. I may never get over it. And now my whole family is a godawful mess.

The only comfort I get comes from Alma. She was Tasha's best friend. We shared our pain over our parents being missing and over losing Tasha, and we fell in love. Now we're married. Some people say we're too young to be married, but we need each other too much to listen to them. Alma saved my life just as much as Nana and her secret house did.

Within a few hours, I've hoed our front yard and the one next door, where the old-lady nurses live. I slug some water and take my hoe to the backyard garden. I've got tons more shit to do by nightfall.

Not that long ago, I was a snot-nosed nerd, spending all my time on computers and building robots, studying science and outer space and being shy.

I never thought I'd become an eighteen-year-old urban farmer in an EMP apocalypse, but here I am.

NEAR DUSK, ALMA CALLS ME for dinner, and I go inside to wash up—or I try to. Washing up is a bad joke around here. We're so short on water, all I can do is wet a soapy rag and wipe my face, hands, and arms. I'm still all sweaty when I sit down at the table, but so's everyone else.

Besides Alma, Uncle Eddie is here, my tweener cousin Milo, and his cutie-pie sister Mazie, who's seven. Our neighbor Jack Jeffers is getting Nana settled. She needs a lot of help since her stroke, and Jack loves her and takes care of her.

Us kids have had to grow up fast and become like pioneers, except we don't have horses or covered wagons. We have Nana's secret house, though—or it used to be secret—full of food and seeds and guns and every kind of tool you can think of. A lot of the food is gone now, but that house and the stuff inside it are the smartest thing Nana ever did. Smartest thing anyone ever did, if you ask me.

She didn't just feed our family. She fed all the neighbors, too—the ones who didn't leave to look for food and water before Nana told everyone about her stockpiles. And she organized neighbors to farm the yards and the land around us.

The most brilliant thing about it: she didn't tell Grandpa about the house full of stuff. If Grandpa had known, he would've stopped her, and by now, we'd all be dead.

I haven't even taken a bite of supper when a loud whistle pierces the air outside, and a bunch of yelling comes from the front street. Someone's emergency whistle, a referee's whistle, sharp and shrill and scary as fuck.

Uncle Eddie and I shoot to our feet.

"Stay here and get down," I tell the others as Eddie and I bolt to the coat closet for guns. "Jack, keep them safe."

Eddie and I grab our rifles, and we slip out the front door. There's a lot of weight and heft to a rifle, a deadly vibe. Nothing like the joysticks I'm used to. The yelling outside has stopped, but my heartbeat's all erratic. I can't see anyone in the fading daylight, but that whistle shrieks again, down the block to our right. Within minutes, it'll be crazy dark out here. No streetlights, no moon yet, and so far, no northern lights.

"What's going on, you think?" Uncle Eddie asks.

"I'll go see. You stay here and guard the house."

"You can't go alone!"

The front door jerks open. I almost crap my pants, it startles me so much, but it's Milo with a pistol in his hand.

"I'll protect the old folks and girls," he says, all ironic, like he's suddenly in a cowboy movie or some shit. He's a good enough shot to be in a cowboy movie, even though he just turned fourteen.

"Stay hidden," I say to Milo, and Uncle Eddie and I step off the stoop. We stick close to the house, passing the garage door, stopping to scan the space between our house and the neighbors', and then skirting the front of that house.

"He's going that way, toward Bea's!" some guy, maybe Silas Barnes, yells from down the block.

"We're down here!" Eddie calls out. "Where is he? What do you need?"

"Stop him. He stole our last jug of water and a rabbit." That's Harvey Zizzo's high-pitched voice. He and his wife raise rabbits in their garage.

"Is he armed?" I shout.

"Don't know," Harvey hollers back.

I can't see shit. Where's this guy supposed to be?

"Stay quiet," Uncle Eddie mutters. "Maybe he'll make a noise."

We stand still, partly hidden by a small tree. It's all I can do to squelch the whining sounds trying to escape from my throat. The last bit of sunlight seeps slowly away.

"He's not making noise," I whisper in Eddie's ear. "Should we do something?"

He picks up a rock from the ground. "Get ready."

I aim my rifle down the street, between the dead cars. Eddie skips the rock across the sidewalk and into the road. A second passes, and then footsteps pound down the sidewalk and away from us. We take off running.

Up ahead, a tall silhouette appears. A guy running with a five-gallon water bottle on his shoulder, slowing him down.

"Halt!" Eddie barks. "Set down the water and the rabbit or I'll shoot you dead."

"Fuck!" says the thief as he freezes in place. I can barely see that he's wearing a flannel shirt, hanging open, not buttoned. In this heat, the only reason for a heavy shirt is to hide things, like weapons.

"Fuck is right," I say. "My gun's on you, too. Put the water down. Now!"

The guy turns sideways, rolling the water bottle off his shoulder and to the ground. He has a long, dark beard growing out of a super-skinny face, his eyes buried under a mess of wild hair.

Silas and Harvey run up from the other side of the guy, pointing guns at him, too.

"Hands up," I say. "Don't move."

"Where's the rabbit?" Uncle Eddie asks.

"Inside my shirt." The thief's voice is all scratchy. "Please, can't I keep it? My kids are starving." Then he starts wailing.

This jerk has hungry kids. I'm tempted to let him go with the rabbit, but I worry it will make more people come here to steal from us.

"Hands up high, to the sky!" I poke my rifle toward him. "Stop bawling!"

The guy shoots his hands into the air, whimpering. "I'm trying to stop. It'll take a minute."

"Just be quiet about it. Harvey, reach under his shirt and get your rabbit."

"I guess he killed it," Harvey says. "It's not moving."

I think Harvey might cry about his dead rabbit. Honestly, I could cry for a week about the whole freaking thing. I'm sick of seeing starving people and not being able to help them.

"How are we gonna punish this guy?" Silas asks.

"Letting him starve. How 'bout that?" Sarcasm drips from my voice. Like there could be a punishment worse than watching his kids starve.

"Shit, I'm already starving." The guy's shaking all over, as though the effort of holding his hands in the air is too much for him.

"You want us to come up with more punishment? Do you?" I ask. "Harvey, get your rabbit."

Eddie and I keep our rifles aimed at the thief's head while Harvey pushes the guy's shirt aside. A lifeless white rabbit is poking out of a fanny pack. Harvey gasps and reaches in to free the rabbit.

"It's only a bunny." Harvey's shaking as much as or more than the thief.

"Eddie, check him for weapons," I say.

My uncle pats the guy down. "He's got a knife." Eddie pulls something red out of the guy's shirt pocket.

"Shit, it's just a Swiss Army knife." This guy's voice sounds like something is wrong with it. Probably thirsty as fuck. "I was hoping I'd find a raccoon or a squirrel."

"So, you thought you'd steal a rabbit instead?" I ask.

"He killed a bunny," Harvey says. "It's not even big enough to eat."

I look Harvey in the eye and slowly take the rabbit from his hands. "It's too little for adults to eat, Harvey. Let him feed his kids with it." I shove the bunny at the thief. He stares down at it with his hands still in the air. "Take it and get out of here before I shoot your ass."

The guy bursts into tears again and grabs the rabbit, hugging it to his chest. "Thank you," he says in that scratchy voice, like someone took a scouring pad to his throat.

"If you come back, I will shoot you dead without giving you a chance to say shit. Understand?"

"Yes," says the thief, scrambling away but staring back at us.

"Wait. Your knife." Uncle Eddie tosses the knife to the thief. He and his kids won't survive without that knife. It's not like he could kill us with a Swiss Army knife.

"Thank you," the man rasps out. "You did me a favor. I want to do one for you."

"What kind of favor could you do for us?" I'm aiming my rifle again.

"Don't shoot!" The thief is shaking so hard he's about to drop the rabbit that he's clutching by its ears. "It's something you should know."

"Like what?" Eddie asks in a menacing voice.

"Some guys came through my neighborhood, waving guns, terrorizing us. Stole our water. Said they were coming over here, that you guys are rich. That's how I got the idea to come here."

"How many guys?" I ask. "What do they look like?"

"Two big guys. One with a big frizzy beard, one bald with lots of tattoos. They wanted us to go with them, but we weren't gonna team up with those guys. People get more desperate, though, someone will join them. Then you're in for trouble."

Uncle Eddie, Harvey, Silas, and I give each other the side-eye.

"Thanks for telling us." I lower my rifle. "Now, go!" The thief takes off running.

"Just what we need," Silas says.

"Seems like things are getting worse out there," Uncle Eddie says. "More starving people. If they ever band together…"

"We need a damned fort to live inside," I say.

"Yeah," says Eddie, "but we can't build a wall around this whole neighborhood. I'm going to increase the patrols. We haven't been doing them in the daytime, but now I think we have to."

"Like we have time for that," I mutter.

"We have no choice, Keno."

"I know it. I'm just pissed about it."

Uncle Eddie pats me on the back. "I hear ya, man."

Wavery bands of green light suddenly shoot up into the sky along the northern horizon. We all stare at them for a minute, but we're getting half-used to it, like it's normal to have dancing lights in the sky when you're three thousand miles farther south than Scandinavia.

My brain is scrambling, thinking about how to protect Alma and my cousins; Nana and Jack; my uncle, aunt, and grandpa, who are pissed at us; and my mom, who won't talk to me anymore.

Even though we're a little cut-off from the rest of the city and we have the park, railroad tracks, and empty houses around us to give us a buffer zone, we've always known that people are out there lurking, people we need to fear. Now we know that two particular guys are plotting against us.

And that skinny, freaked-out guy with no clue how to survive in this world, stealing a baby rabbit for his starving kids, armed with nothing but a Swiss Army knife? That's just…

Fuck! Dinner's waiting for us, but my appetite is gone.

CHAPTER 2

I'm pedaling my bicycle like a demon, taking Tasha home from the only clinic we've found to get her checked out.

"Hurry, Keno. Go faster!" Tasha's yelling into my ear from the bike cart behind me. "Chas is gonna catch us!"

"I'm trying! Hold on!" I hunker down and pump harder, huffing for breath, my leg muscles burning.

I turn a corner, and Tasha hollers, "Woohoo! We're getting away!" She's laughing into my ear, squeezing my shoulder. "Best brother ever."

I peek back to see her pink cheeks, her grin, the pure glee in her eyes. My pretty sister with her long, dark hair. I'm protecting her from the asshole who made her pregnant and won't leave her alone. I'm proud of myself as I lock eyes with her and give her the biggest smile I've got.

I turn my eyes back to the road and keep pumping, racing the bike faster than I thought it could go with the bike cart attached and my sister inside.

"I'm glad they can't give me an abortion," Tasha says. "I love babies!"

I reach back and squeeze her hand. Then, suddenly, the corner into our neighborhood is in front of us. I brake and turn the handlebars, and I lose control. The bike is tumbling and crashing with the cart, and Tasha is flying through the air, hitting the concrete on her stomach. I scrape myself off the pavement, and Tasha is bleeding.

I scoop her into my arms and run, both of us covered in her blood.

***

I CRY OUT AND SHOOT up in bed, shaking and dripping with sweat. Alma pulls me to her, and I latch on. She's used to me doing this. She strokes me, saying, "Shh, baby. Shh." She doesn't tell me it's all right, because she knows that it's not.

BY BREAKFAST TIME, UNCLE EDDIE has the whole neighborhood organized for more patrolling. He assigns Alma the morning shift for tomorrow, and I've got the afternoon today. He says we'll have the same schedule every four days on top of our nighttime patrols, when we take turns going out in teams of two.

"I'm thinking of adding more people at night," Eddie says.

"Then we're gonna need more patrollers," I say. "We've only got—what? Thirteen or fourteen men, a handful of women?"

"Jack's going to train more people," Eddie says.

"Like who?"

"Old people. Women. Teens like Milo."

"Milo's just a kid."

"Keno, he's the only person in the neighborhood who's killed anyone before. He can handle it."

"I know he can shoot, but don't you worry about what kind of person he'll grow into with so much shooting?"

"It worries me sick, but we need a safe place to live if he's going to grow up at all."

Eddie's my mom's stepbrother. He's only been home for a few months after walking with his brother two hundred miles to Waco and back to search for Mom and Grandpa and for Milo and Mazie's parents, Aunt Jeri and Uncle Tom. The four of them had gone to a football game up in Dallas. Grandpa had called us from the road when they were heading home and almost to Waco, just minutes before the sun went ballistic, and that was the last we'd heard from any of them.

Nana had been keeping Mazie, Milo, Tasha, and me for a long weekend but hadn't planned on being in charge of us for months and months with no help, no power, no outside communication. Nana never complained, though. She just kept right on taking care of us when the world fell apart.

No one got found in Waco. Eddie and his brother, my Uncle Pete, got held hostage by the National Guard up there until they escaped. When they finally made it home in late summer, Nana had just had a stroke and couldn't talk, and Tasha had been dead for months.

Uncle Pete had to leave town again, but I feel a lot safer now that Eddie is back. After Nana's stroke, I was the oldest able-bodied, able-minded person in the family. That was petrifying. I don't know what I would've done if Eddie hadn't been here six weeks ago when Mom and the rest of them finally came home after being missing for more than a year. We'd thought for sure they were dead.

We were so glad to see them, crying and hugging. But then they started spouting insane bullshit, screaming at us that we'd done everything wrong when they didn't know shit about it. And when Mom found out that Tasha was dead, she collapsed, but not before she blamed me.

THIS MORNING, AS SOON AS Jack gets Nana settled on the patio and kisses her goodbye, I go to hang out with her. I need to get to work in the gardens, but first, I need comfort from my grandmother.

Now that Nana's a little better from her stroke, Jack brings her over every morning to stay with whoever's here while the rest of us go out to work. Alma loves, loves, loves to cook, so she's usually the one to stay home.

They were lovers before her stroke, Nana and Jack. With Grandpa gone so long, I think it hit Nana how much she hated the way he treated her. He was a dick to her all the time, acting like she was stupid, the one thing that Nana is not.

I was pissed at her for sleeping with Jack at first, until I thought about how hard it would be to stay married to a dick like Grandpa. Jack treats my Nana right. I love that about him.

As Jack walks away, he says, "Keno, we need to start thinking about getting more gasoline for the rototillers soon. I'd like to talk to you about it."

"Sure. Maybe some evening this week, we can talk."

Jack nods with a little wave and walks away.

We've had enough gas up until now, because Nana stockpiled so much and then the men siphoned it from the seventy or eighty cars we have in the neighborhood. All the people who left had to leave their cars behind. We still have about ten jugs, which will go a long way with rototillers, but we'll need more before long.

"Keno," Nana says with a sigh when I hold her hand and kiss her cheek. Since she got better, she remembers our names again.

"Hey, Nana." I sit down beside her, keeping hold of her hand. "How you doin' today?"

"Okay," she says. She won't say she's good, because we all know she's wasting away to nothing. Nana will always tell the truth, no matter how many words she's lost.

"Your mother?" she says like a question, and I wince.

"She's still not talking to me. I don't know what to do."

"Wait," she says.

"I have to wait, don't I?"

Nana nods, but I feel her pouring love into me. "Your dreams?"

"Still there. Still bad."

Sitting here with Nana, I might be reading my own wishes into things, but I feel like she understands me and the grief I'm dealing with, the crushing worry. Her eyes are full of sympathy. They give me courage, like she believes in me.

"We had to chase away a guy last night who was stealing water and a rabbit. He said his kids were starving."

Nana's eyes get big. "Oh no," she says.

"I wanted to take him and his kids in, but I didn't feel like we could. Our food stock is running low."

"I wish..." She takes a deep breath. "Wish I bought more."

"Nana, you bought enough food to feed all fifty people in the neighborhood for more than a year. We still have some left. You don't need to feel bad."

"Not enough," she says, and she looks away.

"I just..." I pause until she faces me again. "I wonder if it's bad karma that we didn't help that guy and his kids. If the help he could give us would pay back whatever food and water they would use."

"Don't know," she says, her face sinking into a sad sort of smirk.

"We gave him the rabbit—"

"Good."

"But we didn't give him water. We're so short on water right now."

"There's more," Nana says, and my mouth falls open.

"More water?"

She nods at me. My heart starts racing.

"I didn't know we had more. Where is it?"

Nana's face crumples into a mass of wrinkles, and her breath speeds up. She's shaking her head at me.

I don't want to upset her. I give her a minute. Even though some kind of gymnastic event is going on inside my chest, I make my voice extra gentle. "Nana, do you know where more water is?"

She lets out a moan that startles me, and tears shoot into her eyes. She's shaking her head back and forth, back and forth. "I… I… I can't!" She swats her head with her fingers. "I can't…"

I stand up and grab hold of her hand before she can hit herself again. "You can't remember? That's okay." I pet her head and shoulders, stroke her arms. "It's really okay. Now that we know about it, maybe we can find it."

"I don't know."

"Did you hide it?" I ask, and she nods. Oh, God, she's hidden it even from herself. I hug Nana, and I kiss her on each cheek while she shudders all over. "Don't worry. You did great. We'll find it."

She seems to be trying to smile at me, but it's coming out more like a strained frown.

"Good morning, Miss Bea," Alma says as she steps outside from the house. She looks at me, with my arms around my grandmother and a frown on my face that Nana can't see. She looks at Nana with her teary eyes. And then Alma starts singing that Bob Marley song, "Don't Worry About a Thing." Nana's face lights up.

Alma can take a simple song and give it so much passion. I get all enthralled by her singing. She takes Nana's hand and swings it, doing a little dance. We all grin.

When the song is done, Nana has settled down. If my mom would ever talk to me again, she would say that Alma is emotionally intelligent. I'd say she's brilliant.

"I haven't heard that song in forever," I say.

"My mom used to sing it to me when I was a kid. Both my parents sang all the time."

"No wonder you're so good at it." I settle back into sitting with Nana while I marvel at Alma as she works with her pots of herbs.

Before Tasha died and after the second solar pulse—when we were all scared the sun would kill us—Nana told me it was my job to take care of the other kids if she ever couldn't do it herself. I should've seen it as a clue that she wasn't feeling so great, but that part sailed right past me. I was busy freaking out and trying to act all cool at the same time.

I've stepped up like she asked me to, but I don't always feel up to the task.

Now, I'm suddenly realizing that Nana probably didn't always feel up to it either, but she did it because of her love for us. I want to be like Nana that way: driven by great love.

"Nana, you're my hero," I say, and she squeezes the crap out of my hand.

Her eyes gleam at me when she says, "And you are mine."

AS SOON AS I LEAVE Nana, I go straight to the Mint's attic to see if there's water stored up there, but there's not. There's stovepipe, plumbing pipe, and some lumber, though. That's good to know.

Then I go to our attic at home, but there's no water there, either. Mostly old keepsakes and papers. I find a couple of boxes of new cotton underwear, socks, and long johns for different sizes. I drop those down from the attic before I close it up.

Shit, where could Nana have hidden water?

I find Jack in his pinto-bean garden.

"Hey, Jack. Do you have any idea where Nana could have hidden some water? She says she hid some, but she can't remember where."

Jack gapes at me from across the garden, then walks up close. "Are you sure you understood her right? That she understood you?"

"Pretty sure. She was pretty lucid this morning. She didn't hide anything here at your place, did she?"

"Not that I know of. I don't see how she could've without me knowing."

"I tried the attics at our house and the Mint. Guess I could look in the cellar over there."

"Good idea."

"Doesn't seem like there's room in that cellar. She wouldn't have stored it behind walls, would she?"

"I don't think so, but there's no telling." Jack shakes his head.

Geez, Nana, what did you do? She's always been the smartest person around. Now, it seems like she's outsmarted herself.

CHAPTER 3

I've never patrolled in the daytime before, and it's hard. Everywhere I look, I see work that needs to be done. Even though I'm sticking to the outer edges of the neighborhood, people who are working in gardens and building outhouses and rain-barrel systems keep trying to get me involved. I pull down my ballcap and hold my rifle more menacingly while I tramp around in the sun. From now on, I'm keeping a loaded pistol on me even when I'm not patrolling, after what the rabbit thief told us. There's no end to the dangers around here.

When I'm done with patrolling and on my way home, I see Mom working in the Mint's backyard, right behind our yard. It's the house on Mint Lane where Nana stored the food, tools, and seeds. Now that we've eaten so much of the food, there's room for Mom and them to live there. We call it the Mint since it stores the neighborhood treasure—we still keep what's left of the bulk food there, plus tools for people to share.

Mom's helping Grandpa in the Mint's potato garden.

I stand in the shadows across the street and watch my mother. She's very close to the place where Chas Matheson shoved a gun into my neck. Chas—the so-called father of Tasha's baby. What a joke, Chas being a father, except it's not funny.

So many people have died, but Tasha was only fifteen.

I don't want to think about Tasha's death. I don't want to think about the baby who would have been my niece or nephew but died with her. I don't want to think about Chas shoving a rifle into my neck and Milo blasting Chas's brains out to save me.

Milo was only thirteen, and now he's got Chas's exploding brains stuck in his mind for the rest of his life. Those brains are stuck in my head, too. I'm scared to death I'll need to kill someone, and after seeing what that looks like, I don't know if I can do it.

Before I know what I'm doing, I'm heading toward Mom. I go into our yard at home and stop at the hedge between our house and the Mint.

I gaze at my dark-haired mother where she's digging up potatoes and looking crushed. She's too skinny after being locked up like a criminal for a year by the asshole National Guard in Waco. She keeps sighing deep sighs while she works. She's only thirty-eight, but she seems older now.

I want my pretty mother back. I want to hold her and cry. I need her so bad.

Grandpa goes inside the Mint, leaving Mom alone.

"Mom?"

She doesn't look at me, but she stiffens up. Shit.

"Mom, are you ever gonna talk to me again?"

She stabs her spade into the dirt and stands up with her back to me. "Please. I asked you to leave me alone."

"I get that you're mad and have to blame someone about Tasha, but I need you to forgive me. Please!"

Mom swivels her head toward me but doesn't meet my eyes. "You let your sister get pregnant and die. I don't know how to forgive you for that."

"God, Mom. I didn't 'let' her! I would've died myself to save her."

Grandpa rushes out the Mint's back door, waving a spade in the air. "Leave your mother alone, boy!"

"Did you even let anyone tell you how it happened, Mom?" I'm just yelling and crying now, out of my mind. "I took Tasha to a clinic in the bike cart I built. But that asshole Chas Matheson was chasing us and Tasha didn't want to talk to him, so I raced us away."

Mom's face is frozen like a mask of horror.

"But I turned too sharp, and Tasha fell out of the cart. She landed on her stomach—"

"Shut up!" Mom cries, and she throws her hands over her ears.

"—and she bled to death. So, yeah, maybe it is my fault."

"Stop it!" Mom runs toward the far side of the Mint, and I yell louder.

"I beat the crap out of Chas after the funeral. I thought it would make me feel better, Mom. But I felt worse. Do you want to know why? Because there was nothing left for me to do for Tasha after that. Not a damned fucking thing."

Mom is out of my sight. Grandpa's snarling at me and leaning forward, like he's ready to launch himself at me.

I throw my hands in the air and scream as loud as I can. "You're not the only one who misses Tasha and who's mad at the world that she's gone!"

I whip around, run past Alma on the patio, and blast out the front gate.

"Keno! Wait!" Alma hollers from behind me, but I can't stop.

I don't even know where I'm going. It's getting dark out here, and I'm just running.

"Please stop, Keno!" Alma calls from half a block behind me, but I keep racing down the street. Neighbors stare at me as I run past, but I ignore them, even Bobby Carlisle, who's heading out for patrol with his Kalashnikov.

"He all right?" Bobby shouts to Alma as she runs past him. "Get home. It's dark."

"Give us some time, okay?"

"Only a little," he says.

I'm two long blocks from home, and I plunge into the park on the east side of our neighborhood. I plop down on the bottom end of the slide, slapping my hands over my eyes and catching my breath.

Crickets are chirping like maniacs, and there's a chorus of tree frogs coming from the empty swimming pool that's covered in slime. It's peaceful out here. If I could stay here for a year, maybe I could calm down.

"Your mom's still mad, I guess?" Alma says as she reaches me. Her black-brown eyes lock onto mine, and I want to fall into the depths of them. She takes my hand and pulls me up. I scoop her strong little body into my arms. She strokes my back and then leads me over to sit on the swings.

"I knew it was my fault. I told you!"

"Keno, it's not!"

"Mom thinks it is."

"She didn't mean that. It's her grief talking."

"No, Alma. She means it." I yank at my hair, tears spewing out of me, all the grief and shame rushing back like it never receded.

"Stop it!" She's got a grip on my arm that won't quit. "I know how much you loved Tasha, whether anyone else knows it or not. Your Nana knows it. Uncle Eddie knows it." Alma soothes me while I shudder and cry.

My mind's flooded with images of Tasha. Blood all over her and all over me when I carried her home in my arms.

Carried her home to die. Tasha crying, "Don't let me die!" But the nurses didn't live here then, and none of us knew how to save her—not Nana, not our neighbor Sonja, and definitely not me.

"All this time," I blubber out, "when I dreamed Mom might come home someday, I thought she would comfort me... that we would comfort each other."

"I'm so sorry," Alma says softly, turning my face toward her. I can hardly see her through the tears and snot rolling out of me, but I feel her love, stronger than the sun and worthier of my trust than that ball of fire that fucked up our lives. "I've got you, baby."

I stand up and hug Alma to me until I can't breathe, my tears running into her soft black hair. It takes me a while to slow down.

Alma steps back and gives me a cute, crooked smile. "Race you to the monkey bars!" She takes off quick, getting a head start. I speed after her, but she beats me there and scrambles to the top of the bars. "I win!"

"You're fast," I say, and we laugh. I climb up from the inside, swinging myself around, but I'm too tall for these kiddie bars. Alma's upside-down face is suddenly in front of me, surprising the heck out of me. She's hanging from her knees above me.

"Hey, babe. Your face is all red," I tell her.

"My mom said it's good for your complexion."

"Is it? I better try it then." I feel for the Glock in my hip pocket. Still there, still loaded, safe and secure. I climb up and hang from my knees beside her, only, since I'm taller, my head hangs lower than hers. "Can't really look you in the eyes this way," I say. "Does my complexion look better now?"

"A beautiful shade of pink."

A huge sliver of moon rises to the east, lighting up the park and Alma's face with an orange-yellow glow. We pull ourselves up and sit wrapped together on top of the monkey bars like we rule the planet, gazing into our dark subdivision, on the southern edge of our emptied-out city, in the middle of the scary-as-fuck world.

"Keno? Alma?" Bobby Carlisle calls from the street.

"Yeah, Bobby?" I shout.

"Y'all come home. Now!" Uh-oh.

"We're coming." I jump down from the bars, and Alma slides into my arms.

"Watch out for those trees behind you," Bobby says.

Oh shit. The tree line.

The crickets and tree frogs have gone silent. I hear Bobby cock his rifle thirty yards away. For a split second, Alma and I gape at each other, and then we run.

When we reach Bobby in the street with his Kalashnikov aimed into the park, I stand between Alma and whatever danger Bobby sees. I scan the trees behind the swings and monkey bars, half a football field away.

Before the sun zapped us, those trees would've seemed pretty. Tonight, they're creepy. I've been too worked up about Tasha and Mom to even think about watching the tree line. As bad as things sometimes get around here, I'm still not totally used to life post-apocalypse and the never-ending vigilance.

"I don't see—"

"Shh!" Bobby aims his rifle at something.

I shudder and run my eyes back and forth among the trees. With all the different-sized trunks in the deep shadows, people could be hiding in there and blending in.

"There!" Bobby hisses, pointing to the north edge of the trees. And I see—what? Feet. Two pairs of feet—one in boots, one in white sneakers. At least that's what I think I see, but it's so far away. Then the feet with the sneakers move, and metal flashes in the moonlight. Behind me, Alma gasps. I pull my Glock, flick off the safety, and aim.

"Run home, kids. Now!" Bobby whispers.

"But, Bobby, you need backup."

"Then get to cover. I'm firing a warning shot."

I grab hold of Alma's waist, and we take off across the street. I catch a glance from Bobby as we duck behind a dead SUV.

BOOM-BOOM-BOOM-BOOM-BOOM!

Shit, that was five shots. I raise up enough to see dirt flying near those feet in the trees. The feet jump around then disappear.

I point my Glock again and feel for Alma to be sure she's still ducking. "Stay down," I say.

"I'm staying."

And we wait, Bobby and I with our guns aimed, Alma crouched with her hands over her ears. The eerie green lights rise up to sway a surreal dance in the northern sky, and still we wait.

At last, Bobby lowers his rifle. "Y'all go home. This isn't a safe place for a therapy session."

"'Kay, we're going, smartass," I say with a smirk. He chuckles, and we sprint for home.

When we tell Uncle Eddie what happened, he grabs his rifle and heads toward the door.

"Told you we need more nighttime patrollers," he says. "I'm gonna organize folks to scour our perimeter every morning and evening—to check the woods in the park, the train tracks, the field behind Jack's house."

"I'll take some shifts."

"Good. You can bring Milo."

I just sigh.

AFTER LYING IN BED WIDE awake for a couple of hours with green light pulsing through the window and Alma cuddled up sleeping beside me, I slip out of bed and go downstairs.

I'm wandering around in a daze when I see Nana's wind-up radio. Makes me think of her before her stroke, when she would listen at night for news that might tell her what happened to my mom and the rest of the family. I saw her crying once when she thought she was alone. Made me love her even more.

The radio's got AM, FM, and seven short-wave bands. Being cut off from the rest of the world makes us hungry for news, but the only broadcast Nana ever found is this guy named Rick, who gets on his short-wave every night from more than a hundred miles away.

I take the radio to the patio, wind it up, and listen while green lights swirl overhead.

We got ourselves a wild light show goin' on around here. I imagine if you can hear me, you got one, too. It's a crazy universe, people. I just hope there's still room in it for us.

Most of you know that I'm Rick, I am ab-so-lutely skinny as a stick, and I'm comin' to you live from Clifton, Texas, thirty miles west of Waco. Farm country, U.S.A. Our little town has been goin' through some shit, folks—people dyin' left and right. We're not s'posed to cuss on ham radios, but I'm way past carin' 'bout that. If someone comes to arrest me, maybe they'll feed my ass. I mean, I hardly even have an ass anymore.

Ooo–wee! Sorry, folks.

A couple of ranchers here have old diesel tractors that still run, but the rest of us work the ground with horses or by hand. Folks are tryin' to breed more work horses, but it's gonna take years before we'll have enough. And feedin' those horses will be hard as hell. I'm just gonna keep pushin' my plow by hand. I can handle my few acres of garden that way.

I had to fight with birds over my figs. Next year, I'm campin' out around my fig trees and will spend my days chasin' off birds. Maybe I'll catch me some quail or some doves. Now that's some good eatin' there.

Sorry to go on about food, folks, when I know some of y'all don't have much. It's just, I'm hungry, and I got food on the brain. Sometimes, I think life without cheeseburgers may not be worth livin'.

Cheeseburgers, movies, and my mama. That's what I miss most.

CHAPTER 4

Uncle Eddie rousts me and Milo out of bed more than an hour before dawn to go patrol the neighborhood perimeter, to check the places beyond our streets and yards where the nighttime patrollers don't go. Damn, it's early. I only slept a few hours.

The northern lights are still strobing in the sky, but they're fading. Milo and I are all bleary-eyed as we trot along the train tracks. We go about a mile to the drainage pond and back without seeing anyone. There's evidence that people once cooked on the other side of the tracks, but the empty cans are rusty. It probably happened before the sun zapped us.

While we cross the neighborhood to go to the park, I ask Milo, "Did you ever work it out with your parents to let you stay at our house?" They've been hassling him to move into the Mint with them ever since they came home, but so far, he's managed to squirm out of it.

"They said I could stay," he says.

"Cool, man. How'd you get them to do that?"

He stops still, catching his breath, and looks me in the eye as I stop, too.

"I told them I killed Chas."

"Shit. They didn't know that already?"

"Nope. Dad told Mom that I'm a man now, so I can stay where I want."

"They must be mind-blown," I say. "They might change their minds when they come back to Earth."

"They might, but I'm not moving."

"Yeah, I wouldn't want to fight with you over it." I bump his shoulder with my fist and grin at him. "I never knew a fourteen-year-old man before."

"Shut up!" Milo shoots me a dirty look and takes off toward the park.

For months after Tasha died, Milo brooded and moped around all cranky, refusing to discuss it, while the rest of us cried and moaned and talked about Tasha, comforting each other and "processing our grief," as Nana called it.

The thing that finally got him out of that hole was shooting Chas. Milo said it was like helping Tasha, and, crazy as it seems, it brought him back to himself. I probably don't need to worry about the kid as much as I do.

We scour the park side of the stand of trees, not finding much—boot and sneaker tracks in the dirt at the place we saw the feet; a spent bullet embedded at the bottom of a tree. Bobby's bullet, I assume.

As Milo and I tromp deeper into the woods, I say, "Now that Nana can't run the neighborhood and tell us what to focus on anymore, we need to start thinking like she did. Looking at the big picture and thinking ahead about stuff we need and how to get it."

"Shouldn't we be quiet?" he mutters.

"I don't see why. The goal is to chase off whoever might be in the woods, just like we do when people come onto our streets begging for food."

Milo snorts. "Man, that's different. Bad guys won't go away. They'll hide and stay to cause trouble when we aren't looking."

"That's true. But how do we know those feet Bobby shot at belonged to bad guys?"

Milo shakes his head at me. "Just be quiet. Okay?"

So, now that he thinks he's a man, he thinks he can boss me around? I'll have to get his ass about that soon, but for now, I shut up.

We keep going, moving aside bushes and low-hanging branches to be sure we don't miss anything. We come out the back side of the trees and stare toward the eastern horizon as the sun starts to rise.

"My mom's super pissed at Nana," Milo says.

"Why? Because of Tasha?"

"Probably that, too, but mostly because she left Grandpa."

"Why is that any of your mom's business? Nana's a grown-up. She can choose who she loves."

Milo sighs. "Mom wants her parents to stay together."

"Well, when I was little, I wanted my parents to stay together, too, but we don't always get what we want, do we? Your mom needs to get over it."

He smirks. "Yeah, in your dreams."

We stand there a minute, watching the sun come up. A thin line of black smoke rises above the treetops a few miles east of here.

"Look, Milo. Something's burning over there."

"Probably another house."

"Idiot scumbags who burn down houses. I'll never understand them. C'mon. Let's go home."

RIGHT AS WE FINISH EATING the breakfast of eggs and oatmeal that Alma cooked for us on the grill, we hear Grandpa hollering on the Mint's patio, "This is not right!"

I step outside to see Aunt Jeri and Uncle Tom talking to Grandpa, but I can't hear their words.

Grandpa backs away from them. "Teenagers should live with their parents!"

"Hank," Uncle Tom shouts, "do not tell us how to raise our kids. This is what's happening, so get used to it."

"This family's gone straight to Hell!" Grandpa whips his face around to glare at me, like he needs a new target, but I step back into the house.

Seems more like Hell has come to us, if you ask me.

THAT NIGHT, ALMA AND I hang out with Uncle Eddie where he's sprawled on a mattress on the floor of Nana's old bedroom, listening to Rick on the radio.

GOT MYSELF SOME NEW FRIENDS: *the three Jackson kids from next door—well, out here, next door's half a mile away. Anyhow, these kids brought me some blackberries they picked, just outta the kindness of their hearts. Almost made me cry when Becky—she's the littlest one—gave me a hug.*

Her brother Jed—he's about twelve—says he wants to go huntin' with me someday. He's killed rabbits before, but I'm gonna show him how to get some quail. And that Timmy is a cut-up, always pullin' tricks on his brother. I've gotten where I really look forward to seein' those kids. I gave them some of my figs and potatoes, made a little wooden doll for Becky. They're a bright spot in my life—one of the only bright spots I got.

One thing that's not so bright is these radio people who keep talkin' bout FEMA camps, FEMA camps. There's all these rumors on the radios that the gov'ment's herding people into camps, but so far, no one I know has seen one.

I ask them, "Do you know anyone who got taken to
one? Do you even know anyone who disappeared?"
"Well, no," they say.
"Why would the gov'ment bother?" is what I wonder.
People been talkin' about FEMA camps for twenty years.
I ain't believin' it 'til I see it for myself.

Uncle Eddie clicks off the radio and blows out his candle.
He whacks at his pillow and rolls over with his back to us.

"Doesn't seem like the government's organized enough
to have FEMA camps," he says.

"They're not," says Alma.

And that's what scares the bejesus out of me.

No government, evil invaders, running out of water, bad
weather, no medicine, no outside help. I could go on all night.

CHAPTER 5

After dinner the next evening, Alma and I go to our room to change into long-sleeve shirts before we go do patrol duty. Being shirtless, we can't resist feeling each other up. I just want to roll around in bed with Alma and kiss her all over and get hard and come inside her, but we don't have time. All this responsibility crushes us sometimes.

My dick isn't crushed, though. It's so hard it hurts me. Alma with her beautiful breasts all bare and calling to me. Man!

I turn away and try to think of other shit, like Grandpa. He's a dick-crusher.

OUT ON THE FRONT STOOP, I load two bolt-action rifles. The half-moon's already out, so I can see all right. Sometimes the dark is almost opaque. Seems like even Hell wouldn't be as dark as that, what with the hellfire and all. Though now, these rogue northern lights give us a little relief from the darkness.

"This gun has a bigger kick than the ones we've been shooting." I hand Alma a rifle.

"Does it?" she says, like she's saying, "No shit, Sherlock." She's a good shooter, Alma. We used to practice together, but we can't waste bullets on practice anymore. If we ever see a squirrel, we'll shoot it to eat, but people already killed all the squirrels around us. I hope squirrels are surviving somewhere. I wouldn't like a world with no squirrels in it.

Alma puts her warm hand on my face, I kiss her cheek, and then we head out to patrol around the edges of our neighborhood. It's four big blocks—people call them square blocks, but they're long rectangles. Some guys walk in opposite directions, but Alma and I, we go together. We'd be too worried about each other if we didn't.

Uncle Eddie's idea of having more patrollers at night isn't working out. Between adding daytime patrols and scouting our perimeter, people won't do extra night shifts. And all the new people Jack was going to train have good reasons why they can't patrol—kids, age, illness, whatever.

"These northern lights bug the crap out of me," I tell Alma. "What are they doing here? They're supposed to be tied to magnetic poles. I saw this show a couple years ago that said the north pole was drifting north, not south. So how did they end up here? The poles can't drift around randomly. That's impossible."

"I don't know, baby. They worry me, too, but we need to be quiet."

"They make me feel like something bad is gonna happen. What do you call that? Fore-something."

"Foreboding?"

"That's it. I'll be quiet now and just stew in my foreboding."

"Silly." Alma reaches up and ruffles my hair.

When we patrol and we can't cuddle on account of guns, Alma and I could talk all night. It's not a good idea for us to talk much when we're patrolling, though. We get all involved and forget to listen for anyone who might be sneaking around, hunting for food or water, or worse: getting ready to kill us for it.

We walk along with our rifles in the night. It's cool out here but not cold. There's a green sheen swirling across the half-moon with no pattern to the timing.

Alma stops and raises her gun.

"Hear that?" she whispers.

"No, what?" I've got my gun up, too, and I'm pivoting around, searching. I want to hide Alma, but she would never let me.

"Over there." She points at the corner by the park. And I hear a jangly noise, like car keys. No one drives cars now, though, except a few old junkers that still run. The solar pulse only spared cars that didn't have internal computers—there aren't too many of those.

The noise gets louder, closer. I aim my rifle into the shadows, where I can't see a thing. The noise jangles again. Even closer now.

I'm about to tell Alma to run when two dogs come bounding from the shadows. They still have dog tags making that noise. Shit, we've seen some mean-ass dogs lately, so I keep my rifle aimed at the one in front. He's brown, like a big retriever.

But his tail is wagging, and he's making friendly chuffing sounds—not snarling or barking. He's skinny and raggedy, and he stops and whirls in a circle when he sees the rifles. A little black curly dog skids to a stop and lets out a whimper. He has the saddest eyes I've ever seen on a dog.

Alma lowers her rifle. I relax my grip but keep mine up, in case.

"Y'all dogs better get out of here before someone kills you and eats you," I say. But as soon as the dogs hear my voice and it isn't yelling or pissed off, they wag their tails and step toward us. The brown one actually grins. Someone who loved that dog probably taught him how to do that. He thinks if he grins at us, we'll feed him. And he might be right. I'm a sucker for a cute dog.

"Shit."

"Aww… look at them," Alma says. "They're sweet dogs, and they're starving."

"So are lots of people."

She crouches down to the dogs, reaching out to pet them. The dogs look at other and then scamper up to Alma.

"Careful," I tell her. "They might be hungry enough to bite you."

"You won't bite me, will you?" She's all honeyed and friendly, like she's talking to a cute baby. She fluffs up the black one's hair. He tries to jump into her lap, but she laughs and says, "Nope. Can't do that." The other dog turns in circles in front of her, waiting his turn. I would wait in line for Alma and whirl in circles in excitement. I would. She pets the brown dog, too.

"You know what's gonna happen, don't you?" I reach down to help Alma to her feet. "They're gonna be in love with you, and they'll follow us around. Then we'll—"

"I know." She looks at me with pain in her eyes. All the dogs that used to live around here ran away or died, except the one who stays with June and Charlotte. Those old ladies are all skinny, but they feed their rations to that dog and treat him like their child.

"Better get back to patrolling," I say.

"I know that, too."

We give each other sad looks, holding our rifles in front of us, pointing the barrels away from each other. We turn the corner with dogs on our heels. The little black one whimpers a lot, not loud, but a kind of continuous squeaking. He has to be hurting from hunger, skinny as he is. But with all that squeaking, we might not hear something or somebody dangerous.

"Wait a second." I take off my rucksack and pull out the three tortillas that Alma packed for us to eat after we've been out here for hours making ourselves hungry. Alma always gives me two tortillas, and she only eats one. She says it's because I'm bigger, and I am. But I always try to get her to take one of mine. She never does, though.

I give the dogs slurps of water from my bottle. I tear up two tortillas. We don't have anything to put on them. We're out of honey until we can harvest more from Nana's bees that live in an outside wall of the Mint.

The dogs go kind of crazy when they see the tortillas. They're jumping around, pawing at me and yipping. "This other one's for Alma." I set tortilla pieces on the sidewalk, where the dogs gobble them up almost before they hit the ground.

"Give them mine, too," Alma says.

"Oh, Alma. Really?"

"Yes, really." She straps her arms over her chest, rifle and all. I can't say no to my fierce wife, who happens to be armed at the moment. I split the last tortilla into pieces and give them to the dogs.

"Thank you." Alma hops into the air so she can reach my cheek to kiss it.

"Ha. Be careful jumping with that gun."

For the rest of the night, Alma and I tromp about the neighborhood, going all the way around ten or twelve times, the dogs practically glued to us. At one point, they start sniffing something in the storm drain, probably a dead rat or skunk—I hope it's dead, if it's a skunk.

I poke Alma's arm and whisper, "Run!"

We take off running, trying to get away from those cute, hungry dogs. We zip around a corner and hide behind a half-wall next to the sidewalk, catching our breath and laughing. We try to be quiet, which only makes us laugh harder.

Pretty soon, here come the dogs. They run up to Alma where she's crouched behind the wall and lick her all over. I'm the one who fed them, but they know that Alma has more love to give them than I do. Where she gets it, I don't know.

"Blackie! Brownie!" she says to the dogs.

"Don't give them names. They're gonna break your heart."

"That's okay. Everyone needs a name."

I pull Alma up, clutching her to me. "Don't you worry that if you give your heart away so much, it could get damaged?" I'm searching her eyes while I say this. She crinkles them and steps back.

"Silly, that's not how love works." When I keep gaping at her, she says, "Don't worry. I'll never run out of love for you." And she means it. It's all a guy could hope for, really—a beautiful woman to say that to you and mean it.

Me and Alma and the dogs make one more circuit around the blocks. The sky's getting lighter. As we get back near Nana's house, the sun peeks over the horizon behind us, turning the world all pink and sparkly. Kind of beautiful. Too beautiful to do what I have to do next.

"Go on inside, Alma. I'll be right back." She knows where I'm going. She stares at me from the front stoop but doesn't ask me not to go. I duck my eyes from her. "Please go on," I mutter. "I won't be long."

She steps inside, peering at me and closing me out. Alma is brave, but sometimes, she hates being brave.

"Come on," I say to the dogs, who've been watching the door where Alma disappeared. I can't call them by their names. It's too hard.

I go down the side street and cross it to Jack's house. Woodsmoke's coming from his backyard. Smells like he's scrambling eggs. I go around to the back of the house.

"Hey, Jack."

"Morning, Keno," Jack says. Then he sees the dogs, who run up to him at the smell of food. "Oh." That's all Jack says. He lets the dogs jump up on his legs while he makes sweet noises and scratches them behind their ears.

"Sorry, Jack. We couldn't get them to go away. We tried hiding, but it didn't work."

"Probably fell in love with you," Jack says, and his eyes are so sad I want to break something.

"It's Alma," I say. "Everyone falls in love with Alma."

"We do. Watch the dogs for a minute while I take Bea her breakfast and tell her what's going on."

"Sure, Jack. Whatever you need."

He carries the eggs inside. I flop down in a beat-up lawn chair while the dogs climb my legs and wag their tails and whimper at me. I pet the dogs a little, but I can't look at them.

Jack's talking to Nana inside the house. I can't tell if she's answering him or not. She talks so quiet now. Nana is fading away. That's what I'm afraid of and can see plain as day. I hope I can handle losing her, because I will lose her, and the thought of it makes me want to give up. Just freaking quit. I would never quit on Alma, though, or my cousins, or my mom, even though she quit on me.

I'm nodding off in the chair with dogs climbing on me. Finally, Jack comes back. "I'll take it from here," he says.

"Thank you."

The dogs look back and forth between Jack and me as I walk away. He tells them to stay.

***

AT HOME, UNCLE EDDIE'S EATING oatmeal.

"Hi." I glance around the room. "Did Alma go up?"

"Yes, but she had oatmeal first. You should have some, too."

"I can't eat right now."

"But, Keno, you need to."

I give my uncle a tired smile. As I turn around to go up—a gunshot. Then another. I flinch all up and down my spine. "Fuck!"

I glimpse back at Eddie and start to explain, but he says, "Alma told me. Go on to bed, honey. You look whipped."

I drag my ass up the stairs. At least those dogs got some Alma love before they died. Alma love will carry me through eternity. I believe that.

Jack loves dogs and insists on being the one to shoot them so they don't suffer. He knows if he doesn't kill the dogs, then someone else will, and they won't be humane about it. Either that or the dogs will hide out from people and starve. Plus, I'm sad to say that we need the meat. I won't eat those particular dogs, though, not after I knew them.

Jack says a clean shot to the head stops dogs' brains so they don't feel the pain. I hope that's true, because I'm about to explode, and if I thought those dogs felt themselves get shot, I would hurl up everything I ever ate in my life and empty myself out clear down to my toes. Then I'd collapse, and Alma would have to scrape me off the floor, an empty sack of skin.

I'm so sick of people dying, and cute dogs with waggy tails. I don't know how much longer I can take this shit. I have to take it, though, for Alma, for my family. Fuck!

CHAPTER 6

D ays later, Milo shakes me awake long before dawn.
"What? It's not time to patrol the woods yet." I throw
my pillow over my face.

"Shh… get dressed. Come downstairs," Milo says. "I need
your help."

"Grrrrr…" I scratch my dirty scalp and climb woozily out
of bed, trying not to wake Alma.

I carry my clothes and shoes to the game room and throw
them on, basically dressing in my sleep. Milo meets me at the
bottom of the stairs, hands me a rifle, and opens the front
door. As soon as we go through it, I'm after his ass.

"What's going on? Why do you need me?"

"I have this great idea." Though I can barely see his face
in the pulsing skylights, I can tell the kid is beaming.

"It'd better be a great idea if you got me up hours before
dawn."

"It is. Come on."

"I'm not moving until you explain."

Milo gets up in my face, nose to nose. "Remember those
offices they were building before the sun zapped us, on the
other side of South First?"

"No, but if you say so."

"It's behind that Mexican market, La Familia."

"What about it?"

"They had tons of building stuff—big stacks of boards
and bricks and cement." He throws his arms wide. "And

they had a bulldozer and backhoe always parked there. I bet they have gas."

"How do you know this?"

"'Cause I used to wonder why they left that shit out there all the time. It looked like it would be easy to steal."

"It's on a main road. People would have to haul it away in trucks."

"Yeah, but who would notice or care?"

"I don't know, man. What's your point?"

"You said we need to start thinking like Nana, about stuff we're gonna need and how to get it. We need boards to build outhouses, don't we?"

"We do."

"So, let's go see what's there. Maybe we can get gas for the rototillers." His enthusiasm is starting to pull me in.

"It's probably diesel, if it's even still there."

"Didn't Jack say he has a diesel tiller?"

"He might have."

"Okay, so let's check it out. If they have stuff we want, we'll bring people over to get it."

"Shit, dude. It's two miles away. We can't leave the neighborhood anymore, especially at night. Too damn dangerous."

"Well, we can't steal gas during the day."

I let out a loud sigh. "I guess it won't hurt to scout it out. We'd probably need wagons to carry back fuel or anything else."

"They'll make too much noise. Let's just sneak over there and look."

I shake my head and start jogging down the road. Milo jogs up beside me.

"Next time you have a brilliant idea, save it for morning. If it's a good one, we can do it the next day with a plan."

"Yeah, but once I thought of it, I wanted to hurry. I don't want someone else to get it."

"Dude, it's been there more than a year. It's probably long gone."

Our way partly lit by the swirling aurora, we jog about halfway there, past the park with who-knows-what going on in those woods. Our feet make too much noise, slapping against the pavement, so we slow down, walking fast but quiet the rest of the way.

I don't know why Nana never had us check construction sites, except she always wanted us kids to stay home. I think Silas and some other guys got plywood from one, but that's all I've heard of. Somebody got lumber to build outhouses from somewhere. There's so much I don't know about the things our neighbors have done to keep us alive. I'm only now waking up to pay better attention.

Ahead of us at the South First intersection, stalled and vandalized cars fill the streets. Behind the Mexican market with its windows busted out, there's a shell of an office building about four stories high—no siding, just an open view of girders, pipes, and subflooring with long runs of wiring dangling loose. Such a damn waste, as was so much of our lives before the sun zapped us.

A bulldozer and a backhoe are parked alongside the building. We creep warily onto the lot and up to a pile of lumber that's been looted down to scraps. Still, scraps can be useful, and there are a few sheets of warped plywood we could put to work.

Bags of concrete have been rained on so much that they're hard as boulders. Looks like someone busted up most of the cement blocks, but a few good bricks are scattered around.

Milo's about to step inside the building shell.

"Wait!" I whisper, too loud. "We need to be sure no one's in there."

Milo's shoulders slump, and he takes a big breath. Then he whirls around to face me. "Hey, smell that smoke?"

"Probably someone's cookfire."

"Kinda early for that," he mutters, and we take bigger whiffs.

"Shit," I say. "Smells like tires."

We scan our surroundings until I see a glow above the trees in the neighborhood behind the office structure. I tap Milo on the shoulder and point, putting my finger over my mouth. Milo gulps, and I nod toward a stand of trees between us and the fire. We raise our rifles and slink into the trees. We ought to get out of here, but I've got to know what this is and whether it's a threat.

On the other side of the trees, we hit fencing for a row of backyards. We skirt along the fence until we find a break between two burned houses. We scoot close to the street in the shadows and watch. The fire's a few blocks down a low hill, past a school, on the other side of a creek. The wind's blowing the tire smoke away from us, but it still stinks like ass.

It's crazy-dangerous to get closer, but we're drawn to this fire like moths. The lights in the sky make me jumpy, but they throw off moving shadows that give our own movement some cover.

Without talking about it, we start acting like scouts we've seen in war movies. I crouch and run ahead while Milo guards the rear, and then he stoops down and runs past me while I watch his back. We get a block from the fire, near the creek and its bridge, and we duck behind a hedge in front of a house with busted windows. We peek over the top of the hedge.

And there it is. A stack of burning tires. Behind it, four scruffy guys in camo are milling around in full gear with big-ass automatic rifles and bulletproof vests. One guy has a bandolier full of bullets strapped across his chest. Jesus.

I grab Milo by the shoulder and speak into his ear. "Go back the way we came. Run through the grass, but stay low." And we take off.

We don't stop to catch our breath until we reach the construction site, and we crouch down huffing and puffing in the semi-cover of the building shell. Two five-gallon jugs of some kind of fuel are in a dark corner. We grab them—they're only half-full—then we jog down Dittmar toward home. The sky's getting lighter, and the northern lights are dimming.

"We better patrol the park woods before we go home," I say. "It's time."

"Yep. Time." Milo veers toward the back side of the park.

We comb through the woods with our rifles, lugging our jugs of fuel. We don't see anyone, but we're breathing so loud that any intruders would've scattered by now. We come out of the trees, and I plop down on a picnic table.

"Shit, man," I say. "Was that some kind of militia? Why were four guys burning tires this time of night? How many other guys are over there sleeping? What the fuck are they up to?"

Milo sits down in the dead grass. "Maybe they're guys guarding their neighborhood?"

"In camouflage with burning tires? What are we going to do about them? We can't go back over there to spy on them. They could kill us."

"Stay away from them," Milo says, wincing.

"They're more than three miles away, but that's too close. We can't go past the park anymore. We don't want them to notice us."

"But there's stuff at the building site."

"Not any stuff worth dying over. Let's get home. I'm starving."

I also need a nap, but I'm not gonna get one.

I CAN'T GET THE NEIGHBORS to understand how scary these guys could be. Everyone, even Uncle Eddie, seems to think they're just men guarding their neighborhood and going overboard about it. Plus, Eddie's all mad at us for leaving here in the first place.

"Lots of guys in Texas collect guns and military gear," Jack says. "This new life gives them a chance to use it. They aren't smart like you and your grandmother. They feel helpless, and dressing up like warriors makes them feel safer."

"Remember how the men here used to burn fires and hang out all night when this first started?" Silas asks. "Before your nana got us organized?"

"Maybe that's all it is, but what's to keep those guys from taking it further?"

No one has an answer for that.

The consensus of the neighbors is that we should keep to our side of the park from now on and stay alert. It's not enough, but no one's listening to me. Maybe we need to pack up and leave, but where could we go with all these old people and kids? Maybe I'll give up sleeping and patrol to our east all night every night.

It doesn't help for me to worry so much, but worrying is my specialty.

***

THAT AFTERNOON, I'M SHARPENING TOOLS in the open garage. I don't notice Alma's little brothers approaching until they roll a bicycle up our driveway. One of those BMX bikes that tweener kids like Pedro and Chris love so much. You can pop great wheelies with a BMX.

"Hey, guys. What's up?"

Chris, who's thirteen, gives me a little smile while Pedro, who's eleven, looks at the ground. These guys are my brothers-in-law, but they're so shy I feel like I barely know them.

"Can you fix this bike?" Chris asks.

"I can try. What's wrong with it?"

Chris jiggles the handlebars to show me a wobble in the front wheel. "Wheel's loose or somethin'."

"Or somethin'." I take hold of the handlebars, jiggling them again. Then I flip the bike over to stand it upside down, and I turn the wheel. "Looks like the wheel hub's loose. I'll show you how to fix it." As I dig around for wrenches, I ask, "How you guys doing? Are things going okay living with the Barneses?"

Pedro doesn't say anything. He frowns hard, like maybe he might cry. He does this every time I try to talk to him.

But Chris says, "Shit, yeah. We have our own bedrooms. We always had to share a bedroom before." That Chris is an upbeat kid, but I wonder what's up with Pedro.

"I didn't have a room until me and Alma got married," I say. "I slept in the upstairs den across from my uncle."

"Wow. Your house is so big. I thought all you kids would get your own rooms."

"Yeah, well, one of the rooms was Tasha's."

"Oh." Chris looks down with an embarrassed frown. I want to ruffle his hair to make him feel better, but it's a stupid thing that adults do to kids, and I don't want to be a stupid adult.

"Let me show you how to fix a loose hub." I take off the bike wheel, and Chris bends down to watch me. Pedro slips down to the street to kick a can between the dead cars.

"Is Pedro all right?" I whisper to Chris. "Does he ever talk?"

"He used to talk before… you know." Chris crumples his forehead. "Not so much anymore."

"So, he stopped when the sun zapped us?"

"Not at first."

"Did something happen to make him stop?"

Chris shrugs. "I guess it's 'cause our parents never came home."

"Poor guy," I say, knowing how Pedro must feel, since my mom was missing for so long and still isn't "here" for me. My dad's off in California, I guess, where he's been since I was twelve. If he's even alive. You can't count on people being alive anymore. "You seem to be doin' all right, Chris."

He puffs out his chest. "I have to be. I'm the man of the house now."

I bump Chris's shoulder with mine. "Good man." Chris blushes, and I finish tightening the hub and rehanging the wheel. "There you go."

Chris spins the wheel, then flips the bike upright and jiggles the handlebars. No wobble. A grin spreads across his face.

"Thanks, Keno!" Chris mounts the bike and pedals away toward the Barneses' house, where these Ibanez boys live, and where Alma lived until we got married. Pedro follows Chris, kicking his can.

Alma stops hoeing corn in the Barneses' front yard to check out the bike with her brothers. I lose my breath just looking at her, with her sleek black hair falling to her shoulders and the love shining on her face for her brothers. When her parents didn't come home after the solar pulse, she didn't have any adults to help her, but she kept Chris and Pedro alive. I can't imagine how hard that was. But I know that it caused her a lot of pain, and her pain is my pain, too.

Several months after the sun zapped us, Tasha and I went to our mom's house with Nana and a bunch of neighbors to get supplies. Tasha found Alma and her brothers alone, and Nana said we should bring them to our neighborhood to protect them. Silas and Doris Barnes took them in. Nana would never leave children to fend for themselves.

Only Alma and I, Uncle Eddie, and Milo live in Nana's house now. We asked Chris and Pedro to move in with us, but Pedro didn't want to. He wouldn't say why, but we think he's afraid of living with new people. And Chris wants to look out for Pedro.

"Plus," Chris said, "Doris and Silas really like us. They'd be sad if we moved out." I think Alma was a little hurt by this, but she didn't show it to her brothers.

This house seems pretty empty now, and sometimes, that makes me ache. For a while, it was stuffed with people. Stuffed to the gills, as Nana would say, if she could talk like herself again instead of like a simple person. I don't think she's simple in her mind, though. She's still thinking the same smart shit she always did; she just can't tell us much about it anymore.

CHAPTER 7

Grandpa will not stop being a dick. He's out there in the Mint's backyard, screaming at someone right now. He's got a damned shotgun, and he means business.

Uncle Eddie and I frown at each other in our dining room. Eddie blows out a blast of air. "We better go see what the hell he's doing."

I'd rather finish my breakfast. I give Alma a look, and she rolls her eyes. I want to kiss her, but Eddie's already halfway to the Mint's backyard.

Grandpa's been keeping people out of the Mint's garage all week, and we need to get food and tools out of there. He's been home for two months, and he's more of a dick every day.

"I said, 'Get the hell out of my yard!'" Grandpa's howling, waving his fucking shotgun at Phil Hendrix, who must have gone over there for tools. Phil looks freaked, backing away with his hands in the air.

"It's not your yard, Dad!" Eddie yells as we slip through the hedge between our two backyards. "Leave Phil alone!"

"Shut up, son! Get your pansy ass out of here."

"This pansy ass is gonna whip yours to Hell and back if you don't put down the goddamned gun."

Uncle Eddie's all muscled-up like a wrestler. If he says he's gonna whip your ass, you'd better run. Grandpa never used to complain about Eddie being gay, but now that the old man's so angry, he must be letting out whatever shit he's been holding inside for freaking ever.

If we don't get Grandpa under control, the neighbors are gonna run him out of town on a rail. Shit, I might help them.

"Dad!" Mom calls from an upstairs Mint window. "Cut it out. Put the gun down!"

"Don't tell me what to do!" He's like a brat kid gone out of control, my grandpa, except he's got a gun and he's meaner.

While Grandpa's glaring at Mom in the window, Uncle Eddie motions for me to sneak behind the old fart.

"Don't try to get the gun, just pin down his arms."

As Grandpa turns to re-aim the shotgun at Phil, me and Uncle Eddie crowd up on Grandpa and trap him so he can't move.

"What the hell?" he shouts, his skinny shoulders scrunched up between us.

"Put the gun down," I say, nice and even-like, trying to be all mellow while my heart's chugging like a speeding train.

"Down, Dad," Eddie says. "I'll back away, but if you don't put down the gun, I'll knock you to the ground and rub your face in the dirt." Uncle Eddie would do it, too.

Grandpa must believe this, because he lets go of the shotgun, and it falls to the dirt. The ground's so hard from no rain that the gun bounces. I dive away from it.

"Duck!" Eddie hollers, and he sticks his foot on the gun to make it stop bouncing. The gun doesn't fire, but it could have. Crazy bastard Grandpa.

Phil's flat on the ground, his hands over his head, like that would stop a shotgun shell. Aunt Jeri and Uncle Tom run out the Mint's back door with their mouths hanging open. Mazie's watching, bug-eyed, through the bay windows. I hate for her to see this shit.

Grandpa was stunned for a minute, but now he's mad as a hornet. He shoves Eddie.

"What the blazes? Attacking an old man! What's wrong with you, boy?"

"Dad, you're a menace to the neighborhood." Uncle Eddie inches closer to Grandpa's face. "I'm taking your guns. They're Mama Bea's guns anyway."

"Bea's guns, my ass! There's community property in Texas. Those guns are mine, too."

"Possession is nine-tenths of the law, and since I'm stronger than you, the guns are mine now."

"You don't respect the laws God made for us. Damned queer."

Eddie sighs so deep I think he'll never quit sighing. He picks up the shotgun, cracking it open to eject the shells.

"Nice, Dad. Real fucking nice. So, I should give up being a gay man, and I should be a prick like you?" I would melt into a puddle if Uncle Eddie ever stared at me the way he's staring at Grandpa. For once, the old man doesn't know what to say.

"Jeri, Tom, where are the other guns?" Eddie asks with his mouth sideways, still staring holes through Grandpa.

"Now, Eddie, we don't need to go that far. He didn't shoot anyone." Why is Aunt Jeri defending Grandpa? He's a total bully, and there's no compromising with that shit.

"I'm taking Mom's guns," Uncle Eddie says. "You can hold on to one for protection, but you have to keep it locked away from dickhead over here."

Tom gets it. He nods and goes inside. Phil brushes himself off and starts slinking away.

"You okay, Phil?" Eddie asks.

"I'm good." Phil's either awfully hot or he's blushing.

"It's not fair to take the guns from Dad!" Jeri whines. "Mom dumped him like he was nothing. He's already lost everything."

"We've all lost everything," Eddie says. "No one else is threatening to shoot people over it."

Aunt Jeri yammers on about Nana hurting Grandpa and everyone ganging up on him, her voice getting more and more heated. I tune her out, the way I have to do if I'm going to have any peace around here.

Uncle Tom comes back with a couple of Glocks and two bolt-action rifles—I forgot those guns were over here. He's got the AR-15 strapped over his shoulder.

"I'm keeping the semi-automatic," he says.

Uncle Eddie nods. He's sad and disgusted. Me too. We take the guns and turn around to go home.

Mom hollers from her window, "I have a gun, but I'm not telling you guys where it is."

Shit, Mom. Why don't you just invite Grandpa in to rampage through your room and throw your shit around, looking for your stupid gun? She's not usually so clueless, but this is the new Mom, the wounded and pissed-off Mom. I guess she's siding with Grandpa, too, still blaming us about Tasha.

She blames Nana as much as or more than she blames me. I hope Mom gets past that shit soon. Nana may not live much longer, and Mom will be screwed up forever if she doesn't forgive Nana while she's still alive.

"You're gonna leave me here without a gun?" Grandpa cries out. "What am I supposed to do about these prowlers?"

"What prowlers?" Eddie and I both ask.

"These damn people skulking around here day and night, looking for stuff to steal."

"Grandpa," I shout, "they aren't freaking prowlers. That was Phil. He's a neighbor coming to get tools. Neighbors need stuff from the Mint to do their jobs and to feed you."

"Well, they can't have it! This is not a charity. I need those tools."

"Everyone needs them. That's why we share them."

"I don't care what everyone else needs."

I want to punch Grandpa, but I walk away seething.

"Time to get to the gardens. We're late," I holler to everyone, including the neighbors who are standing around watching. I'm supposed to be in charge of the gardening, like I have any control over these people, especially the ones related to me.

I'm still all shaky inside when we come into our yard with the guns. I make sure they're not loaded then set them on the patio table, and Alma jumps into my arms. The minute she touches me, I already feel better.

We're still hugging when Jack comes around the west side of the house with his scruffy white mustache, pushing my tiny, wasting-away Nana in the wheelchair.

Jack parks Nana on the patio. Winter weather in Central Texas goes back and forth between warm and cold, but it's warm today, so Nana will want to stay on the patio. That makes it easier for Alma to watch over her while Alma harvests greens from our garden before a frost comes and kills them off.

Nana is like the family treasure. Sometimes I say these things, and Alma tells me I sound like Nana. I was embarrassed at first, until Alma said, "I love it that you admire your grandmother so much."

Nana throws her arms out to Eddie, and he stoops down to be sucked into them.

I look away. I'm afraid Uncle Eddie will cry, and I won't know what to do if he does. Grandpa saying all that shit must hurt Eddie something fierce. My dad was hardly ever around, but at least he didn't call me names, act like I'm not even human.

"Do you think Grandpa's losing it?" I say to whoever wants to listen. "Like he's getting all senile?"

"Might be coming down with dementia," Jack says.

"He's a jackass," Nana says. Ha! That's Nana's word for a dick.

Uncle Eddie backs away from Nana. "Dad can't have a gun anymore. That's all I know."

"We have to get back into the Mint," I say. "People need shit in there. We haven't had bread for a week." I never used to cuss around my grandparents until this apocalypse. Nana doesn't want us to be rude, but she doesn't care about casual cussing anymore. She was married to Grandpa for thirty years, and he never stops cussing.

"Let's think on it," Jack says. "We can talk about it at dinner tonight. Got to get those pinto beans harvested before a frost comes."

"I'll be planting winter wheat in the park," Eddie says. "With Phil."

Milo comes outside just as Mazie scampers into our yard to join us. They're going to collect firewood from the park, which I'm hoping will be safe, since it's daylight, and Phil and Eddie will be there.

"Take a gun," I tell Milo. "You two need to help me with the tomatoes after lunch."

"Can we eat a tomato?" Mazie wants to know. That girl loves tomatoes.

"If you help me, you can eat a tomato. The rest of them have to be canned."

Alma nods sideways for me to follow her inside. I would follow Alma to Mars if she asked me to.

As soon as we get in the door, Alma grabs me and French kisses me. If I had my way, I would spend all day kissing Alma, but there's too much work to be done, so I have to stop.

"You okay, Keno?"

"I'm good." I'm trying to stop feeling rattled.

"Poor Eddie. Grandpa was so mean to him. And there's not any other gay men around for Eddie to talk to."

"Uncle Eddie's got his eye on Phil," I say.

"I didn't know Phil was gay."

"He seems to like Eddie an awful lot."

"Everyone loves Eddie. He's so good-looking, he's almost pretty." She has that funny grin of hers, all crooked and cute.

"He is awful pretty, isn't he?" I smile and kiss Alma again, then I grab my buckets, tools, and water bottle, and I head down the block to the tomato garden in old Mr. Bellows's backyard.

CHAPTER 8

It's too hot for December in this tomato garden, but at least it's not summer.

We had a lot of trouble with our tomatoes earlier this year—some kind of blight or fungus. Now we're trying this heirloom variety. They're healthy and juicy, more orange than red, but we have to save seeds for the spring, and I've got no idea how to do that. Jack thinks he can figure it out. We'll be out of tomatoes forever if he can't.

Maybe we could find seeds or abandoned tomato plants in another neighborhood, but we can't leave this one anymore.

I'm picking juicy tomatoes and piling them up in buckets, but I can't get my mind off Grandpa. What does he think he's doing, anyway? Some idiotic power-trip bullshit. Like he thinks if he controls everything, then Nana leaving him and lying to him won't hurt so much? Like that's going to work—like he didn't deserve to be lied to.

If you're gonna be a dick, people are gonna lie to you. It's a rule of life, or it ought to be.

This crazy life we live could turn anyone into a dick, but Grandpa had a head start. Even as a little kid, I knew I never wanted to be anything like him.

MILO AND MAZIE FINALLY SHOW up to help with the tomatoes after I have most of them picked.

"Where have you been? I told you to come after lunch." The kids are still growing, so they get lunches every day. The adults, not so much. Milo's grown four or five inches in the last few months, and he's gonna pass my six feet any day.

"Sorry," Milo says. "We had to help Alma bring herbs into the house for the winter."

"I forgot about the herbs. I shoulda done that this morning." Alma has filled half the patio and part of the yard with pots of herbs and medicinal plants. She dug some out of the woods, and neighbors gave her more. She's learning how to make poultices and teas. She thinks they'll help us the next time someone gets sick.

"She has so-o-o many herbs," Mazie says. "We had to fill all the southern windows with them, even the windows upstairs."

"Very cool. So, I want you guys to pick those tomatoes down there, and I'll finish the other end."

We get to work. For Mazie, that includes jabbering at Milo; for him, it's half-listening to his sister and teasing her. Work gives me a chance to think.

I wanted to be an environmental scientist, but that'll never happen now. The solar pulse blew all the giant transformers in the country, and Nana said that no one kept spares. It could be decades before the grid comes back, if it ever does. By then, the whole society will have to be rebuilt before anyone can go to college.

I've been digging through Nana's books and pulling out any that might help me figure out how to get us some electricity. She has hundreds of books, all over both her houses, but I need technical details, and I haven't found too many yet. I'd like to ask Nana about it, but I hate to frustrate her when she probably won't be able to answer me. It's the water I need to know about first.

I wanted to fix Nana's solar panels that she was so smart to have. She thought she'd set them up to generate electricity without the grid. But the manual says the system won't work off-grid unless it's attached to some kind of big-assed lead-acid battery. I have hope, though, that I can figure something out, maybe with car batteries, if I can only find instructions somewhere in those books.

Nana was mad that the solar sales guy didn't tell her about the battery. I don't get why she didn't know, since she's been an environmentalist all her life. She could've afforded the crazy-expensive battery plus a bunch of spares. She was a millionaire before money got worthless. Grandpa didn't know she inherited all that money. None of us did.

For months, I've been spending all my time growing food, but winter's here again and I should have more time to search for answers. Refrigeration is what we need most, so the food we grow won't go to waste before we can eat it. Those canning jar lids that seal—we're going to run out of them in less than a year. We could starve without freezers.

If I have to build ten windmills out of scraps, I'm going to find a way to get freezers working—I hope by spring, when the winter veggies come in.

I'M PICKING THE LAST FEW tomatoes at my end of the garden when Mazie hollers, "Stop it!" I spin around to see Milo chasing Mazie and squirting water at her from his drinking bottle. I open my mouth to tell him to stop just as he catches her and dumps two whole liters of water on her head.

"Milo! Are you insane?" Anger and alarm propel me across the garden. I grab him by the shoulders. "Stop that shit, man! You're wasting water!"

"Milo, you're mean!" Mazie cries, wiping water off her face, shaking it from her hair, water that should've been Milo's drinking ration for the rest of today and into tomorrow.

"Shit, I was only having fun," Milo croaks, wrenching himself away from me. "Can't even have fun in this shithole."

"How'd you like to go without water until tomorrow? You wasted your ration. Now whose water are you gonna drink? Mazie's? Nana's?"

Milo's face crumples and his shoulders sink, his defiance falling away. "Shit," he mutters.

"Shit is right." I step back from him, trying to calm down. "You need to limit yourself to one cup of water until morning. I don't want you getting dehydrated, but you've got to feel how stupid that was."

"I'm sorry. Okay?" He whirls around and stomps toward the gate, like he's leaving.

"Get back here. We've got shit to do, and you're helping!"

Milo stops past the edge of the garden and plops to the ground on his butt, facing the cedar fence like he's putting himself in time-out. Time-out is probably a good idea.

"Mazie, are you all right?"

"I can give Milo my water."

"Aww, you're sweet. But I want him to think about what he did."

"But I don't want him to be thirsty," she says with trembly lips.

I wrap Mazie in a hug. Though it pains me to say it, I add, "If you forgive him, I guess I should, too."

"You should. You love him, don't you?"

"Mazie, you blow my mind. I do love that punk kid." I kiss Mazie's cheek and squeeze her. Then I walk over to Milo and sit down, staring at the fence with him.

We've been getting most of our water from the drainage pond by the railroad tracks on the western edge of our area—not the place where the train crashed and left so much poison in the ground, but upstream about a mile. We've also built rain-barrel systems with house gutters running into them to catch rain. We have about five systems already, but we never have enough rain. And with Mom and them home, we have more people using water. If we don't get several good rains this winter, we could go completely dry. Totally terrifying.

The neighbors could turn on us about this, about bringing in more people and using more resources. Especially with Grandpa being such a dick.

"Sorry I got so mad," I say to Milo. "I've been crazy-worried about the water."

"Why didn't you tell me it was so low?" He looks at me like I've hurt him.

"I didn't want to worry you."

"That's bullshit."

"No, I really didn't—"

"It's bullshit to try not to worry me. Aren't we in this together? Don't you need my help?" His eyes are boring into mine.

"Is that what you want, for me to tell you everything? I know your dad said you're a man now, but you're really just a kid."

"So are you."

I flop back into the dead grass. "That's true, but I'm supposed to be a man. I didn't mean to leave you out. If I get all busy and forget to tell you stuff, remind me, okay?"

"'Kay," he says, nodding at me like a man would.

"You could also learn to look at things and think them through for yourself. No one told me we were low on water. I figured it out by looking and thinking."

"I didn't think of that," he says.

"That's 'cause you're a kid." I poke him in the ribs with my elbow, and he swats at my head. "C'mon. Let's put straw on this garden for mulch."

Mazie runs over to hug Milo, and he ruffles her damp hair. The three of us grab big bunches of straw that we got from the park after no one mowed the grass for a year.

Together, we pile straw about a foot thick on the garden, and then we stomp the straw down so it won't blow away. I hope it rains soon to pack the straw better—also to make it less likely to catch fire from cinders blowing out of chimneys or grills. A bad fire could take out the whole neighborhood.

"Can I have my tomato now?" Mazie asks me. She's so cute with her straight blond hair all messed up with straw in it. The straw sorta blends in with her hair. She looks like a pixie who's been rolling in hay.

"Yup, I promised you a tomato, didn't I?" I hand her a good-looking orange one.

"Thanks." She grins so big it makes me laugh, and she takes a huge bite. Juice squirts out over half her face.

"Don't you want to take it home to wash it and put salt on it?"

"Nope. I like it this way." Obviously.

"A little dirt never hurt no one," Milo asks.

"A little dirt never hurt 'anyone,'" I say. Nana wants us to have dignity and good grammar, and to carry knowledge and civilization to the future. I don't know if there will be a future. It doesn't seem like it, but I act like there is one, just because.

"I get a tomato, too, don't I?" Milo asks.

"Pick one out. Then grab buckets, and we'll take them to the canning house." That's the house next door to us where

Nana's friends June and Charlotte, the nurses, live. They do most of the canning, but they're older than rocks, so I figure someone else will have to do it before long.

CHAPTER 9

At home, I lead Alma into the old laundry room and shut the door so we can kiss without everyone watching. She's been cooking and she tastes like jalapeños, which makes me hungry and horny at the same time. I really, really don't want to let go of her, and I know she doesn't want me to.

We get back to the dinner table just as Uncle Eddie comes in with Phil. They're grinning at each other and sort of glowing. I knew something was up with those two.

Alma has cooked us beans, tortillas, and lots of collard greens. Alma can whip out tortillas like a factory, only hers are better. She makes them just right: not too thick, not too thin. And her homemade salsa is so freaking good.

"So," I say while we're dishing up our food, "what are we gonna do about Grandpa and getting into the Mint?"

Phil gives Uncle Eddie a sad, sympathetic look. He must know what it's like to get trashed for being gay. Probably why he didn't tell anybody.

Uncle Eddie sighs. "I'd like to take Dad out back and shoot him."

"You can't shoot Grandpa!" Mazie cries.

"I know," Eddie says. "Sometimes I want to, though."

"That's mean."

"Well, Grandpa's mean," Milo says.

"It's just a saying," I tell everyone. "Uncle Eddie's not shooting anybody."

"Talk to him," Nana says, and we look at her, surprised. "All of you." She sweeps her good hand around the table, toward each of us. "Together. Just family."

"Me too?" Mazie asks.

"Not me. I'm not goin'," Milo says.

"You're going." I point my fork at Milo. I notice I'm doing this and put the fork down. I'm not his dad, even if I feel like I am sometimes.

"There's not enough of us, Mom," Eddie says. "There's only me, Keno, Alma, and the kids."

"I'll go," Nana says. Wow, that shocks me, and everyone else, from the look of them.

"But he's so mad at you, Mom. He might refuse to talk to you."

She half-smiles. "I'll make peace."

I want to ask how she plans to do that when she can't talk much, but it would be disrespectful. Besides, Nana has her ways of getting what she wants.

Jack says, "When are you doing this?"

"Tomorrow," Nana says. "Morning."

People mutter their agreements, and I'm just glad as hell we're not going tonight.

We scarf up our dinner in silence. I don't want to talk. I just want to eat. We finish and rinse our plates in a dish pan with only a little water in it. If you ever don't rinse your plate around here, someone will yell at you, and I do as much yelling about plates as anyone. We cannot waste water by letting food dry on plates. Not a drop.

I shoo Mazie and Milo over to the Mint. Mazie needs to get home, and Milo needs to visit at least once in a while. It's more exciting for the kids at our house, but they owe their parents some respect.

Jack and Nana head home, and Alma looks like she's about to cry. She shakes her head, blinking, turns around, and hurries upstairs.

"Um…" I look at Uncle Eddie and the dinner mess, pointing my thumb toward the stairs.

"Go see about Alma. I'll get the dishes," Eddie says.

"I'll help," says Phil.

"Thanks, guys."

UPSTAIRS, I STOP AT THE bathroom to wash my face and to pee in an enamel pot that Nana calls a chamber pot. I don't have a lot of pee, like I used to. Sometimes, my pee's so yellow it burns me. Alma says I should drink more water, and I should, but we don't have enough, so I don't.

In our room, I yank off my clothes, leaving them where they land on the floor. I fall into bed beside Alma, and when I crawl under the covers, she's naked. Her cheeks are wet and her eyes are red. I can't stand seeing Alma cry, so I grab her with all my strength.

"I love you so much," I say, brushing hair from her face. "What's wrong, baby?"

"Sometimes I watch you with your family, and I miss my mom and dad so much I feel stabbed in the chest."

"I'm so sorry." I kiss tears off her cheeks.

"I don't know how they'll ever find us."

"I thought you left our address in their house for them."

"That's true. I did. I just wish they'd hurry up and find it."

"I'm here for you, Alma. I'll always be here for you." I put my hand on her heart. "Is this where it hurts?"

She snuggles into my hand. "Make love to me," she says.

Alma needs me right now. She is hurting. She kisses me hard and long and good, like she's channeling her pain into love. Then she rolls me to my back and climbs on top of me. She grabs for me, and I'm already hard and reaching for her. She kisses me there and I almost come, but I hold it in. I need to be inside her and she needs me there.

She sits down on me, and I go all the way in to a deep new place. Oh God, everywhere she touches me heals me. I can't believe how good she feels and how much I need her and want her and have to have her. I'm dying a little right now, with her all wet and slick and moving up and down on me more and more and faster and faster.

I want to cry out, but I can't because people. So, I cry out in my throat, and she hums and quivers all over, and it's too good. It's too—too—too good and I can't, I just can't, but I do it. I come. I feel Alma vibrating inside and coming with me and our juices spilling out of her and onto me.

Holy shit, and I mean holy holy. Because that, this—this right here—this is love.

I clutch Alma to me, and I kiss her so much. I say, "I love you," and she says it back and kisses me on my face and chest. I slip out from inside her. She wipes us off, and then she scoots around until she's plastered to my side. I tingle where she touches me. I want to keep making love, but my body has other ideas, and I start falling straight to sleep.

Then Alma raises up a little. "Keno?"

I open one eye and look at her sideways. "Yeah?"

"I think…" She glances at the ceiling for a second, and then she drops her eyes until they're boring into mine. And she says, a little louder, "Baby, I think I'm pregnant."

What?!

I shoot up in bed and bust out crying, pulling Alma up and holding her so tight our lungs are crushed. I keep holding her until I freak out for air. She's crying, too. We don't say anything. We can't. There's too much to say and too much emotion to say it.

Euphoria, anxiety, happiness, dread—it seems impossible to feel so many extreme emotions at once. I hold Alma's face in my hands and rest my forehead on hers.

Finally, I say, "Are you sure?"

"Pretty sure. I haven't had a period for two months."

"You'd think I would've noticed that."

"Guys don't notice that stuff."

"I thought I would. I thought I'd be different because I love you so much."

"It's okay, Keno. Two months can fly by."

"I guess they did. So how do you feel? Do you need to barf? It's not morning yet. Tasha always barfed in the morning."

I wish I'd never said that. Tasha died from being pregnant with no doctors around. Alma can't die. I won't let her.

We stare into each other's eyes. Alma's face is puckered up. So is mine. I shake my head, sniff my nose. I'm not going to cry anymore about this. Not in front of Alma.

"I'm not sick," Alma says. "But my breasts are bigger and kind of sore."

I touch my fingertip to one of her breasts, then I squeeze it a tiny bit. I don't want to hurt her, but I want to see what they feel like.

"It does feel different. Not harder, but—"

"Firmer," she says.

"That's it. Firmer. I didn't notice that when we were all busy having orgasms." I put my hands over both her breasts.

"Does this happen when women get pregnant? I never knew about this before."

Alma laughs. "Yeah, it happens. My mom told me."

"My mom never told me shit, except how to use condoms."

"She probably told Tasha about what it's like to be pregnant."

"Maybe, but I kinda doubt it. Tasha was so young."

In our apocalyptic world, the difference between Tasha being fifteen and Alma being eighteen, though barely, seems enormous.

"So, do we need to stop making love while you're pregnant?" I pull my hands away.

Alma musses my hair that's already poking out everywhere. "I think it's fine."

"Do you just think that, or do you know?"

"Pretty sure. But if it will make you feel better, I'll ask other women about it." Alma runs her finger down my cheek. "But let's don't tell anyone yet."

"Sure, if you want. But why?"

"Let's get used to the idea first. Just you and me."

"That's brilliant," I say. "I'm too crazy to talk about it anyway."

"Exactly. We need time to find the words. And the courage."

I take a deep breath, like a backwards sigh. "This is gonna take a ton of courage."

"Yep." She flops back on the bed, and I flop down beside her. She turns her back to me and scooches against me to sit in my lying-down lap.

We say "I love you" a bunch of times, and then her breathing changes, and I know she's asleep. I don't sleep, though. How could I? I'm gonna be a dad! I'm gonna have a little kid running around.

I'm so freaking happy, and I'm scared to death. Raising a baby in the middle of all this danger—Jesus! I'm half-paralyzed with my eyes wide open.

I LIE HERE CLUTCHING ALMA in her sleep. I drift in and out all night, and now it's morning. We only have one working clock in the house, and its battery won't last much longer. But from where the sun hangs in the sky, I'd guess it's around seven. One thing I learned how to do since the sun flipped out is to tell time from it—not the exact time, but it's not like we have school bells to beat into class.

I feel kind of sick about the pregnancy, worrying about how the birth will be, how there are no doctors, but Alma's belly will grow and grow. She'll have to eat more. What if we don't have enough food? Or water? That would be worse. If Alma barfs a lot like Tasha did, I'll take care of her, I will, but all that barf without enough water to clean it up right? Sick.

Nana, Jack, Eddie, and the kids are probably waiting for us so we can go talk to Grandpa. Wish I could get out of it, but Milo will point a fork at me if I try.

I don't want to wake Alma up. Pretty sure she needs extra sleep, but I don't know shit about what she needs. They should've taught us kids more about how this works.

Too bad Alma can't go. Having her there would keep me from going apeshit. She'd help the whole talk, too, because as mean as Grandpa is, he likes Alma.

During those first days they were back, Grandpa sat around seething, about to blow a gasket over Tasha dying and about Nana leaving him and lying to him about her inheritance and the Mint full of food and supplies. I felt sorry for Grandpa then. It was a whole lot to handle, even if he did deserve for Nana to leave him and to lie to him.

I was over at the Mint for days, dismantling shelves and moving stuff around so they could live in the house. Every time Grandpa saw me, he'd say shit like, "What's wrong with you, getting married so young?" or "Have you lost your mind, boy?"

He was so skinny when he got here—they all were—and with him being so old, he looked like death. Stank like it, too, like the rat that died inside the wall at Mom's house when I was ten.

But Alma wasn't afraid. She would fuss over Grandpa, bringing him home-cooked meals and clean clothes, washcloths and soap and bowls of water.

"How can you do that, Alma?" I asked. "He's so pissed off I'm scared he'll grab me and choke me."

"He's a sad, skinny old man who needs help and a good bath. His heart is broken."

She was so amazing that even Grandpa—stunned as he was—couldn't help but appreciate what she did for him.

Once, he said "Thank you" to Alma, and he started crying and shaking.

Christ, he looked like he had so much pain I didn't know how he could breathe. When I saw Grandpa crying like that, I watched him until I couldn't take it anymore, and then I carried stuff to the garage and stayed out there organizing it.

I'll love Alma forever for doing things for Grandpa I never thought of. She is wise.

And now she's pregnant. She'll be a wise mother, if I can keep her alive, and I will keep her alive if I have to die to do it.

***

DOWNSTAIRS, I TELL EVERYONE THAT Alma's sleeping in. I find tortillas and cold beans in the warm fridge that we use as a cabinet now. I make burritos on two plates, then take Alma's plate upstairs with some water. I watch to make sure she's breathing, and then I skitter down the stairs.

"Let me eat, then we can go," I say to my family. Milo groans.

"Dad's awful quiet today," Uncle Eddie says. "No telling what he's up to."

Phil's not here. He's probably working on the wheat. We have to grow wheat in the winter in Texas, but we're running late with the planting. I hope Uncle Tom's helping Phil with the other rototiller—they have one can of gasoline left until we get into the Mint's garage. Planting wheat all over that park is a huge job. And it's so important for us to get more wheat before the bulk flour runs out.

"Everyone ready?" I ask after I rinse my plate.

"Wait," Nana says. "We need… um, peace offering." That is smart as hell.

"What kind of peace offering?" Uncle Eddie asks.

Nana puts her finger to her chin and smiles. "Chair." She makes up and down motions with her hands going in opposite directions.

"The rocking chair," Mazie says. She always understands Nana better than the rest of us do. Nana might've died from her stroke if Mazie hadn't talked to her constantly until she finally talked back. Mazie is kind of a magical kid.

"Yes. It's Grandpa's chair," I say, and Nana grins.

"Yeah, and he wouldn't let anyone else sit in it," Milo says. I swear, Milo keeps a list in his head of all the ways that Grandpa is mean. He never forgets a one of them. But it's true that Grandpa used to yell at anyone who sat in his precious chair, even Nana, or especially her.

"Let's get this done." I pick up the big rocker. "Ready, Nana?"

"Yes, thank you." Nana's always polite, even now. She used to tell us about going to charm school, like Southern girls did back then. Nana wants us to be charming, too. We try, but we're not as good at it as she is.

Jack strokes Nana's shoulder, and she pats his hand. They love each other as much as me and Alma do, only they're all old.

CHAPTER 10

I can't wrap my head around talking to Grandpa, emotional as I feel. We go down the sidewalk that runs beside our yard and the Mint's. One whole end of the block is Nana's. No, ours. The houses and yards belong to the whole family, even nutso Grandpa. Nana told us.

We stop when we reach the Mint's entrance sidewalk, clearing our noses, smoothing the dirty clothes we have to wear.

I turn to face the Mint, and Grandpa and Aunt Jeri are scowling at us from separate windows. Uh-oh. I should've gone to find Uncle Tom before we headed over here so he could help with these hotheads, but it's too late now.

Jeri opens the front door with Grandpa behind her.

"What are y'all doing here?" she says, like she owns the place and we're trespassers. What's wrong with her? She's been upset lately, but this is a step beyond.

But Mazie runs up to hug her mama anyway, because Mazie is like that—full of love. Jeri scoops Mazie in the door behind her. Grandpa ignores Mazie when she looks to see if he'll hug her. He wasn't much of a hugger before, but now, a hug from Grandpa ain't happenin'. I just hope he doesn't have a gun.

Milo shuffles to the door with me following. Thinking someone needs to cool the vibes, I say, "Grandpa. Aunt Jeri. We brought a gift."

Grandpa snorts, that old fart. I'm sure he's thinking that it's his chair, he bought it, so it can't be a goddamned gift.

I don't give a crap what he thinks. Jeri pats Milo on the shoulder, but she doesn't say shit to me. Okay, so that's how it's going to be.

As soon as I maneuver the chair through the door and past the people standing around—including my mom, who just ran in the back door—Aunt Jeri steps across the threshold and straps her arms over her chest. She glares at Nana in the wheelchair with Eddie behind it.

"Eddie," Jeri says, "what do you mean by showing your face in our yard and bringing *her* with you?"

Why's Aunt Jeri acting this way? It's freaking me out. What did Nana ever do to her besides take care of her kids for a year when Jeri didn't come home from a damn football game? Talking to Nana like that after all she's done for this family? Such bullshit.

I have to do something, so I say, "It's Nana's house, and she can come in if she wants to." I stick my head out the door. "Nana, would you like to come in your own house now?" I grin at Nana, and she grins back but with pain in her eyes.

"Yes," Nana says. It would be so cool if she could say more. She could tell the truth in just the right way to knock the wind out of Aunt Jeri's meanness.

Uncle Eddie has always been closest to Nana of all the five kids, even closer than Mom and Aunt Jeri, Nana's only kids by birth. Jeri probably hates that about Eddie, since she's not her old self anymore. I guess she thinks we're on Nana's side. But we don't need to have sides.

Eddie backs Nana's wheelchair over the threshold. Jeri huffs and moves aside. Grandpa slaps his forehead and stomps into the dining room to pace while Nana gets settled in the living room.

I set the rocking chair next to Nana. She pats the seat and says, "Hank?"

"What?" he barks.

Mazie, being all innocent, thinks Grandpa needs to have Nana explained to him. "She wants you to sit by her in your rocking chair."

Grandpa growls in his throat. "I'm not sitting next to *her!*"

"Dad," Eddie says, "you were married to Mama Bea for thirty years. She raised your kids for you. You can sit beside her a few more minutes."

"I don't bite," Nana says, and we're all floored. She gives Grandpa the cutest grin, like she probably used to give him when she still loved him.

"I didn't know she could talk like that," Grandpa says. But he heard her say a few whole sentences when he first came home. She didn't say what he wanted her to say, though, so he must have distorted the whole thing in his cracked head.

"Grandpa," I say. "Nana wants to talk to you, and you need to talk to her, so please sit in your chair and get on with it."

My mom comes up and puts her hand on my shoulder. She hasn't touched me since she found out that Tasha was dead. I grab Mom's hand tight and lean down to hug her. I just want to cry and forget about Grandpa's stupid shit.

Mom lets me hug her, sort of cold at first, but finally, she sighs and hugs me back. I feel her crying, but I don't look at her face. Seeing Mom cry would be the end of me for today—for the week, even.

"Come on, Dad," Uncle Eddie says. "Please sit by Mom. We love you, and we need to discuss some things, like a—like a—"

"Family," Nana says, and Grandpa gasps. "Please, Hank."

Did Nana just bat her eyelashes at Grandpa? It was so quick; my eyes could've tricked me.

Grandpa grumbles, but he picks up the rocker and moves it away from Nana. He plops down his skinny creaky butt and starts rocking too fast, all agitated. Okay, that's a start.

"Hank." Nana looks like she might cry. Shit. If everyone starts crying in this room, I might have to leave. "Hank, I'm—I'm—I'm sorry."

"You should be!" Grandpa leans forward like he's fixing to yell at her. I think Nana might get mad, because I would, and she would've before her stroke.

But she nods and says, "I know."

Wow. I didn't think she'd be that sorry. Grandpa gave her every reason to do what she did. But Nana's probably sorry she hurt Grandpa, knowing her. Likely, she's sorry she spent thirty years with him and it didn't work out like either one of them wanted it to. I'm going to be extra careful my whole life in my marriage to Alma so that nothing this screwed-up ever happens to us. Because look how many people get hurt by this shit.

No one's moving. Everyone's barely breathing. Finally, Eddie says, "Dad, do you have anything to say to Mom?"

Grandpa lets out a loud sigh. He leans back in the chair and starts rocking again, only slower this time.

Nana waves at Mazie to come to her.

Mazie runs over. "You need help, Nana?" God, it's so sweet, I could cry over just that. Nana nods and unlocks her wheelchair brakes. She inches up in front of Grandpa. He leans the rocker back about as far as he can get without tipping over backward. Nana pats Mazie's head.

"You, Hank. You," Nana says, and she points at Grandpa's chest. His eyelids are stretched wide. She shakes her head all exaggerated, puts her hands to her heart and moves them away from her then back, points to herself, and looks at Mazie.

"You," Mazie says, "don't? Didn't? Something that means no. Her heart? Love? Then Nana. You didn't love her, that's what she said. Didn't you love Nana, Grandpa?"

Grandpa's mouth falls open, and his eyes look all wild, darting around. Maybe he's trying to see what the rest of us think, but we're waiting to hear him.

"I loved you," he says to Nana, and he leans a hair closer. "I loved you a lot for a long time." Now his voice is cracking, and my eyes start looking for the exits. "I loved you for years, Bea, but somewhere in the middle of it, I stopped."

Tears spring to his eyes and he closes them, his face puckered with deep wrinkles. He's going to start blubbering out loud any minute. Even Milo is about to cry.

The rest of us shouldn't be watching this. It's way too personal between Nana and Grandpa, and it's about how their marriage went to Hell. But Nana needs our help to communicate with Grandpa so he can go on living without being such a dick.

Mazie is like an ambassador angel. She climbs into Grandpa's lap, surprising him and forcing him to think for a second about someone besides himself. She puts her little arms around his neck and hugs him. He doesn't hug her back, but he supports her to keep her from falling, and he just cries and cries.

Nana pats Grandpa's knee. "It's okay… It's okay." She's trying to tell him he'll be all right. But she's got tears on her face, too. Because she used to love Grandpa a whole lot, and it's just so freaking sad when love ends and there's nothing left at all.

"Y'all go home," Grandpa says, crying even more, his face so contorted it's got to hurt him. He can't accept comfort. He wants to wallow in it, seems like.

Aunt Jeri and Mom are watching from the couch, where they have a good view of the whole proceedings. Mom's wiping her wet cheeks with her fingers, but Jeri's all stone-faced.

I hug Grandpa. He's the most broke-up person around. Nana spent the whole time he was gone being torn up and deciding to leave him. Grandpa hasn't had time to let go yet. Even if he didn't love Nana, he never admitted it to himself before. He relied on her, and that's a kind of love, too. Now Nana's with Jack. Plus, she could die soon, and none of us will be able to rely on her except in our minds. I know what she would say: rely on each other. And she would be right.

Milo stumbles a bit when he leans in to hug Grandpa, knocking me further into the old man, and Mazie cries out, "Hey, you're smooshing me!"

We laugh and back up to let Mazie out of this hug-cluster. Grandpa even laughs a teeny bit. I feel kind of hysterical, half-laughing, half-crying, not knowing which way to turn.

"Better go," Nana says, and a weird relief washes over me.

"Wait, Mom." My mother rushes over to hug Nana. "I'm sorry I blamed you."

Next thing I know, everyone's crying again. I wipe my hands under my eyes and flick tears off my fingers. Biggest bunch of bawling people I ever saw. I'm glad I'm older now. If this shit had happened a couple of years ago, I would've been so grossed out I might've never talked to any of these people again. Milo looks kind of green, like he might puke. It is pretty pukey.

Finally, we file out the front door. It doesn't seem like we solved a thing, except maybe we gave Grandpa a start on getting over it. But I have a sick feeling that he's never going to change. He's been a dick his whole life. Don't know why he'd stop now.

We didn't even get to talk about letting people into the Mint's garage. I'm sick of tortillas. I want some bread. Plus, we're running out of flour to make tortillas unless we can get to the bulk food bins. Alma needs her tortillas now more than ever.

Alma! I almost forgot about her. How could I do that? Uncle Eddie's already got Nana to the big sidewalk.

"You got this?" I ask him. "I need to see about Alma."

"I got it. But what's wrong with Alma?"

It's probably two hundred degrees on the surface of my cheeks. I rush away, hollering back, "Nothing. I just want to see her." I run as fast as I can to the front door and fumble around for my key. Then I fly up the stairs. I hear Alma in the bedroom, squeaking the bed frame. Thank you, Jesus.

Jesus probably didn't have shit to do with Alma being alive in the bedroom, but I thank Jesus anyway, just because.

CHAPTER 11

When Jack brings Nana over the next morning, I ask if he'll teach me how to siphon gas, and he wants to know why.

"Grandpa's not letting us get gas for the tillers from the Mint, so we need to get some of our own."

"What are you gonna do? We already siphoned all the gas in the cars around here."

"Take some guys and go to other neighborhoods, or down the main roads."

"Cars on main roads have been looted down to scrap metal. People already took the gas. We never got a chance to have our talk about it, but I've got a better way. Let's go to my house."

Jack kisses Nana goodbye, and then he takes me to his garage.

"You know I used to manage the H-E-B grocery on Slaughter Lane," he says.

"I remember."

"They have a gas station in the parking lot, and when they got a new hand-pump for their underground storage tanks, they sold me the old pump for fifty bucks."

Jack reaches into a corner and pulls out a hefty device with a hand crank on it and a piece of pipe shooting out the bottom. He grabs a coil of hosing off a shelf.

"You attach this hose to this pipe, then thread the hose into the underground tank, and pump." He thrusts the pump and hose out toward me. "Here. It's a gift for the cause."

"Holy shit! Thank you. I didn't know you had this."

"Some of us men used it a couple of times at the beginning of this thing, back when your Nana didn't want you boys to leave home at night."

"Seems like all the gas would be gone by now," I say.

"It could be. But I don't think many people have the means to pump it."

"Probably somebody does. Like those guys who had the GTO and old truck that still ran."

"Yep, and whoever drives trucks up and down Menchaca sometimes. Some storage tanks will be empty, but there are probably fifteen gas stations within two miles of here."

Jack gathers up a bunch of empty gas cans and threads a length of rope through the handles, tying a double-knot.

"To carry them home," he says. "You'll need these and any other gas cans you can find." He explains all the different kinds of caps the underground tanks can have and the various tools you use to get in.

Jack sits down on an upturned plastic bucket, and I notice how he's sagging a lot, with more wrinkles around his eyes, like this life is wearing him out. He explains that each station will have three or four tanks for diesel and different grades of gas. Then he tells me we need motor oil, too, and says to look in the pits under the repair bays at lube and mechanic shops.

"For a lot of these tanks," he says, "even if they're locked, you can get in through the hole for the dipstick that measures how much fuel is left in the tank. You should check the dipstick first, anyhow. You don't want to pump from a tank that's real low. That fuel will gunk up the machinery."

"Wish you could go with us to show us how to do it."

"Yeah, but I need to stay with Bea."

"I appreciate that," I say, wondering if he'll be able to take care of her much longer. He looks like someone needs to take care of him.

I take the pump and hose and pick up the string of gas cans. "Thanks, man. Don't know what we'd do without you."

BEFORE I START WORK IN the gardens, I go to our garage and grease the wheels and handle joints on the four wagons we've got over here. There are two more wagons at the Mint, six in all. We call them wagons, but they're garden carts—much longer, wider, and deeper than a kid's wagon, with wooden side rails and big-ass wheels that can handle a heavy load. I tighten bolts until not one wagon squeaks or rattles. I fill three of them with Jack's gas cans and ours.

Then I pad up the fourth wagon with rags to keep tools from clanking together—the hand pump and hose, hacksaw, crowbar, pipe wrench, hammer, plus the only two flashlights I can find that still have working batteries. Last of all, I add four loaded rifles and some bottles of water, and I lock the garage up tight.

As I work in gardens for the rest of the day, I run into Milo and my friend Max. He's the only other guy my age in the neighborhood—a tall, skinny guy with dark hair who might be more of a nerd than I ever was. I recruit these two to go with me tonight and ask them to meet me at our garage after dark.

I need one more person to pull the fourth wagon, but out of the fifty people here, I can't think of anyone who isn't patrolling tonight, or isn't too slow or too old or too young, or who doesn't have a twisted ankle or some other thing that rules them out.

Shit. I might have to pull two wagons—either that or get less gas. Hard to guess how heavy the wagons will be when the gas cans are full.

•••

ALMA'S NOT THRILLED ABOUT ME going, but she understands how much we need gas. I hate that I have to put her through so much worry. I'm supposed to be taking care of her instead of driving up her stress load.

I go to the garage a little early and test the wagons, trying to decide whether or not I should pull two of them. I'm leaning toward pulling only one so I can move faster. But then I think of Greta. She's a middle-aged woman who's pretty strong and usually gung-ho about helping. Why didn't I think of her sooner? I'm about to go ask her when Milo shows up with his stocky friend Danny, who's a little older than him, maybe fifteen. These guys love to play soccer in the street at night, screaming out cuss words in the dark.

"I brought Danny," Milo says. "You need another guy, right?"

"How'd you know that?"

"You have four wagons and only three guys."

"Noticed that, did you? You might be growing up."

"Hey, fuck you," he mutters, and he gives me a shove.

"I was only kidding." Guess it's a bad idea to tease him in front of another guy.

Max trots up to the garage and looks over the scruffy crew and the wagons loaded with gas cans. "Wow. We're gonna get that much gas?"

"If we can. We need as much as we can get. If this works out, we'll go back every so often until we drain every gas station around us."

"And if it doesn't work out?" Max asks, fretting with the dark hair hanging in his eyes.

"Then we're fucked."

My three helpers gulp at me, their eyes a little buggy.

"Not totally fucked, but we'd have to work the ground by hand. Everyone, grab a wagon. Let's get some gas and save ourselves a shit ton of work."

We roll east down our street. It's cloudy, so there's not much light from the moon and stars. I hope the northern lights don't come out from behind the clouds and put us under a spotlight.

"We need motor oil, too," I say, "so I'm thinking we should try that Valero station on William Cannon first. It's got a lube shop next door. There's a street across from the park that we can take through the abandoned neighborhood north of us—at least I hope it's abandoned."

I explain the other places we can try and how we'll go in a circle to end up at home.

As we turn into the abandoned neighborhood, I say, "No talking at all, okay? No coughing or loud breathing. When we get to a station, we may have to talk a little, but Jack told me how to get to the gas, so I'll point and give you directions without words."

From what I can see of the guys' faces, they look serious and determined to do this right. That's all I could ask of this ragtag group of kids.

***

AT THE VALERO STATION, IT takes us a while to figure out what we're doing. We're clumsy, and we have to break one of the storage-tank caps. Every tank is empty down to the dregs, except for the diesel. We manage to get three ten-gallon cans of that.

As long as we make it home with the diesel, we'll have one good working tiller, so that's a relief. But the lube shop next door is half-burned-down, and from the look of the blackened basement, it seems like the oil stored down there is what fueled the fire. What the hell is wrong with people to waste so much stuff that we need to survive? And who's doing all this burning? Those guys in camo or random berserkers? Kids that no one cares about anymore?

Silently, we head down William Cannon toward the Shell station at the corner of Menchaca, sticking to the shadows as much as we can.

The street used to be Manchaca, and everyone called it Man-Chack, which never made sense. But the city changed the name not long before the sun zapped us to match the historical spelling of some hero of the Texas Revolution, like it's a good idea to honor men who helped steal Texas from Mexico. But people around here are proud of that shit—at least white people are. Nana and almost every other adult kept on calling the street Man-Chack, which would be fine if they would spell it that way in the first place.

I'm thinking all this shit to keep my mind off the spine-chilling quiet. We haven't seen one other person, but my Spidey-Senses have me on alert that others are slinking around where we can't see them. They could be following us, so I guard the rear of our little wagon train, walking backward with my rifle in front of me. I don't see anyone.

Still, the hairs on the back of my neck will not settle down, like they're antennae picking up evil vibes and warning me to watch the fuck out.

I stop walking, and the other guys stop, too. I look at them with my finger to my lips, and we listen and scan our surroundings. But I don't hear or see a thing, and the others don't seem to, either. There's not even any wind to rustle the leaves, like the eerie calm before a storm. I shake my head, cringing, and we move on.

After walking another quarter-hour, give or take, we're finally close enough for me to see the Menchaca intersection with the binoculars, but there's no gas station. What the—?

I motion for Milo, Danny, and Max to put their heads close to me. "Sorry, I screwed up," I murmur. "The station I'm thinking of must be behind us a mile on South First. Too close to the camo guys to go there. Let's hit the stations on Menchaca and get closer to home."

We cut across a shopping-center parking lot where we've got the cover of two strips of looted shops, we come out on Menchaca, and we angle across it to a convenience store with gas pumps. We find the storage tanks behind the store, where the pavement butts up to a stretch of woods.

I motion to Milo to guard our backs while the rest of us open a tank of unleaded gas. The dipstick tells us the tank is half-full. Score! We insert the run of hose into the tank. Max gets to pumping while Danny and I fill every gas can and jug we've got, the three of us grinning.

We're loading gas cans into wagons while Max extracts the hose and lets gas drain into the last open can. Then Milo cocks his rifle. Shit!

We freeze and jerk our faces toward Milo, where he's aiming into the trees. A deer with a big rack of antlers takes off bounding through the woods.

"I can shoot it," Milo mutters, still aiming.

"Don't!" I say. "You'll call attention to us."

"I want some deer meat," Milo argues, moving the rifle to follow the deer.

"Milo, you can't!"

"Shouldn't y'all be quiet?" Max asks, all nervous, biting at his lip.

Milo sighs and lowers his gun. I watch the deer bound out of sight, my stomach knotting up. A deer that big could feed the whole neighborhood for days.

"We need a sound suppressor for your gun," I say, "then we could come get it another night. Let's get this gas home."

"Wait," Danny says, and he steps over to pop open the store's back door with the crowbar, as though he opens locked metal doors every day. He's a muscly little sucker, but not much of a thinker.

I motion that Danny and I will go in and that Max and Milo should stand guard, one on each end of the store's back side.

Crap, it's dark in here, like a windowless storeroom. I almost light a match, but I think better of it, since we've been handling gas, and I pull out my flashlight. A jumble of half-crushed boxes and papers is strewn across the floor. We rifle through the boxes, but they're empty. As my eyes adjust, I see shelves in the far corner—twelve-packs of Cokes that we've got no room for in the wagons. But I go to grab us each a Coke, and I half-trip on a box poking out from under the shelves. There's something heavy in that box. I rip it open and shine the flashlight inside. Motor oil, a whole case of quart bottles. I don't know if it's the right weight of oil, but I'm taking it.

Danny grabs for the Cokes and comes away with two twelve-packs.

"There's no room for that," I say, but he rushes out the door with the Cokes while I snatch up the box of oil.

I fill my rucksack with bottles of motor oil, and Danny wedges the Cokes into the tool wagon. The clouds above are thinning out, and stars are throwing more light on the ground. The northern lights are still behind the clouds, but they're turning the clouds green. We hurry to the other side of Menchaca, where there are more trees for cover, and we make our way toward home.

Up ahead, there's an open parking lot for a church. I slow down, looking for a safe way to cross the lot, and someone shouts, "Woo-hoo!" I raise my gun, arms trembling. Sounded like it came from behind the church.

"Be quiet, idiot!" some man barks.

We duck and creep backward into the bushes, pulling our wagons under cover with us. My heart's kicking me in the chest, and the other guys look like theirs are, too.

Feet are trampling through the gravelly church parking lot, and we're not breathing. Max has his eyes closed, and his lips are moving, like he's praying.

I lie flat on the ground so I can see beneath the branches in front of me. Three men on the move, loaded down with duffle bags. I hold up three fingers for my team to see. The men come out of the shadows, strapped with rifles, one carrying a pistol and darting his eyes around. They're all wearing camo, and those rifles have sound suppressors on them. Christ! If they come this way, we're toast.

The chubbiest man slides to a stop where the gravel driveway meets the street. "Man, who woulda thought a church would have so much food?" he says. The other two stop as well, and then the one with the pistol steps into the street, scanning it in both directions.

"They've got their Sunday brunches and Wednesday-night potlucks," another guy with a deep voice says. "Didn't you ever go to church?"

"You're kidding, right?"

"Shut up, both of you," says the guy with the pistol. He's got dark, greasy-looking hair, best I can see. "You're workin' my last nerve."

"Yes, sir," says the deep-voiced one. "Been a long time since we got so much in one haul."

"Look here what I got," says the chubby guy, and he pulls a big cross from inside his camo jacket. Is that real gold? Stealing a cross from a church? That's all kinds of wrong.

"Heathen." The leader with the pistol grins. "Let's get while the gettin' is good."

They trot away from us, heading south on Menchaca, and I release a breath, but quietly. They're on their way to Dittmar, the same street we have to go down to get home. If they're part of the camo guys we saw—And why wouldn't they be?—then Dittmar would be their quickest way home. We may have to wait them out.

"I shot the preacher," Chubby sings out, "but I didn't shoot the deputy."

The leader wheels around and points his pistol at Chubby's head. "I told you to shut up!"

Chubby freezes and throws up his hands. "Okay. Sorry."

The leader leans up in Chubby's face. "Just nod. Don't talk." And Chubby nods. The leader motions for Chubby to go ahead and then falls in behind, with the pistol only inches from Chubby's back.

That fucker's threatening his own guy.

I slip ahead and watch with the binoculars. When the camo men disappear over a rise past Dittmar, I come back to the wagons.

I whisper, "Think they shot the preacher?"

"Should we go look?" Milo mutters.

"If they shot him," I say, "they probably killed him. And if he's alive, what would we do with a preacher who's been shot?"

"Come on," Milo says, and he slides out from under the bushes. That kid has a keen sense of justice, keener than mine.

"Okay, but Danny and Max, stay here. Don't leave unless someone's coming for you."

"I wanna go with you," Danny says.

"No, man. Help Max guard the wagons."

Rifles up, Milo and I slip across the gravel lot, around to the back of the church. The door is wide open. Warily, I stick my head inside and almost choke on the stink of death. Oh fuck!

Milo shoots his flashlight beam into a hallway, and there's a corpse on the ground with its head bashed in. I whirl away, gagging. Milo starts to step inside.

"Wait. No," I sputter.

"I'm goin' to look for the preacher."

"That probably is the preacher. He's got a suit on. Can't see his collar, but he's been dead for a while."

Milo's staring down at the corpse. "There's worms on it."

"Maggots, man." I pull his arm, and we run.

I don't know how long it takes a corpse to rot that far, but if the men in camo killed him, they didn't do it tonight.

WE FINALLY GET HOME IN time to sleep a while before morning, not that I expect to sleep after that. We park the wagons full of gas in our garage. I bring a couple of Cokes inside for Alma, who meets me at the top of the stairs.

"You've been awake all night?" I ask while I hug her with relief.

"I half-slept until I heard you open the garage."

"Aww, baby." I search her face and try to pet the worry away. "Let's get you to bed." I'm waiting until morning to tell her about the looters in camo and the corpse. She needs to sleep.

"You brought me Cokes?" She grins a sleepy grin.

I just hope I don't stink like a corpse.

CHAPTER 12

The men in camo live three miles east of us, and now we've seen them a mile and a half to our northwest. They're hemming us in. It's so claustrophobic I want to scream.

It makes my brain go numb to think about these guys. It's a threat so potentially huge it could paralyze me if I dwell on it. Kind of like worrying about environmental collapse and nuclear war—you have to go on living in spite of it all.

I wish I knew if they killed the man in the church, but I'm sure they're not the only bad guys around. That corpse didn't keep the camo guys from robbing the church—cold-ass motherfuckers.

In the back of my mind, I never stop stewing about these guys, but by morning, I'm also obsessed with the problem in front of my face: Grandpa not letting us into the Mint.

Alma goes next door to make salsa for canning. Silas needs help harvesting lentils today, so I send Milo on over, and I go to the Mint to try another tactic on the old man.

I don't know how to expect him to act today. He's crouched in the Mint's garden, digging up potatoes with a sharp spade. If he's losing it, he could bludgeon me with that spade.

"Hi, Grandpa. How you doin'?"

Grandpa mutters, "I'm fine," but we both know he doesn't mean it.

I sit on the patio bench. While Grandpa digs potatoes, I talk to him about the tools and the ingredients for bread and for canning that are inside the Mint, and how they belong to the whole neighborhood, and we need a way for people to get them. Grandpa keeps his back to me but turns his head and twists his mouth.

"Why are you feeding so many goddamned people? It's wrong. And where's your little wife? I never saw her yesterday."

"Alma was exhausted. She wanted to come because she likes you, but I didn't want to wake her up."

My mom would call this a white lie. Alma's nice to Grandpa because she's nice to everyone, but she doesn't exactly like him. I figure it can't hurt to let him think people like him more than they do. I'm trying to butter up the old fart and get some cooperation out of him.

"Grandpa, while you were gone, we needed our neighbors to help guard the Mint so everything wouldn't get stolen by crazy people with guns, like those guys who did steal a bunch of it. And we needed the neighbors to help us farm. We couldn't grow everything we needed in one yard or even two. Plus, we were afraid that someone—if they saw us sneaking in at night to get the food, they would take it away from us.

"Nana had this brilliant idea to make a deal with the neighbors. She's already made the deal, and we have to stick by it—to trade them food for farming work, for building outhouses and rain-barrel systems."

"Bea gave away every goddamned thing and didn't think once about the rest of us," Grandpa says.

This makes me mad, sick mad. Nana thought about all of us every day of her life. But there's no point arguing with Grandpa about it. He's probably always gonna hate her, like my mom hated my dad forever after he left us.

"Nana didn't give everything away. She has stuff hidden in the Mint cellar for the family."

Grandpa drops his spade and whirls around, shooting to his feet to glare at me. "The Mint has a cellar?"

Damn. I guess no one told him about the cellar. But who can tell shit to an old jackass who doesn't listen?

"I gotta get to work, but what if I come back tonight after dinner? I'll show you how to get down to the cellar and all the cool stuff that's in it. I'll bring Alma, too. She's never been down there before. How does that sound?" I'm thinking if I do him a favor, he might make a deal. I also want to look for Nana's hidden water down there.

"Shit, I forgot about it," Grandpa says, "but that must be what they built in this yard when we all went to Big Bend years ago. Bea lied to me about that, too." He picks up the spade, frowning again, the craggy lines in his cheeks and forehead craggier than ever.

I sigh so loud that he looks at me funny.

"Grandpa, I get it that you're mad because Nana lied to you. That must be hard to take. But it's all in the past, and she said she's sorry, and it's real hard for her to talk, but she still said it. Plus, whatever way Nana made all this happen—the Mint and the food and seeds and tools and honeybees and the cellar— aren't you glad she did it? If she didn't, none of us would be alive."

Grandpa studies me with his arms folded in front of his skinny waist, not like he's mad at me so much, but like he's mad in general. I wish he would listen to me like he's listening to a grown man who makes sense. I don't feel much like a grown man, except I'm gonna be a dad, so I have to be one. And I'm tired to death of Grandpa being a dick. I want him to act like a grown-up for once.

He keeps studying me and not saying anything. I get up to go. "Can I send people over today for tools and stuff to can the food and make the bread? Please, can I?"

"Shit. Y'all don't care about me. Why should I care about what you all think you need?"

And now I can't help it. I'm pissed.

"Shit, Grandpa! How do you think you have water right now? Who grew the beans and veggies you had for dinner? And who planted that garden you're digging potatoes out of? Not you, that's for sure. Why should we feed you if you're gonna be a dick?"

Grandpa rears back like he might try to hit me, so I leave, glaring back at him like if he pushes me, I might hit him. I won't, but I want him to think I will.

We won't be getting any flour today. Now I don't know if I should show Grandpa the damned cellar or not. He'll probably find a way to screw that up, too.

Weeks ago, Silas pushed his cars to the street so we could store different kinds of beans in his garage. We can do that with more garages and starve Grandpa out, force him to cooperate, if it comes to that.

"Jack!" I holler when I make a side-trip to his house on my way to Silas's.

"What? Who's yelling?"

I run into Jack's backyard that's filled with pinto beans growing up poles. Old Mr. Bellows is there with Max and Greta, the only single woman in the neighborhood except for Mom.

"Jack, do you have any flour left? Can you make biscuits for dinner? Grandpa's still being a dick, and we're almost out of flour, and Alma's busy making salsa for canning, so I don't know what we'll eat."

Jack stands up from behind a row of pinto beans. "Don't worry. I already have a big pot of these pinto beans cooking."

"Cool. Maybe Alma will bring salsa home."

"We can hope," Jack says, and he goes back to work. I'm just glad as hell that most people here are a thousand times nicer than Grandpa.

LATE THIS DECEMBER AFTERNOON, IT'S already getting dark. I feel like I haven't worked long enough yet, but it's hard to see. We got about half the lentils harvested and piled up in Silas's garage, still in their pods inside a pen he built out of worn-out plywood.

Alma brings lots of salsa home. I scrounge a couple of straggler tomatoes and a little head of lettuce out of our garden so we can have a touch of salad with our beans and biscuits. These biscuits of Jack's are so damned good, I could eat a ton of them, and I might before dinner's over.

Once I've eaten enough to calm my growling stomach, I want to ask my family whether I should show Grandpa the cellar after our crazy meeting. I'm just getting started with my story, still taking bites of food.

"Keno!" Grandpa hollers from the Mint's backyard.

"What now?" I give Alma my please-save-me face while I jump up from the table and go out the back door.

"What?" I yell to Grandpa. "I'm eating!"

"Stop eating and get over here."

Shit. "Why? I'm hungry."

"Because I said so!" Grandpa shouts, as if doing what he says is ever a good idea.

"Give me a minute. You're not on fire, are you? Because you're acting like you are."

"No, but hurry, for God's sake!"

I have a string of cuss words in my head so long that I can't think them all fast enough before I'm back in the house, shoveling the last beans out of my bowl, sticking a biscuit between my teeth, and pulling on my hoodie.

"What does he want?" Uncle Eddie asks.

I yank the biscuit out of my mouth. "No clue. He wants me to hurry because he said so."

"I'm going, too." Milo is protective of me. He already has one hoodie on, but it's freaking cold out, so he puts on another one.

"Uncle Eddie," I say, "after you eat, maybe you'd better help Silas get the rest of the lentils in. It's cold enough that it might freeze. I'll come help after I see what Dickhead wants." We just call Grandpa Dickhead now, and everyone knows who we're talking about.

"Shit. I guess it *could* freeze," Eddie says. "I'll go over to Silas's in a minute."

"I better get back to the pinto beans," Jack says.

"I'll come with you, Jack," Phil says.

"I'll watch Nana," Mazie says.

Everyone's wolfing down the rest of their dinners. Nana's face is crumpled and her eyes are darting around, like we're confusing her with all this activity. I don't have time to explain it to her, and it's wrong not to explain what's going on to Nana.

"Mazie, will you tell Nana what's up?"

Mazie nods with her mouth full.

"I'll clean up dinner, then go to Silas's," Alma says. I whirl around with my eyes all big, trying to ask her silently if that's a good idea, being pregnant and picking lentils in the freezing cold night. She smiles and nods toward the back door for me to go on. I make my eyes wider for a quick second to let her know I'm not sure about this.

"Bring lanterns," I say to the table. We don't have much kerosene left, but we'll need the lanterns to harvest at night even if the moon is full because of shadows from the houses and cedar fences. I grin and swivel around to face my family. "Wish me luck! Let's go, Milo."

"You're gonna need some luck," Eddie says.

CHAPTER 13

The steel door to the Mint's garage is wide open, and wind's whipping around inside. We have to lift garage doors by hand now—no electric openers. I didn't think Grandpa would be strong enough to lift this big-ass door to the three-car garage, but he probably lifted it when he was pissed off, like he is again now, because who knows why.

"Goddamn lock!" Grandpa's saying. He's got bolt cutters, trying to snap a lock off a door in the back of the garage. I never noticed that door with a lock before. Too much stuff must have been stacked in front of it until we ate most of the food that was stored in here. Plus, the woodstoves, rototillers, and lots of tools are out in the neighborhood, helping to keep everyone alive.

"What do you want, Grandpa? We need to finish harvesting. It might freeze tonight."

Milo and I stand under the rolled-up garage door, staring past tools, wagons, and bulk food barrels in the shadows to where Grandpa's crouched with a flashlight and fuming. He's ignoring us.

"Can't you do that in the daytime so you don't waste batteries?"

"Hell no, I can't," he barks. "Get over here and help me!"

"Why are you trying to break that lock? Did you even *try* to find the key? I bet you didn't."

"I need to get into this cellar to see what's in there."

"That's not the cellar!" Milo shouts.

Grandpa drops the bolt cutters, and they bounce and hit him in the shin. He hardly notices. "Where's the cellar then, and what the hell's in here?"

"Don't know what's in there," I say. "Never saw that door with the lock before."

"Me neither," Milo says. "The cellar door's in the pantry."

"I didn't see it in there," Grandpa says, like Milo's lying.

"You probably never go in the pantry," I say. "How would you see it?"

Grandpa stares at me with his face all balled up. Finally, he says, "I need to know what's behind this door. I don't like having shit in my house that I don't know is there."

It's Nana's house, not yours is what I want to say, but I don't.

I pick up the bolt cutters, but Grandpa's frozen in front of the door. "Move over," I say. "Let me try." I squeeze between him and the door. I don't have time for this shit.

My mind's racing so fast, thinking about freezes and lentils and pinto beans and Alma being pregnant, working in the cold in the dark. I feel like throwing down the bolt cutters, breaking them to shit, and hurrying to help Alma, leaving Grandpa to deal with his crap on his own. He's creating a bogus emergency in the middle of a real one, and I kind of hate him for it. I figure I'll open the damned door and leave him with it.

I snap the lock off the hasp like it's nothing, and it falls. I flick the hasp, and Milo yanks the mystery door open. Grandpa crowds me out, trying to see inside. He shoots the flashlight beam through the doorway into a closet with a high ceiling. There's something big and shiny inside.

"What is that?" I ask, forgetting that I was gonna leave. This is some kind of important-looking thing. Something with a long red handle shooting out near the top.

Grandpa jostles Milo against the doorjamb and jumps into the closet, shining his dim flashlight around this big thing.

"It's a pump! A big goddamned hand pump sticking out of the concrete!" Grandpa's all out of breath, and I'm getting that way myself. So is Milo.

"What the fuck does it pump?" Milo asks, and Grandpa shoots him the evil eye.

"Don't know. Could be gasoline or kerosene." Then, for once, Grandpa wants to know what I think. "Should we pump it?" His voice is suddenly quiet, as though he's in awe or afraid.

"I don't know." I lick my cracked lips and run my hands backward through my dirty hair until my fingers get tangled in hair knots. I'm kind of mind-blown, imagining that it could be fuel under that pump and all the shit we could do with more fuel.

"It could explode!" Milo hollers, which causes Uncle Tom to rush into the garage from the house.

"What're y'all doing?" Tom shouts. He's half out of breath, too. "You scared me."

"Come look," I say. Tom crowds up behind Grandpa and lets out a whistle that hurts my ears. So, of course, Aunt Jeri and Mom rush into the garage, asking a stream of questions that I can't listen to or answer.

Because Grandpa's saying, "Get a bucket, and let's see what's in here." Now that's the kind of thing I'd like to see Grandpa do, think of practical shit like buckets when you're about to pump a big handle and don't know what will come out.

"Great idea, a bucket." I run to the other end of the garage to grab a metal bucket out of a stack. The wind's all blowing, making it freaking cold in here. I want to shut the garage door, but it will be dark if I block the moonlight. I don't have time, anyway, because of Alma and lentils that are about to freeze.

"Hurry up, boy!" Grandpa yells.

I want to yell something smart-alecky, but I figure he's just excited, like we all are.

"I'm coming!" I run back with the bucket and thrust it at Tom.

"Milo, you hold the bucket," Uncle Tom says to his son, making Milo more excited.

This is the most thrilling thing that's happened in a long time, except for Alma being pregnant, and the rest of them don't know about that yet.

"Hank, get back and let me pump it," Tom says. Grandpa scowls, or maybe that's how his face looks all the time after scowling for years. He steps out of the closet, Tom goes in, and we crowd around.

Grandpa shakes the flashlight, which is about to go out any second, and those may be the last batteries we have for it. But this shit is important. He shines what light is left on Tom and the pump handle, and then he steps back and leans against me so the light can fill the whole closet. His heart is pounding, making my heart pound faster, too. I put my hand on his shoulder. He takes a sighing breath.

Uncle Tom pushes the red handle up in the air. It goes almost to the ceiling. He's about to push the handle down when Grandpa hollers, "Wait! We might need to prime it."

"Maybe," Tom says, "but how do we know what to prime it with?" He examines the pump on its top and sides. "I don't see a place to prime it. Do you, Hank?"

I don't know what they're talking about with priming. It seems like I've heard of it, but—

"No," Grandpa says, so quiet I can hardly hear him even though he's leaning against me.

Uncle Tom and Grandpa scratch their chins and muss their already fucked-up hair. "Guess I'll pump it and see what happens," Tom says.

"It might take a while," Grandpa says, and Tom pushes the handle down hard and fast. Nothing happens.

"It might take a while. I told you."

"We get it, Hank. Hold your horses."

Tom starts pumping harder and faster, getting into a rhythm, up and down, up and down. We're all making noises in our throats and fidgeting around. Grandpa hunches forward to see better, shaking the flashlight. I sort of miss him leaning on me, making peace by touching without words.

Pumping, pumping, up and down, up and down. Uncle Tom's getting red in the face, and I'm starting to think, shit, maybe there's nothing in it.

But Milo says, "I hear something." He's crouched down holding the bucket, and he crams his ear against the body of the pump. "It's gurgling!" he shouts.

"Gurgling," we repeat, hoping that whatever's gurgling is good.

Tom rubs his hands on his pants and starts pumping again, getting the handle going so fast I wonder if it would keep pumping without him.

"Still gurgling," Milo reports.

"Come on already," Aunt Jeri says. She just has to say something. But she doesn't sound bitchy. She sounds like a little kid.

"It's louder!" Milo hollers, and I hear it now, too. Holy shit, come on already, I think.

Loud gurgling and sputtering, and out from the spout comes a giant splash of something clear and wet. Uncle Tom stops. We hold our breaths while he and Milo fall to their knees, running their hands through whatever came out of the pump. They sniff their hands. Then Milo sticks his hand in the wet stuff again and licks it.

"Don't, Milo!" I shout, but he jumps up and starts dancing around.

"It's water! It's freaking water!"

Oh my God, no one can believe that it's water. We crowd up to put our hands in the wet stuff and touch it and smell it ourselves. Liquid runs out of the closet and onto the garage floor.

Tom tastes his fingers and hollers, "It *is* water! It really is!" I finally get enough on my fingers to taste it. From smelling my fingers, I already know it's water, but I have to taste it, and when I do, I drop to the floor on my butt.

Nana, you're brilliant! You did hide water, under the ground. How did you think of that?

I don't know how much water it is, but with the pump so big, I'm guessing it's a lot. And even if it's not much, it's still water, crazy-beautiful water, and we can live longer and maybe there'll be enough for Alma and the baby to stay alive and keep making me happy. I start crying after being so long without enough water, with yellow pee that burns me and dry-ass throats and the grass all dead like Tasha.

I think about Native Americans protesting oil pipelines that were poisoning their water, and how Nana gave them money when they said the smartest thing anyone ever said in the history of the world:

"Water is life."

Freaking sad-ass, beautiful life. I can't believe it, and I can't stop crying.

Everyone's crying and hugging each other. Even Jeri's hugging people. Grandpa goes over and leans on the tool bench, I think because he's worn out from excitement. I get up and hug people, too, but I'm remembering Alma and the lentils and the freeze. I realize how cold I am in this garage after sitting on the cement floor. Aunt Jeri hugs me. Mom dances me around a little, and then—

Grandpa hollers, real pissed-off, "I'm not sharing this water with anyone but this family!" He's got a pistol in his hand that he must've stashed somewhere.

We fall still, stop breathing, staring at Grandpa, my heart thumping in my throat.

I can't stop myself, and I don't even try. I yell as loud as I can yell.

"Fuck, Grandpa! This is *not* your goddamned water! It's Nana's. It's ours. And we're sharing it if I have to lock you in the cellar for the rest of your life. Give me the fricking gun!"

"I won't!" he screams, all red in the face.

This is so fucking wrong! I'm thinking of tackling his ass even if it breaks every brittle bone in his body. I don't even care if it kills him. He's a menace to the whole world.

Everyone can see what I'm thinking of doing. Milo's about to launch himself at Grandpa whether anyone helps him or not. That would be a fairer fight for Grandpa, but Milo might get shot, and I can't let that happen. Milo saved me from getting shot. I love Milo and I can't grab hold of my runaway mind.

Uncle Tom rushes up and grabs me. He's the strongest one to stop me. Mom grabs Milo even though he's stronger than she is, but she has to stop him somehow. She thinks he won't hit her, but I'm not sure he won't. Jeri starts screaming, "All of you, stop it!"

No one listens to her.

And Grandpa waves the gun at us. "Get back! Get the hell back!"

Oh my God, he might really shoot us.

"I hate you for this, Grandpa. I fucking hate you! Pointing a gun at your family? Milo's just a kid, for Christ's sake. Put down the gun! I will kill you before I let you shoot it!"

"I'm not a fucking kid!" Milo screeches, and he's not, but who cares? Milo cares, that's who cares, even with a gun pointed at him by his grandfather. Milo's hysterical—we all are—and I'm about to puke, but I can't. Grandpa might start shooting.

"Fuck!" I yell at the top of my lungs.

Tom shoves me backward toward the open garage door. Mom's pulling on Milo in the same direction, but Milo's not moving. Then Jeri grabs Milo's other arm and starts tugging him, too. Grandpa's waving the gun around, not knowing where to point it.

Tom has me almost to the garage door going backward when that big bear of a man Bobby Carlisle runs up the driveway with his Kalashnikov aimed into the garage.

"The hell are you people doing? Keno?"

Bobby steps sideways to look deeper inside, where Mom and Aunt Jeri are tugging on Milo and Milo's wailing and pulling them back. Then Bobby sees Grandpa with the gun.

Bobby aims his rifle at Grandpa so fast I don't know how he does it.

"Hank! Put the gun down! *Now!*"

From the look he gives Bobby, I think Grandpa won't do it, that he might try to shoot Bobby and Bobby will kill him and it will almost be a relief, except it won't be.

"Down, Hank! Right the fuck now! I swear to God I'll shoot you dead!"

I don't know if Bobby's a Marine, but he sounds like one. He looks like one. Even Grandpa can see it. He raises his hands all meek-like and holds out the gun. Tom jumps forward to take it before Grandpa changes his cracked, crazy motherfucking mind.

"Goddamn it!" I cry. Tom and Bobby tie Grandpa's hands behind his back with rope. "Let's put the old fuck in the goddamn cellar."

"What cellar?" Uncle Tom, Mom, and Jeri all ask.

"Yeah, what cellar?" Bobby asks. And I realize that Bobby doesn't know about the cellar even though he's been here since the sun zapped us. Almost no one has cellars around here, with the shallow soil and the high water table. Nana didn't tell any neighbors about her cellar except Jack, who wouldn't tell, Sonja, who's in Mexico, and Darla Belding, who's dead now.

"I'll show you." I should be keeping the cellar a secret from Bobby, but I've already blown that. "Don't tell anyone about the cellar, okay?" Bobby raises his eyebrows and nods.

"You can't put Dad in a cellar!" Aunt Jeri's crying, tugging on people's arms. "You can't!"

I rush into the house, heading toward the pantry. Why the hell didn't someone who lives here notice the big wheel in the pantry that opens the wall to the cellar stairs? I guess they didn't have food to put in the pantry since they could put stuff in the empty fridge like a cabinet and maybe feel better, like in the backs of their minds, the fridge is still a fridge.

Everyone follows me, with Jeri bitching all the way. Tom and Bobby are in the rear, pulling Grandpa so fast that his feet aren't touching the floor. I grab the key from a high pantry shelf and unlock the cellar door, then turn the big wheel in the pantry wall. Milo helps me turn it faster until the wall opens to a big hole of darkness. I fumble around inside the blackness until I find the wind-up flashlight that Nana keeps there, so people can see to get down the cement stairs to where the candles and lanterns are.

"I'll wind it," Milo says, and he grabs for the flashlight, but I yank it back from him.

"No, you won't. You break wind-up shit."

"Shit, it was only o-o-n-n-c-c-e!"

"That's one time too many." I get the light wound up and switch it on. People ooh and aah when I shine the flashlight down the steep stairs. They've probably never seen a wind-up flashlight and the amazing bright light it makes, like a head-light. Plus, the cellar is huge and nice inside.

"I'm not going in that hole in the ground!" Grandpa screeches.

I step up into his face. "Shut up or I'll put a gag in your mouth. I swear to fucking God I will!"

"Don't say 'fucking God!'" Aunt Jeri yells.

I whirl around to her. "Really? You're gonna scold me for cussing when Grandpa just tried to kill us? That's what's important to you right now—cuss words?" I turn to face the others. "Wait here. I'll get some light going."

Jeri's squealing like a stuck pig, Mom's covering her ears, and Grandpa's growling, but they're not saying shit.

I go down into the cellar, which stinks like something rotten, probably a dead rat. I find kitchen matches, and I light three candles. I don't want Grandpa having fuel from a lantern anywhere near him. I don't like him having candles and matches either, but I can't torture him by putting him in a dungeon with no light. Then I see the guns Nana stored down here.

"Milo, Mom," I holler up the stairs, "come help me carry shit out of here so Grandpa can't hurt someone with it."

Milo rushes down with Mom right behind him. I load them up with guns, ammo, and lanterns. I look around for other shit that might be dangerous. I snatch up a tool box, pull out the whole damned silverware drawer, and I carry it all up the stairs.

"You can take him down now," I say to Uncle Tom and Bobby. "You'll have to watch him. I can't leave him down there with no light, so he'll have matches. He could burn the house down. Plus, there's probably other dangerous shit down there that I don't know about and didn't find."

"Shit. Maybe I'll stay down there with him tonight," Tom says.

"I guess untie him at some point so he can go to the bathroom—unless he starts acting crazy again."

"How's he gonna go to the bathroom?" Tom asks. "Is there a thunder jug?"

"A what?"

"You know. A pot to pee and poop in."

"That's a gross name for it," I say. "There's a composting toilet."

"Really? Underground? And it works and everything?"

"Sure, it works. Nana was freaking brilliant to get this stuff built."

"True that," Uncle Tom says, like he's suddenly a teenager from the past.

"Thanks, Tom. And thank you, Bobby, for saving us from this lunatic."

Tom starts dragging Grandpa down the stairs.

"Bobby, Mom, we're harvesting pinto beans and lentils tonight. We're afraid it's gonna freeze. Can you guys help us?" I don't even ask Aunt Jeri to help.

"I'll get my coat." Mom darts away.

"Shit, a freeze? Sure, I'll help," Bobby says. "Let me go home and get my jacket and tell Melba. Should I get anyone else?"

"Sure. Get everyone who's not patrolling or watching kids. Jack probably needs the most help. Pinto beans—we need as many as we can get."

"You got that right." Bobby rushes out the front door, taking his Kalashnikov with him.

"Good freaking night!" I call down the cellar stairs. "And Tom, you better hide these guns we brought up before you let Grandpa out of there."

Mom comes back wearing a coat. I grab two lanterns from the pile of stuff we just carried up.

"Erin, you can't go out in this cold!" Jeri cries, like she didn't just witness us talking about harvesting before a damned freeze. "Milo can't go. I won't let him!"

"Shut up, Aunt Jeri. I've had enough of your bitching. Bitch again and I will gag your ass!"

"Well!" she says.

"Don't. Say. Another. Fucking. Word."

Mom shakes her head at me. So, I got mad? Who wouldn't?

Jeri makes a loud *humph* sound, and I run out the door. I'm in the biggest hurry I've ever been in, except when Tasha was bleeding to death in my arms.

CHAPTER 14

Outside on the sidewalk, I stop for a second to think. "Mom, let me check on Mazie and Nana, and I'll be right there." I send one lantern with Milo to Jack's and the other with Mom to Silas's. I'm hoping I can work close to Mom. It would be so nice after this... whatever it was.

I go in the back door at home, and Mazie jumps up from playing Barbie dolls by candlelight at the table. She grabs my hand and pulls me around the kitchen counter, saying, "Shh... Nana's asleep." We get into the old laundry room, and she pulls the door to. "What happened?" she asks. "I heard lots of yelling. Grandpa, you, a bunch of people."

I hug her. She must have been scared here alone in the almost-dark, with the screaming at the Mint and Nana asleep. I hold her away from me to barely see her eyes.

"It's a long story, Tater Tot, but everything's good now. I have to hurry and go harvest food before it freezes. Something great happened, too, in spite of the yelling. It can be a surprise for you. I came to check on you and Nana before I go to Silas's. Is everything all right?"

"Nana had a bad night," Mazie says, and my heart jolts. I think she might cry, which just kills me.

"Nana? What happened? Where is she?"

"Asleep on the couch. I made her a bed with lots of pillows and blankets. I took your pillow and Alma's and Milo's."

"That's great. You take good care of Nana. I'm proud of you."

"But Nana wouldn't stop crying."

"Crying?" That's not like Nana. "Do you know why?"

"She was confused. She didn't know where y'all went. I don't think she knew me." Mazie plops down on the floor and starts bawling.

God, that would be horrible for Mazie. She loves Nana so much, probably more than she loves her own mom. And why was Nana so confused she was crying?

I bend down to hug Mazie. Shit, I need to hurry, but how can I now?

"Mazie, I'm going to check on Nana. Be right back. You did a great job."

I'm dreading checking Nana, and when I see her, she looks so tiny and pale. I don't think she's breathing right, either. Stuttering breaths, I guess that's what you call them. Then no breaths for what seems too long, and then more stutters and coughs. God, Nana. Don't die on me. Not now!

I rush back toward Mazie, but stop and try to act calm before I get to her.

"Mazie, come on back to the dining room, where the candles are. I'm gonna get my mom and your mom to stay with you and Nana, all right?"

"My mom won't come over here," Mazie says.

"She might. She won't want you to be alone when Nana had a hard night."

"Doesn't seem like she'd care."

God, I can't believe poor Mazie has to think like that about her own mother. Problem is: Jeri probably doesn't care.

"It might take a few minutes to get them over here," I say. "Will you be okay until they get back?"

"Yeah," she says, but she doesn't sound sure.

"Why don't you sing songs to make you feel better?" Mazie loves to sing.

"It'll wake Nana up."

I'm wondering if Nana will ever wake up again.

"You won't wake her up if you sing all quiet-like."

"Okay." This little girl is so freaking brave. I never saw anyone braver.

I hug Mazie and kiss her cheek, and I hurry out the door to get Mom. Suddenly, it seems like I'm in charge of taking care of everyone in this family. I'm not even sure I should get Aunt Jeri, now that I think about it. She'll just make shit harder for Mom and Mazie—Nana, too.

"Mom? Where's Mom?" I call out when I zip into Silas's backyard.

"Over here," Mom says from the first row of lentils.

Alma pops her head up from a row farther back.

"I'll be back there in a few minutes, Alma. I love you."

"Love you, too." She stands there watching me. I want to run to Alma, but I have to do this first. I rush down the row to Mom and whisper to her.

"Mom, something's wrong with Nana. Can you go sit with her and Mazie?'

"What's wrong?" my mother asks, all panicky. I take her arm and walk her toward Nana's house. We stop in the middle of the street while I explain. Mom puts her hand to her mouth. Her eyes are shocked and full of tears that just hang there and don't fall out.

"What should I do for Mom?" my mother asks me, like I would know. *I'm only eighteen* is what I feel like saying.

"Maybe watch her? Be sure she keeps breathing. Maybe wake her up at some point to see how she acts? And be sure Mazie's all right. She got scared when Nana was crying and everyone was screaming at the Mint. I'd come with you, but I need to help with the lentils. Do you want me to get Aunt Jeri?"

"Shit, no," Mom says.

"Okay, well, please tell Mazie that her mom was sleeping. I told Mazie I was going to get Jeri, and Mazie said, 'Doesn't seem like she'd care.'"

Mom gasps. "That poor little girl. I don't know what's wrong with Jeri. She used to be so good with her kids. But I've got to move out of there. Jeri and Dad are driving me nuts."

"We'll move you out then. But tonight, please go take care of Nana. And thank you."

"What about Jack?" Mom asks.

"Oh shit. I forgot about Jack. My brain's all screwy."

"No wonder, after that shit with your grandpa."

"Go on over. I'll get Jack."

Mom trots away.

How can I tell Jack about Nana? She seemed fine when we left her earlier. Wait, no, she was confused. She hasn't been confused since she got over her stroke. If she had another one, what could we do for her? Nana, please do not die on me. I need you more than ever right now. Maybe she'll be better after she sleeps.

"Jack? Jack?" I holler when I get to his backyard. There are people all over back here, and I'm relieved about that. But I don't see Jack. "Where's Jack?" I ask Phil.

"He went inside to get stuff to make tea. Why? What's wrong?"

I figure, why worry Phil when he's got so much to do?

"Long story. Right now, I need Jack." I rush into Jack's house through his back door.

"Keno! You scared me. What's up?" Jack's got a tea kettle, a strainer, and a bundle of herbs in his hands. The circles around his eyes are darker than usual, and I hate having to tell him this.

"It's Nana."

Jack drops his armful of stuff to the counter. "What about her?" He drills his eyes straight through me.

"She's, uh, well, Mazie said Nana was confused tonight and kept crying. And Mazie doesn't think Nana knew her."

It's hard to see in here. There's only one candle, but I see the alarm in Jack's eyes. He's already halfway out the door, waiting for me to finish. I try to hurry up.

"Nana's asleep on the couch, but I don't like the way she's breathing."

"Why? How's she breathing?"

"Kind of raggedy. Stuttering some. Then pauses where she doesn't seem like she's breathing at all, then more stuttering breaths."

"Sweet Jesus," Jack says. "Can you tell them where I went?" He nods toward the pinto beans. "I'll get June and Charlotte on the way."

Damn, why didn't I think of the nurses? I should've got them first.

"Sure, Jack. Go. My mom's there, too. I got this."

Jack rushes away stiffly, as though he's in pain. I pinch myself between the eyes and realize my hands are shaking. Shit.

"Hey," I call out when I'm back in Jack's yard. "Jack went to see about Nana. Do y'all need anything before I go help Silas with the lentils?"

Bobby pops his head up, and so does Greta a couple of rows behind him.

"Is your nana all right?" Bobby asks.

"She just needed Jack." No use panicking everyone. Something happening to Nana will be rough on this whole group. When she had the stroke, I didn't know if the neighborhood would hold together without her. Nana was the only person with the right mix of grit and tact to keep us from busting apart.

"I hope she's okay," Bobby says. "This has been a bad night for you."

"Why? What was bad about it?" Greta asks.

"Personal shit," Bobby says.

"What kind of personal shit?"

Come on, Greta. Cool it.

"Well, that would be personal, wouldn't it?"

Man, I love Bobby for saying that. Greta smirks.

"I'll make the tea," Phil says.

I reach down into Jack's woodpile and throw another log on the fire in the grill. "Y'all can warm up while you drink your tea. Think you'll finish with the pinto beans?"

"We might," Bobby says.

"'Kay. I'll be at Silas's if you need anything." I rush away.

I want to check on Nana, but someone will come get me if they need me. And I have got to convince Alma to go to bed.

Harvey and Mark pass by on patrol, all intent on looking for danger. They nod at me, not saying anything, and keep marching down the road. We're so damned vulnerable here. We need to do something about it. Just the anxiety of it could shorten our lives.

When I finally get back to Alma, she says, "I'm staying, Keno. No use trying to talk me out of it."

So I grab a bucket and work beside her, having her sit on my bucket to pick the low stuff while I pick the high stuff. We both throw lentils into her bucket, and I run back and forth to Silas's garage to dump lentil pods into the pen. I help Alma all night, whispering the whole story of what happened in a messed-up way, all out of order.

Alma clucks her tongue, and she gets teary about Nana. She's sighing and soaking up this bullshit. I worry if I should be putting all this stress on her and the baby. I mean, I've got a knot in my stomach that hurts, like a lot.

At dawn, when all the lentils and pinto beans are picked except whatever we missed in the dark, snow starts to fall. We almost never have snow in Austin, and we didn't know this was coming. No weather forecasts. At least the snow should be good for the dry ground, and when it melts off the rooftops, some of it will run into our rain barrels.

Alma whispers, "So Grandpa's locked in the cellar, Uncle Tom's with him, and something's wrong with Nana. Keno, this is bad."

"Yes, it is." I hang my head. I'm about to drop to the ground from exhaustion.

"How long are you gonna keep Grandpa in the cellar?" Alma asks me.

"Fuck if I know."

CHAPTER 15

Alma and I sit on the curb and make out beneath the falling snow in front of God and everybody. We don't care who sees us. I figure people need to see some love in this place. They might not remember what love looks like.

We're trying to drum up courage to go to see Nana.

I hope someone scoured our perimeter this morning. I'm too tired to move.

At last, we go inside, clutching hands. The only noise is coming from Eddie at the patio grill, making breakfast. Jack and Mazie are sitting in chairs they've pulled in front of Nana on the couch. I'm not liking the sad looks on their faces one bit. I stop in the entry and press my face against Alma's. She pets me and squeezes me; she knows what I need.

We walk slowly into the living room and stand behind Jack and Mazie, looking down at Nana, still sleeping with her stuttering breaths, only slower now. That can't be good.

Jack half-glances back at us, and I pat him on the shoulder, leaving my hand there. It seems like a stupid question, but I have to ask. "How is she?"

Jack looks me in the eye and shakes his head very slightly.

"Oh." There's nothing else to say.

Alma asks, "Did you try to wake her up?"

Jack mutters, "Yes," and shakes his head that way again.

Nana looks like an angel right now. I wonder if angels are coaxing her to go with them, if angels even exist. Nana would never leave on purpose, but her body won't cooperate with her. She seems at peace, though, so that's something to hold on to.

When I look up, Mazie's watching us with her face puckered. I pick her up and clutch her to me. This is how we'll have to get through this: by clinging to each other. We're too sad to even cry.

Alma takes Mazie and loves her up. "Did you get any sleep, honey? What do you need?" Mazie shakes her head to everything. No words, no sleep, just sadness.

Alma stands Mazie on the floor. Even though Mazie's skinny, she's seven and getting tall now and heavy, and she's not that much shorter than Alma.

"Go wash up, sweetie, so we can eat," Alma says, and I'm marveling at what a good mother she already is. "Jack, want some breakfast?" she asks.

"Nah, but thanks."

I want to convince him to eat, but I know he can't. If Alma ever dies on me, I'll probably never eat again. I'd want to die, too, like Jack probably does. Like I kind of do.

AFTER BREAKFAST, UNCLE EDDIE CONVINCES Jack to nap in the recliner.

"Don't you need to sleep, Eddie?" Alma asks.

"I'll sleep in this easy chair with one eye open and glued to Mom."

I want to ask how he can do that, but parents say they do it, and I believe them. Being responsible for someone else's fragile life might give you extra psychic powers, but my brain is babbling.

Upstairs, Alma and I take off our hoodies and fall into bed with our clothes on. I get a good glimpse of her chest before she pulls down her shirt, and I want to bury myself in her breasts.

But it's freezing up here, even with the fire downstairs, and by the time we get enough covers over us to warm up, I'm too tired and weighted down with blankets to make love to Alma. I never thought that would happen, but here it is.

"KENO?" MOM'S WHISPERING FROM UP above my face. I think I'm home and she's waking me and Tasha up for school.

I growl. I don't wanna get up for school. I just fell asleep.

"Honey, I'm sorry to wake you, but you'd better come down."

My heart thumps, and I sit up but can't think. "What? Why?"

"It's Mom. Nana."

That's a slap in the face to shock the sleepiness right out of me.

"Why?" I ask again, even though I know why. I'm trying to avoid knowing it a few seconds longer.

"Sweetheart, Nana's going." She smooths down my bed hair. It feels so good to have Mom take care of me, but I hate the reason she's doing it.

"What time is it?"

"Noon? One? Two? I don't know. It's snowing."

"Should I get Alma?" I can't think what to do.

"Yes, but hurry." Mom pauses for a second, studying me, and she stands up. "We need to tell Nana goodbye." Mom ducks out the door, as though she's too sad to keep looking at me after saying that.

"Alma?" I jostle her shoulder. I hate waking her up when she needs sleep so bad, but she'll be sad forever if she misses her chance to tell Nana goodbye. She's like Alma's grand-mother, too. "Alma, I love you. Please wake up."

"Keno?" she mumbles, but she breathes like she's still sleeping.

"Mom says we need to go down to see Nana right now." I give Alma a second to digest that, and then I half-whisper, "I think Nana's about to die."

"What?" Alma shoots up in bed, clutching the blanket to her chest like she's naked except she's not. She needs to clutch something. "I didn't… I mean, I thought… I didn't think it would be this fast."

"Me neither. We better just grab our hoodies and go."

"What about shoes? Do we need shoes?" She can't think what to do, either.

"No shoes now. I'll get 'em later."

She hugs me fast, we throw on our hoodies, and we go. We stop for a second at the top of the stairs, giving each other scared looks. I put my arm around her, and we go down slowly. Alma is trembling, and I think I am, too, but I don't even know.

Everyone else is in the living room. My breath catches at the sight of Nana. She looks smaller, paler, less… um… less substantial.

Jack and Uncle Eddie have hold of Nana's hands, watching her breathe, breathing with her as though they're helping her. Milo's got his arms around Mazie, protecting his little sister and making me proud of him. Mom is at the end of the couch by Nana's feet, gently rubbing her legs through the sheet, breathing with her, too. Alma buries her face in my side, and I stroke her head. Phil's standing by the fireplace, sadly watching over Eddie.

Uncle Tom's clutching Aunt Jeri, and she's crying. Not that I want to see anyone sad, but I'm glad Jeri can let herself cry over losing her mother. I didn't know if she cared about Nana anymore.

Out the back-door window, the yard is covered in snow, about half a foot of it. The sunlight's muted behind the clouds, and everything looks soft, as though the world is covered in a blanket.

Neighbors are out there, standing and sitting, hardly talking, giving us privacy and showing their respects. Nana saved all of us, and they love her, too. Doris Barnes is silently praying. She's the only one I know of in the neighborhood who seriously prays.

I turn back to face my grandmother with her papery-thin skin. She takes a slow breath and then nothing. I hold my breath and count in my head. It's six seconds before she takes another one. I breathe with her, too. Eddie stands and steps back so Alma and I can take his place, but my feet are stuck to the floor.

I can't tell Nana goodbye! I told Tasha goodbye when she was dying, and that was enough for one lifetime. Life shouldn't be so hard! I'm cursing God in my head, but I stop. It's disrespectful to curse God even in your head when someone's dying.

I try to think of anything besides telling Nana goodbye. Alma nudges me forward, so I finally step up and help her sit in the chair. She takes Nana's hand and kisses it. She doesn't hesitate; that's how natural it is for Alma to be loving, even in the face of death. She leans out to put her lips next to Nana's ear.

"*Vaya usted en paz, mi abuela,*" Alma says. She strokes Nana's forehead and kisses her there, petting her hand. Then Alma sits back and looks at me, trembling, with tears on her face. I lay my forehead on hers.

"What does that mean?" I murmur. "What you said in Spanish?"

Alma whispers, "Go in peace, my grandmother."

And that's when I lose it. I let out a whimper that's way too loud. People around me are losing it, too. I didn't mean to start this, but I'm doing it and I can't stop now.

Eddie steps up, his face wet and red. "Tell her goodbye, honey."

Alma says, "I've got you, Keno." And I know she does, but I still can't, and I say it out loud, like a lament.

"I can't!"

Jack stands and squeezes me to him.

"Take a breath and count to three," he says. I try to do it. Jack loves Nana even more than I do, and I need to be strong for him. "That's good, Keno. In, one... two... three. Out, one... two... three. In... Out... Better now?"

I nod, but I am not better, only a teeny bit calmer. Finally, I bend down to Nana and squeeze her hand. And I swear to God, she squeezes it back. I think for a second maybe she won't die. Nobody wants her to. But getting what we want in life is a rare thing, and it could be a muscle spasm. Still, I'm going to believe Nana squeezed my hand on purpose for the rest of my life.

Somehow, this hand squeeze gives me strength, like all the other ways Nana has given me strength. I kiss my tiny, fading grandmother on her cracked lips, and they taste sweet, like I don't know what, but sweet.

I lay my hand on her forehead. "I will love you forever, Nana. I'm going to do all the things you taught me. Alma and I will have babies, cute little babies that will be your great-grandchildren. And we'll take care of the world like you taught us. We'll take care of each other, too." I stop for a moment to think what else I need to say while there's still time—time that's rushing away too fast.

"Nana, please watch over us from Heaven, if there is one, and keep us on the right track. Because... because... you are the best grandmother any kids ever had, and I'll be grateful to you forever."

It's probably my imagination, but I think Nana smiles, like the corners of her mouth turn up the littlest bit, and the wrinkles around her eyes relax. She's going. I hope my words help her, because I really just want to dive under the ground and die with her.

"We found the water, Nana." She would want to know that. I kiss her cheek and let go of her hand. I step back to crouch beside Alma while she runs her hand through my hair, hugging my arm.

Mazie and Milo go up and kiss Nana, too. Mazie's saying all kinds of sweet stuff, but she says it so fast and quiet—as though she doesn't want to bother Nana but also wants to hurry and tell her everything. Then Mazie says, "You can go up to Heaven and take care of Tasha. She's probably lonely up there."

I let out a wail and curl into a ball. The kids and Alma cry out loud, too. Jack's hugging Nana goodbye, and so are Uncle Eddie, Mom, Uncle Tom, Aunt Jeri. Nana's still breathing, only slower, and then it hits me.

Grandpa.

I jump up and go to Phil. He's the only person here who's not doubled over crying. I whisper, "Do you think someone should get Grandpa?"

Phil lets out a super-soft whistle. "I don't know. Do you?"

"Will you go get him and bring whoever's with him to keep Grandpa under control?"

"Sure." Phil starts to hurry out the back door, but I grab his arm.

"Tell Grandpa... Tell him what's happening and to hurry. But also tell him if he says one single thing that isn't sweet, I'll put a gag on him for the rest of his life."

Phil gulps. "Whatever you want." And he's gone, tromping fast across the snowy backyard like he's in a foot race and he's winning.

We keep watching Nana, holding our breath when she does, inhaling and exhaling with her. Now it's seven or eight seconds between breaths, and now it's eight or nine. I think with every breath this will be the last, but so far, new ones keep happening.

Then the back door opens. It's Phil and Silas, holding Grandpa between them. Grandpa looks sheepish and scared, like a wrinkled-up little boy who's been bad. I swear he's shorter than he used to be, and so skinny I don't know how he can stand up.

Jack caresses Nana's head once more, and then he stands and gestures toward the chair like an usher.

"Hank." He nods at Grandpa.

"Jack." Grandpa winces. He looks back to Eddie. "Is she... is she—"

"She's still breathing, Dad, but probably not for long." Grandpa drops his head, and Eddie takes his arm and helps him sit.

Grandpa peeks at Nana and shakes his head, wiping his hand across his whole face. He looks back to Alma and grabs her hand. I can tell that this surprises her—it surprises the heck out of me—but she doesn't let on.

"Can I, you know, touch her?" Grandpa asks Alma.

"Yes. You can tell her goodbye."

Grandpa lets go of Alma. He touches his pointing finger to Nana's hand, like he's testing it to see if he needs a hot pad. He latches on to her hand with both of his.

"Bea," he says. "You were a good wife. Real good. I was a jackass to you, but you didn't deserve it. I hated that you left me, but I'm glad you got to be happy for a while. I hope you can forgive me. I think you might've, but I don't know."

Grandpa closes his eyes, resting his forehead on Nana's hand. She breathes again after I don't know how long—I forgot to count. I can't believe what Grandpa's saying. Probably nobody can. And he's saying it in front of us like we're not even here. It's his last chance and he knows it, the poor, messed-up guy. Losing Nana the way he did is such an enormous mistake, he'll probably never get over it.

Grandpa scoots the chair closer to Nana. He leans over and kisses her cheek. "It's not true that I quit loving you, Bea. I forgot how to love you right, and I will always regret it. But I thank you for being a good wife and for raising my kids. I'm sorry I made you suffer."

What did Grandpa do, write a speech for Nana and memorize it before he got here?

He looks around like he's lost, and he probably is. I get up, take his arm, and walk him to the back door. He's kind of an intruder here. But Grandpa was a big part of Nana's life. She loved him for decades, and he deserved a chance to say goodbye, but it's time for him to go.

He knows it. He follows my lead to the door and looks back, wiping his face with his hand again, as though he's wiping it with a big rag. "Goodbye, Bea. Night, everyone."

I choke back a sob. As Phil and Silas walk Grandpa to the Mint, I realize it's getting dark. I don't know if we've been having this vigil for lots of hours or if it was later than Mom said when we got here. It doesn't matter. I kind of want to go eat or pee or do anything, take Alma upstairs and make love to her even, to stop feeling so sad for a minute or two. But I'm not leaving Nana for one second. Not yet. Because before long, we'll be without her forever.

Night falls and Phil lights some candles. Nana had a ton of candles, but they're running low now. We don't have enough beeswax to make candles for everyone, and those candles burn super fast. What we need is electricity.

And that's when I know how I'm going to honor Nana. I'll get us power someway somehow. Windmills? Solar panels? There's got to be a way, and I will find it. That's how Nana would want to be honored, by bringing more light to our world. She is full of light, my Nana, even now, while she's breathing her last breaths.

I scoot over to lean against the wall. Alma leans there with me, resting her head on my shoulder while I run my hand over her hair.

Pretty soon I'm dozing off, though I'm mad at myself for doing it. Alma's stretching her eyelids wide, trying to stay awake.

I may have been asleep for a couple minutes when Mom and Aunt Jeri gasp. Uncle Eddie lets out a cry.

Jack stands, leans over, and puts his ear to Nana's chest. And he listens for like a whole minute. He raises up, trembling all over, and wags his head.

"She's gone." He crumples to the floor like a deflating balloon. I sit forward to cradle Jack in my arms while he moans and sobs and shakes all over. I moan and sob with him. Alma has a grip on my arm that's comforting and also trembling.

This is it, what we've been dreading, and it's worse than I thought it would be.

Mazie runs over and tugs on Nana's arm, saying, "Nana, come back. Please come back. Don't leave me here!" She screeches out soft little cries. Oh, man, we all want Nana back, and we feel like Mazie does, only we're too grown-up to do what she's doing.

Milo hugs Mazie tight until she has to let go of Nana and hug him back. They sit down on the floor and bawl. Jeri wails into Tom's shirt. Mom looks lost and needs someone to hug her, so I motion her over to us. She sits down by Alma, and the only two women I truly love in this world now that Nana is gone, they clutch each other and cry.

Phil's comforting Uncle Eddie, who's crying so hard I'm afraid he'll have a heart attack. Phil's afraid, too, from the look of him. He walks Eddie into the dining room and tries to give him water, but he won't take it. Phil hugs Eddie hard, and they slide down to the floor, too.

Because hugging tight for a long time while you're sobbing is easier on the floor. Because we're all flattened now that Nana is gone.

And the world is so empty with Nana not in it that I can't remember how to breathe.

CHAPTER 16

We're burying my beautiful Nana on the day after she died, and I'm so sad I hardly know how I got here. I have a bad case of numb zombie brain.

Mom and Uncle Eddie stayed up all night making a burial shroud for Nana, washing her, and sewing her into the shroud. By the time I got up, they had washed all the bedding Nana died on and hung it to dry, including the pillows.

I swallowed some oatmeal and put on a wrinkled button-up shirt with a tie, but Alma made herself look extra beautiful in a dress with bright flowers on it—a dress of Nana's.

It's the winter solstice, biting cold and bleak, patches of snow still on the ground. Silas and others dug a grave for Nana on the hillock by the entrance to our subdivision. It's next to Tasha, which only makes it sadder, except I'm glad that Nana and Tasha will be together.

Alma and I cling to each other, holding back sobs, and so many people are here. I haven't seen the whole neighborhood gathered together since back when Nana told the neighbors about the Mint and her stockpiles of food.

I'm so freaking proud of Nana and the way she saved so many people, maybe for generations. To see the respect they have for her, how many of them cry. But all that makes the loss of Nana impossibly huge and the world unbearably hollow without her. She had a presence that changed us all. She was like a rock star, my Nana. The rock star who saved our little piece of the world.

Jack is standing all erect with his head held high, but he's trembling, like constantly. Even his mustache is quivering, and tears are running through the wrinkles on his sad-as-fuck face.

Then there's seeing my crying family. I don't know how I'm staying alive in the middle of this.

Out here on this tiny hilltop, old Mr. Bellows is about to lead us in a prayer when I see Grandpa and Aunt Jeri coming up the hill. My brain's so numb that I didn't realize they weren't here yet. Pretty rude to show up late for a funeral.

As they reach the top of the hill, I see that Grandpa is leaning on some sort of cane. No, that's not a cane. It's a machete. A machete at Nana's funeral? Oh, hell no!

I tap Alma's shoulder so she'll look at me, and then I nod toward Grandpa and trot over to intercept him. I get up inches from his face and mutter at him.

"You can't bring that murderous machete to Nana's funeral. Nana was all about peace."

"Leave him alone," Aunt Jeri growls under her breath. "I'm sick of y'all picking on him."

"No one's picking on him. This is a rule of civilization, of respect."

"Not very civilized anymore, is it?" my aunt says with an ugly-ass sneer.

"We have to try, don't we?" I'm boiling inside. I stare at Jeri until she smirks at me. "Grandpa, give me that machete."

"Like hell!"

I bend down so my eyes are level with his, the way he's all hunched over, and I turn my palms out toward him. What did Nana call this? Placating. I'm placating the old cuss.

"Let's lean the machete against this bush here," I say, and Grandpa finally lets me take it.

Behind me, Mr. Bellows says, "Amen," and the crowd repeats it. I look back to see Alma making her way to the front of the group so she can sing for Nana one last time.

"Mom robbed Dad of everything he had," Aunt Jeri mumbles. "And now you won't even let him have his machete for comfort."

"For comfort?" I'm getting more pissed by the second, but I turn my back on my aunt and grandfather, lean the machete on the bush, and go back to the crowd.

Alma clears her throat. "This is a poem that Miss Bea wrote before her stroke. She showed it to me when I was caring for her, and I made a song out of it. It's her way of telling you goodbye, I think."

Oh my God. Nana is still surprising us from beyond the grave. And Alma flat-out astonishes me when she sings out in a clear but trembly voice that pierces me and heals me at the same time. The song is beautiful, and it's mesmerizing, and I am overwhelmed.

I'm gone, but I'm near
I haven't flown away
I'm gone, but I'm here
I'm with you every day
In your hearts and your minds
Where I've taught you all I know
I've nurtured the seeds
That inside you will grow

A shimmer in the air
A whisper on the wind
This is how you'll know that
My love will never end

I'm gone, but I'm near
I haven't flown away
I'm gone, but I'm here
I'm with you every day

CHAPTER 17

Even though we're raw with grief, Milo and I take a shift patrolling the perimeter just before dusk. It's hard not to sigh out loud or even cry, but we have to do this.

Nana's song and Alma's voice ring in my head. *"I'm gone but I'm near..."*

We walk quietly across the park, checking behind the swimming-pool building, following the path between the wheat field and the playground.

When we get to the woods, I say to Milo, "Want to wait here while I go in?"

"Shit, no," he says.

I make noises in my throat, mocking his tone, and he knocks his hip into mine. We poke our rifle barrels into bushes and clumps of weeds as we pass them.

Halfway to the back side of the park, Milo looks to his right. "What's that?" He points to something lumpy on the ground, ten or so feet away. I skulk up to where he pointed.

"It's a sleeping bag." I kick at it. "There's two of them."

Milo slinks past me and points to the ground. A burned-out campfire, with empty cans around it. He rolls them over with his foot. Two cans with sweet corn labels, two with ranch-style beans. And there's a dirty cooking pot nestled in the dead coals. The smears of bean juice on it look pretty fresh.

"Whoever left this here probably plans to come back," I mutter.

"Looks like it," Milo says.

"Let's take the sleeping bags and get out of here. Make it hard for them to stay again."

We each grab a sleeping bag, wad it up, and trot for home.

"Bobby patrolled the perimeter this morning," I say. "Why didn't he see these guys? They wouldn't have set up camp after daylight."

"Yeah, and where are they now?" Milo asks.

"They could be anywhere. I hope they're not hiding in one of our yards."

"Or an empty house."

At home, the whole family is having dinner together, plus Jack and Phil, Silas and Doris, and Pedro and Chris. Well, Grandpa and Aunt Jeri aren't here, but Uncle Tom and Mazie are.

We show them the sleeping bags, and Mazie squeals, "Eww, cooties!"

"They could have lice," Mom says.

And Jack says, "Cooties *are* lice."

"Seriously?" I ask.

"Stick the bags on the patio," Mom says, "and I'll burn them after dinner."

As much as it pains us to do this on the day when we buried Nana, as soon as we eat, all the men here plus Milo and I roust more neighbors, and we search every yard and empty house we've got.

We pass Bobby on patrol, and Eddie tells him what happened.

"Hey, man," I say. "Didn't you see this camp or these guys when you scoured the woods this morning?"

He narrows his eyes at me. "Are you accusing me of something, Simms?"

"No! What's…? No."

"Good," Bobby says. "I didn't see a thing."

I don't believe him. The only way he could've missed them is if he didn't look.

We don't find any interlopers in our yards and empty houses, so why don't I feel better?

On my way home, I suddenly notice that there's no northern lights tonight. They're just gone? Is some evil cosmic mastermind fucking with our heads? It's getting to be like the damn *X-Files* around here.

ALMA AND I FALL ASLEEP listening to Rick. There's something comforting about hearing him talk, and man, do we ever need comfort right now.

Some of us ham operators been buildin' up a network to spread the news that people bring us. More folks have ways to power radios than you might think—one guy rides a bike on blocks to power his. Another guy has some kind of solar battery setup. Others, like me, have generators and still have gas for them, but that won't last forever.

And I never knew this 'til lately, but there's lots of emergency wind-up radios around for you guys to listen with. Some folks in Clifton tell me they listen every night.

Lately, most of the news is about militias poppin' up all over the country. I don't know what's the point of that. I truly don't. Some people just got to have their power trips. I wouldn't mind if militias would protect us, but most of 'em turn out to be the things we need protection from.

Ah, me. I'm still prayin' for the day when Jesus comes back. I wish He'd hurry up, but I ain't supposed to say that. Like I would know better than Jesus does when He's supposed to do what.

CHAPTER 18

For the next couple days, we stay in our rooms—crying, sighing, sleeping. We only come out to eat and prepare food, and we don't do much of that. My heart feels too heavy to lift out of bed, and I imagine the rest of the family feels the same. I know Alma does.

This morning, I drag myself outside to chop firewood in the sun, trying to get warm. We've fallen behind on our work, and now we need to catch up. Mom and Alma are cleaning up breakfast. They're chatting excitedly in there, but when I come inside, they stop, giving each other furtive looks.

"If I'm interrupting your secrets," I say, flipping my eyes between them, "then I can leave."

Mom purses her lips and scrubs at the counter. "I went to see Jack last night," she says.

"How's he doing?"

"Not good, but he's trying. He told me that we need to get pecans today. Since they've been snowed on, they're going to rot if we leave them on the ground. We may have lost some already. Poor Jack. He was apologizing for forgetting them, getting weepy about it. As if he was supposed to think about pecans in the middle of Mom dy—" A sob interrupts her, and I choke up, too.

"I forgot about the pecans," I say. "I haven't been thinking of them as ours."

"I guess they belong to whoever gets to them first," Mom says.

"I already know you don't want me to go, Keno," Alma says. "But I'm going."

I widen my eyes at her. "Not a good idea, Alma."

"We need the pecans," Mom says, tossing down her dishrag. "For the protein and fat. Hell, we need them for the calories. We're all getting too thin with the rice gone and the flour so low."

"Eddie and Phil will harvest honey in the spring," I say, as though that's going to stop these determined women.

"You don't want us getting malnourished," Alma says. She's got me there.

"Mazie says she'll show us the way to the place," Mom says.

"You're taking Mazie?" I shake my head. "Y'all are nuts."

"We're nutty for pecans." Mom snickers with a snort, which gets a laugh out of Alma, and even out of me. It's surreal to laugh when your heart is like a ball of lead.

The pecan trees we went to last year with Nana are about a mile due south. At least they're not in the direction of the camo-guy homestead, but there are plenty of other threats. And those camo guys aren't exactly staying at home.

The trees are surrounded by rows of storage lockers. Anyone could be lurking there. Plus, they're inside a tall chain-link fence, and I'm not letting Alma climb it when she's pregnant.

"I'm going with you," I say. "Give me fifteen minutes to check on Milo and the other teens cutting firewood. I told them I'd help, but they can start without me."

"You're not the boss of me, Keno," Alma says, like she's ten.

"I know that. I'm your armed guard."

***

I THINK WE'LL NEVER MAKE it to the pecan trees, the way Mazie is dragging along, scuffing her heels on the pavement like she's hypnotized by them. Why doesn't Mom coax Mazie out of this? We're not out for some stroll. We need to knock this out and get home safe.

Finally, we get there, and I cut the chain-link fence with bolt cutters and then pull the wagon up under the tall trees while the women run ahead. They're oohing at the abundance of nuts on the ground.

"I'm going over there to take a leak," I say, pointing behind the storage lockers, but no one pays attention to me. They're down on their knees, stuffing fistfuls of pecans into grocery bags.

"Thanks for the help, Keno," I mutter.

Alma says, "What?"

"Goin' over there to take a leak," I shout a little hotly, and Alma waves.

I go to the back end of a row of lockers where I can see the front sides with their roll-up doors. I notice busted locks on the ground, and I walk down the row. Some of the doors are bashed in and broken to crap. We probably should've raided storage lockers, too. Doubt we'd have found any food, but I bet there was other useful stuff. These doors weren't busted when we came here last year. Looters have been busy.

I get sidetracked looking into lockers, but I don't see anything worth sorting through. What's left is mostly dirty clothes tossed around, suitcases, and furniture that's either junk or too heavy to easily move. I come back to the end of the locker row and empty my overfull bladder, happy for the relief.

Then I hear male voices, talking too loud. Shit!

My fly half-buttoned, I flip the rifle off my shoulder, pointing it in front of me as I run around the corner and stop still. Alma's eyes are riveted to a guy in camo with dark hair who has a camo-covered sidekick behind him.

Camo guys only steps from Alma? Oh, fuck no!

"Alma! You know me. It's Ray." He's got a grin like a gash, and he's got his hands out, sweeping down the length of himself, wriggling his hips like a snake. "How's your squealy little brother?" This scumbag is slimy with something black like motor oil down the front of his camo jacket, and he's stepping closer to my wife.

Mom's inching between Alma and this guy Ray while Alma looks frozen. "Hi," she says quietly.

I keep my rifle in front of me while I hustle to Alma. Both these guys have rifles, but they're slung behind their backs. If they have knives, I bet they're fast with them.

"I didn't know what happened to you," Ray says to Alma. "You disappeared on me."

"Yeah, we moved," she says without looking at him.

Ray's voice gets more menacing, less flirty. "Pretty bad of you to skip out on your debts. Come on back with me, and we'll get them taken care of."

Alma gulps. "I, uh… I—"

"Who's this?" I ask as I step next to Alma, nodding toward Ray, turning to face him, my hand on the trigger guard. This freak is talking like he's her pimp.

"Keno, this is Ray. Ray, Keno." There's a tightness in her voice, like anxiety.

Ray's eyes get hard. He scans me up and down, sizing me up, my heart rate increasing by the second.

"I see." Ray locks eyes with me. Then he looks back to his partner. "Let's go, man. Just wanted to say hi to my little friend Alma." His eyes are hooded and dark when he studies me again, then studies Alma, and says, "Y'all take care now."

Ray and his compadre back up several steps, taking their time to turn around and saunter away, like they haven't got a care in the world.

They're fifteen feet away when Ray looks back. "Y'all need to be careful out here. Hidden dangers are everywhere." And he winks.

He winked? What the fuck does that mean?

"Who is that guy?" I ask Alma. "Did he just threaten us? Is he threatening you?"

"A guy I used to know," she says, hurriedly sticking bags of pecans into the wagon.

An old boyfriend? But he looks twice her age, plus his vibes are skeevy. I gape at Alma until she looks at me again.

"Was he a friend of your dad's?"

"He's nobody. Okay?" Alma glares at me quickly, drops to her knees, and starts scooping up more pecans.

I kneel in front of her, pecans digging into my knees, my hands a foot away from her shoulders and face, wanting to touch her but afraid she doesn't want me to. Mom and Mazie start helping her.

"Why don't we go home?" I ask Alma.

"We need these pecans." She crawls away to scoop up more. I don't like it, but she's not changing her mind.

Y'all need to be careful out here. Hidden dangers are everywhere.

That freak Ray had to be threatening us. What's he gonna do? Wait until we load up pecans, then kill us for them?

I give in and start scooping up pecans, too. The shells are damp, but the meat inside still looks good. We'll have to dry them out right away, or even shell them. That's gonna take a ton of work, but getting Alma home safe comes first.

At last, we have all the pecans the wagon can hold—about twenty bags. Alma's spreading bags out in the wagon and not looking at me.

"Babe, are you all right?" I ask her.

"I'm fine." She doesn't seem fine; she's agitated and far away.

When the wagon is loaded, Alma speed-walks ahead toward home without saying a word. I don't know what she's maddest about—seeing Ray or me asking about him.

Mom heads toward Alma. I take off my jacket and pad the top of the pecans. Then I pick up Mazie, set her on a bed of pecans, and try to catch up with Alma.

Who the fuck is this creep Ray? He makes me think of the hard-ass leader of the camo guys we saw when we got gasoline, but it was too dark that night for me to be sure Ray's the same guy. The heights and shapes seem the same, and the dark hair, though Ray's hair seemed cleaner. So, he washed it? Shit, that guy was ready to kill a member of his own gang.

I pull the wagon alongside Mom. Alma's way ahead of us and showing no signs of slowing down. I ask Mom to pull the wagon so I can be sure no one follows us home.

I walk backward the whole mile home, except when I turn around twice a minute to be sure I can still see Alma up ahead.

AT HOME, ALMA STOMPS INTO the kitchen, smears bean paste on a tortilla, and shoves pieces into her mouth, slugging water between bites. She's still chewing when she makes a similar sandwich for Mazie and then rushes up the stairs.

I make an I-don't-get-it face at Mom and drink water, too. I start to follow Alma upstairs, but she's already heading back down with a basket full of laundry. Water's dripping from her face and hair, like she's dunked her head in a bucket.

"Alma, can we talk about this?"

She looks at my mother. "We have to dry these pecans. How do we dry the pecans?" She's frantic.

"I saw an article in one of my mother's books about it. You do your laundry, and I'll find the book. Then we can take care of the pecans together."

"Okay," Alma says, sighing. Then she looks at me. "As you can see, I've got stuff to do." She blasts out the back door with the laundry, slaps a washtub in front of the rain-barrel spout, and starts filling the tub.

I step outside. "I'll handle the water. It's too heavy for you," I say, and she shrugs.

She dumps soap flakes into the washtub and sticks a washboard in there. The second I move the tub into the dead grass, she's throwing in clothes and scrubbing the shit out of them.

"You're gonna tear your clothes if you keep scrubbing like that," I say. "How 'bout if I scrub, and you explain what just happened?"

"There's nothing to explain," she says flatly.

"He said you have debts."

"I don't owe any debts, and he knows it." Alma scrubs at a T-shirt until she scrapes her knuckle on the washboard. "Shit!"

She's about to keep scrubbing, but I lift her hand from the water, trying to put my face in front of hers, but she's making it hard. "You'll get blood on the clothes. You need a bandage. Take a breath."

She tugs her hand away, sucks on her bleeding knuckle, and then examines it.

"I'll take care of it. You can go to work now." She stands up and goes in the house.

What is wrong with her?

WHEN I COME HOME WITH loads of firewood at dusk, Mom and Alma have pecans drying in trays, pans, and skillets all over downstairs.

"Have some pecan biscuits for dinner," Mom says, "and help us shell these things."

So, I eat a couple of biscuits—they're good. I sit next to Alma, and we shell pecans by candlelight for hours without talking.

Fun times.

PART II

CHAPTER 19

It's seven weeks since Nana died, and it's been one lonely-ass winter. I can hardly look at my family anymore except for Alma. I mean, I look at them, but not for long. It kills me to see them so sad. I hope we'll start smiling someday, but I don't see how.

It took Alma days to start talking to me like normal, and she's not that interested in being close anymore. I tell myself it's the pregnancy, it's the grief—which for her includes grief over her parents—but I feel like there's something deeper, something related to the fiasco pecan hunt and that freak Ray. I'd like to ask Mom for advice, except Alma's still not ready for others to know she's pregnant. I try not to worry, but there's this coldness like fear between us that was never there before. It hurts me, but my workload keeps me distracted.

We've been hunkering down for the winter as much as we can, but we have to beef up our soil with mulch and compost, prep the gardens to replant as soon as the frost danger passes, and keep ourselves warm, fed, and hydrated. We're rotating our crops this year, putting the food we need most—like pinto beans—in the biggest backyards.

One exciting thing happened. While a bunch of us were in the Mint's garage trying to figure out where the pump's water comes from, Alma found two manuals—one for the pump, the other for the ten-thousand-gallon cistern tank it's attached to under the Mint's backyard. Holy shit, that was great. Nana wasn't joking around.

After Eddie and Jack warned us that ten thousand gallons could be gone in no time just from cleaning up the backlog of filth in the neighborhood, we decided to let people take three gallons per person per week from the cistern to go with their other water, and we encouraged them to drink it for their health. The first thing that happened, though: people started turning up with clean hair. I did get a laugh out of that.

Having more water to drink is an enormous relief, especially for Alma and the baby.

IT'S ONLY BEEN A YEAR since Tasha died. Before that, four of the Beldings got poisoned by chemicals that spewed from the wrecked train and one of them got blown up. After Tasha, there was that monster Chas who made her pregnant. Now Nana. That makes eight people dead from only our little neighborhood since the sun zapped us sixteen months ago. No, there's nine. Tasha's baby died, too—my little niece or nephew, I don't know which.

Then there's the people who never came home, like Alma's parents and some people down our block I didn't know. Plus, the folks out in the world we're worried about: Uncle Pete, our neighbor Sonja and her son Cesar, Eddie's brother Uncle Wayne and his girlfriend. And my dad Jimmy Simms out in California, or wherever he is. So many people who left the neighborhood, who didn't have anywhere to go but wandered off anyway and might be dead now—there were dozens of them. And who knows how many people died from the solar ejection itself, between car wrecks and plane crashes and fucked-up hospitals, when all the electronics stopped dead in the same freaking second?

And that's just around here. I figure the solar pulse must have hit the whole daylight side of the planet. That would be all of the United States—or what used to be the United States—Mexico, Canada, Central and South America, the Caribbean Isles. The pulse hit in the middle of the day here. It could've hit the western edge of Europe, too, or part of Africa or the eastern parts of Asia, with all the islands over there. Shit, where's Australia exactly? They might be screwed, or Iceland or Greenland or the science stations in Antarctica where, without electronics, those folks would have died on the spot.

In the months soon after the sun zapped us, I used to stare at Nana's globe and spin it around, thinking about what the EMP did to us. I never tried to figure out exactly where it hit, and I could've made a solid guess. But the thought of it was too overwhelming: all that death—and the suffering that's sometimes worse than death.

I don't know if Nana was right and God's punishing us for ruining the planet. It could be that God is pissed off for eternity and we're stuck with it. But to think like that strips my hope away, and my heart won't beat without hope. It just won't.

We might be doomed, but I'm going to hope forever, no matter the evidence, that we are not.

MAZIE SPENDS MORE AND MORE time over here, even overnight sometimes. It's Mazie who's taking the loss of Nana hardest. She mopes around on her own too often instead of playing with the Zizzo kids. Nana was more of a friend to Mazie than her own mother will ever be. I have to do something for Mazie.

"I have a gift for you, Tater Tot," I say one day when she's sitting alone on our patio, spacing out. I hand her a decorated wooden box with a pair of Nana's earrings inside it, plus a necklace of real gold with a ruby pendant. "These are things of Nana's that you can take care of and save for when you grow up."

"Wow, Keno. Really?" I've never seen such awe on Mazie's face.

"Nana would want you to have them. And I have this that you can wear now." I drop a small necklace of multicolored hippie beads into Mazie's hand—a necklace that Nana wore sometimes for fun. "You'll have to be careful not to break it, but you're pretty big now and I think you can take care of it."

"Sure I can." Mazie puts on the necklace. Her face lights up with the reds and blues of the beads, plus a rush of excitement. Then she latches her arms around my neck and hugs the breath clear out of me. "Will you be my best friend now?"

"I'll be your best friend forever."

"Keno?" The corners of Mazie's lips turn down.

"Yeah?"

"I forgot what tater tots are like."

Aww, man. I cuddle up with Mazie and tell her everything I know about tater tots, and how I started calling her that when she was about three and always wanted more of them.

THE MINT PEOPLE STAY TO themselves now, which is great by me. We moved Mom in here at Nana's house—I guess it's our house, now. Mom sleeps in the old game room with no privacy, but she says she doesn't care; she's just relieved to get away from Jeri and Grandpa. Sometimes she takes Eddie's bed when he stays with Phil.

I don't know what they're doing over at the Mint. We let Grandpa out of the cellar and took the garage keys away from him.

Not sure I'll ever forgive him for threatening to shoot us, but he's been quiet lately, so I'm grateful for that. He could be doing anything, though—like wasting that water, or pumping it into buckets and hiding it under his bed. Thinking about what Grandpa might be up to shuts my brain down. I can't even go there.

Jack hasn't come for dinner since the day of Nana's funeral. Alma and I went to see him a couple of times. He's too goddamned sad to be okay, but Jack is a tough old guy, and he's philosophical. He still does his neighborhood chores, so he's not hiding out or wasting away. That gives me hope for Jack. He seems to know he'll always be sad, and he's resigned to it.

Really, if anyone's going to waste away from heartbreak without Nana in the world, it might be Grandpa. He doesn't have his anger at her to keep him going anymore. He looks half-dead already. I can't think about that, either.

CHAPTER 20

Because I made that promise to Nana about getting us some electricity, and since our food security depends on freezers, I'm spending winter nights digging through Nana's books. I found instructions for building solar arrays and climbed all over the roof when the weather let me.

Our panels are fancy and industrial compared to the ones in the book. Even if we rig up something using our panels with this setup, it will only give us power during sunlight. We can't run freezers with it. I know there's a way to get our panels to generate power around the clock, but I don't have it figured out. Windmills are just as frustrating. We don't have the parts we need to make any of this stuff work.

I wanted us to have freezers in time for the broccoli and greens, the first fresh veggies we'll get in March. But that's not gonna happen. I've tried so damned hard to get freezers running, and I get disappointed every single time.

I'm failing Alma. What if I can't keep her alive? Maybe she knows this. Maybe she's lost faith in me. Man, I hope not.

TONIGHT, EDDIE'S STAYING WITH PHIL, and Mom took Milo and Mazie to visit their parents.

I'm in bed with Alma, and it would be a perfect time to make hot, passionate love, but she's being all cold and stiff. "What is it, Alma?" I ask her. "Is it the grief?" And then a more frightening idea pops into my head. "Is something wrong with the baby? Are you sick?" My hands are poised behind her back where she's facing away from me. I want to touch her and hug her, maybe cry with her. I feel so lonely when she's like this.

She sighs and looks over her shoulder at me. "I'm not sick, and, as far as I know, the baby is fine. You don't need to worry."

"But how can I keep from worrying when you haven't been yourself for weeks?"

"It's not you, Keno. I just don't… I don't feel like talking about it, okay?"

"I don't get that, but if you say so." I slump down in the bed, working my pillow.

Then someone bangs on the front door. Shit. No one does that at night anymore. I yank on some pants and bound down the stairs. It's Silas and Grandpa.

Before I can say a word, Silas blurts out, "I was patrolling and found Hank by the park, swinging this damned machete. Almost shot him before I realized who he was." Silas holds up the enormous machete; it gleams in the moonlight.

"Shit, Grandpa. What were you doing down there? You coulda got killed!"

"No one else is doing anything about prowlers. Figured I'd do it myself."

"Hank," Silas says, "I was watching for prowlers. That's how I found you. We patrol night and day. You oughta know that."

"I'll take the machete," I say to Silas. "Thanks for bringing him home."

"Not a problem. But we can't have him doing this, you know."

"Yup. Grandpa, am I gonna have to lock you in the cellar again? You can't go around doing crazy shit like this."

"How crazy is it to let prowlers roam around here all the time?"

"Shut up, Grandpa, and get in here."

He grumbles, but he steps inside.

"Sorry, Silas."

"Goodnight." Silas walks away, shaking his head.

I close the door and whirl around to Grandpa. Alma's watching from the top of the stairs.

"Grandpa, you have to sleep here so I can keep an eye on you. Go upstairs to the futon."

"Where you puttin' my machete?"

"None of your business. Go upstairs."

"Don't want to climb those stairs."

"If you can walk to the park, you can climb the damn stairs."

"Shit," he says. "You've got no respect for your elders, boy."

"I'll give you respect when you earn it."

Grandpa stands there huffing at me. From the look on his face, he wants to break me in two. The feeling is mutual. He shuffles up the stairs but keeps glaring at me.

"I'll get you some bedding, Grandpa," Alma says.

"See, your little wife has respect."

"Her name is Alma. Don't call her my little wife."

He blows out a lungful of air. "Whatever."

Alma talks to him with genuine cheerfulness while she makes up his bed. Wish she'd be that cheerful with me. I go to the garage and hide the machete under the lumber pile. Then I go upstairs.

"I better sleep on the other futon," I tell Alma, "so I can keep him from leaving again."

"Good idea," she says, like she doesn't care if I sleep with her or not.

Grandpa's already snoring when I get back to him. I make a quick bed and lie there awake for hours before I finally crash.

Come morning, Grandpa is gone, and so is the fucking machete.

I CAN'T PUT ALL MY energy into worrying about why Alma's being cold. I need to focus on keeping her healthy while she's pregnant and nursing. We're reaching the end of Nana's stockpiles.

I hate that we can't help the hungry people out there, but we barely have enough for ourselves. And we have less to eat every day. More home-canned veggies, maybe, but much less flour and cooking oil. The rice ran out months ago, and we'll never have more in this climate. We would need rice paddies and canals and shit.

The old-lady nurses, June and Charlotte, have hollow faces and don't seem to eat much. I think they're losing their appetites. A couple of Zizzo kids have sores on their lips that don't seem to be healing. All the adults have weathered skin, and most appear to be losing more weight.

Then there's the added anxiety about keeping Alma's pregnancy a secret. Everyone's been so damned sad that we've been afraid we'd cause them more worry. But I don't know enough about it to be responsible for Alma's health on my own. At least she's not barfing, but what if she's malnourished? How would I know? Not to mention that she's probably three, maybe four months along, and she's gonna start showing through her clothes any day.

Maybe that's what's wrong with Alma. She's hungry or malnourished, and on top of being pregnant and grieving, it's all too much for her. That would make sense, but it hurts me to think of her going through that.

Plus, I need to know more about this puke Ray. Worrying about him and his camo-guy troop and how to keep us safe from them has me tearing my hair out.

Grandpa insists we have prowlers that our patrollers are missing, and I'm starting to wonder if he's right, despite how nutty he is.

THERE'S NO RELIEF IN THIS apocalypse. We can't veg out in front of the TV or play a computer game to give our minds a break. We don't even have music. All we've got is the radio, and it's not exactly entertaining.

After dinner, Milo's doing his first nighttime patrol with Uncle Eddie, and Mazie's hanging out with her mom. I'm helping Alma and Mom repot herbs on the patio.

Alma's putting dirt into a big clay pot with some kind of face on it.

"That's a cool pot," I say.

"It's my mom's pot. It's pretty, right?"

I stoop down to check out the brick-red pot. "It looks all exotic, but then up close, that face is scary, like some kind of lizard person." I run my finger over the jagged teeth.

"That's Quetzalcoatl, the Aztec god of wind. He's the winged serpent."

"Maybe he'll protect us. He looks fearsome."

"Maybe so."

"What kind of plant are you gonna grow in it?" I ask.

"Lemongrass. If I put it by the back door, it should help keep mosquitoes out of the house. We've got way too many mosquitoes, so I'm going to grow more lemongrass.

I'll set it by both outside doors, on the edges of the patio, maybe even in the house."

"You're so smart," I say. "Got anything for fire ants?"

"Cayenne pepper. I've got some under the live oak tree."

"Are you kidding? I need a ton of it. Fire-ant mounds are popping up in a bunch of the gardens." When those suckers bite you, they sting like fire.

"Then I'll grow you a ton of it… eventually," she says with a smile.

That's the only conversation we've had since we've been out here. No one's in a talkative mood. After a long silence, I wind up the radio so we can listen to Rick.

We've got some big worries, folks.

The National Guard in Waco has gone pure-D rogue. They're actin' like some militia of bad guys in an apocalypse movie. They're mean as hell and too damn close, 'specially since they're spreadin' out, raidin' farms outside of town, killin' anyone who doesn't fork over all their food, and I mean all of it. How do they expect people to grow more food if they ain't got food themselves?

Once they clear out the farms close to Waco, I'm afraid they'll just keep spreadin'. It won't take long for them to get to Clifton, since we're on a main road, less than a two-day march away. Christ Almighty, I don't know what we're gonna do.

On top of all that, rats got into my potatoes. I'm kickin' myself for lettin' that happen. They didn't get all of 'em, but now I'm gonna run out before the next crop is ready. I might start sleepin' with my food to keep the varmints away.

Hang on tight, people. Keep your loved ones and your food close. I'll see ya when I see ya.

Christ! This shit is relentless. I've got to listen to Rick more often. If there's a militia in Austin, Rick might hear about it with his radio network, and he could tell us. Militias killing people for food? Goddamn it!

Those camo guys could be a militia. Shit, I need to know what they're up to. There's too many of them.

"I knew those guys in the Waco National Guard weren't right in the head," Mom says, her expression steely. "They were pretty shitty to us when they held us hostage. But some of them were just boys. I didn't think they'd go as far as killing people for food."

I wrap my arms around my mother, and she shudders. "I'm so glad you got away from them before they completely lost their minds."

"Me, too, honey. You have no idea."

CHAPTER 21

Out on patrol this February night, in the deep dark and shivery cold, I'm having trouble staying awake, even though I'm walking—like I'm on cruise control. All this anxiety saps my energy, I swear it does. Alma's more wide-awake than I am. I'm glad, because without her, when I hit a corner, instead of turning, I might keep going straight off the edge of the world.

I've tried to convince Alma not to patrol while she's pregnant, but she keeps saying, "I don't feel bad. No way I'm letting you patrol by yourself." I've offered to get another partner, but she doesn't believe anyone else will have my back as well as she does.

So, we're out here tonight, but she'll have to stop patrolling sooner or later. I'd like it to be sooner. Alma would like it to be later. We've agreed to disagree. I'm not going to push my will on her. That's what Grandpa did to Nana, and that shit doesn't work. And it especially won't work in Alma's current mystery state of mind.

After we've been out here a couple of hours, the north wind picks up, blowing leaves in the air and freezing us. Random gusts knock over buckets and growing pots to rattle them around. I should be glad it's keeping me awake, but it's stressing the shit out of me.

The wind gusts get stronger. We pull our hats and scarves tighter and cross the street to use the south-facing houses as a windbreak. Chickens squawk here and there, probably spooked by the wind or maybe some animal sneaking around. I wonder if it's an edible animal.

"Let's go check on those chickens in Mr. Bellows's yard," I say to Alma. "Last thing we need is some fox or coyote killing chickens."

She's quiet tonight, alert but lost in whatever thoughts are preoccupying her.

A blast of wind hits us, and something loud bangs behind us. I whip around to see water spilling out of a garbage can that's still bouncing. These days, we use those cans to store gray water, at least in the cans that don't leak. We collect mulch and kindling in the leaky ones.

"Damn. Too late to save the gray water in that can," I say.

"That's too bad," Alma says, and we head into Mr. Bellows's backyard.

The chickens really squawk when they see us.

"What's going on with you guys?" I ask the chickens. "Is it too cold and spooky out here? Y'all need to settle down so people can sleep."

The chickens protest even louder, especially the tall, scrawny rooster.

Alma kneels in front of the chicken coop, clucking her tongue, speaking soothingly. "Shh… It's all right, little chicks. Cuddle up together and get warm. Then you can sleep." She draws out the word "sleep" like a hypnotist would. She keeps clucking quietly and saying, "Shh… Shh," until those chickens settle down. Alma, the chicken whisperer.

I didn't realize this until now, but the chickens in our coop at home almost never squawk. Alma must have worked some chicken hoodoo on them.

We're heading back to the street when a loud clatter erupts, out of sync with the gusts of wind. Sounds like shit breaking—wood or bamboo.

Alma and I shoot looks at each other.

"That way." I point toward the park. "Stay here. I know you don't want to, but please."

"I'll follow you partway," Alma says. "I'm not letting you out of my sight."

"'Kay, but hide." I run toward the park, staying in the grass to make my footsteps quieter. I slow down as I near the park corner, and I peek back to see Alma duck into some bushes in front of Greta's house.

I stop still and listen. It's too quiet, as though the wind is holding its breath. Then footsteps—on the road between our neighborhood and the park. They're heading this way. I back into the shadows, aiming my rifle toward the road. I slowly cock the bolt to send a round into the chamber.

"Why'd you step on those bean poles, dumbass?" a deep voice grumbles, getting closer.

"I couldn't see shit in that yard."

"You always fuck up. Because of you, I only got two chickens!"

"I got this firewood, Joe."

"You can't eat firewood, shithead!"

Then I see them. Two big guys wearing camo jackets, but not any guys I've seen before. One has a huge curly beard and a mass of frizzy hair. He's dangling two lifeless chickens by their necks. The other one's bald with a tatted neck, and his arms are full of chopped firewood. They've got to be the same assholes the rabbit-thief warned us about. But they're camo guys? Do I stop them or just shoot? Shit.

Breathing fast, trying not to, I let them step deeper into the intersection. I want to peek back and check Alma, but I don't dare.

The bearded one is in my sights.

"Get out of here," I yell, "or I'll shoot your ass!"

"Shit! They've got guns!" Whiskers whips around and stares in my direction, and the bald guy crashes into him. They can't see me in the shadows. I could totally kill them right now, but should I? My mind's racing a million thoughts per nanosecond. These guys haven't threatened us exactly, but I want them gone and gone for good.

"Drop the chickens and firewood and go! Now!"

They're not moving. They're darting their eyes around, looking for me. If I talk again, they'll find me.

I need a warning shot. I aim at the street behind the guy with the wood. But I forget about the kick this rifle has, and when I fire, the gun kicks up and to my left.

Crack! My bullet hits a log in the tatted guy's arms, and splinters fly everywhere. The bullet ricochets—

"Shit! My arm!" Whiskers cries, dropping the dead chickens, blood oozing through the upper arm of his jacket. Crap, I didn't mean to hit him. I duck behind a tree and brace myself for them to shoot back. Seconds pass. I'm holding my breath. But more seconds tick by, and no one fires. Do they even have guns?

I peek out to see the bad guys halfway down the block with Baldy in the lead.

"Hey, fuckwads!" I holler. "If you come back here, I'll kill you."

"Go fuck yourself!" Whiskers yells.

"You hurt bad, Joe?" Baldy calls back to his buddy from the corner of Dittmar, a long block away.

"Just grazed, but shit!"

I wince when he says this, but he runs faster. I watch until they turn right on Dittmar Road, heading east, in the direction of the camo-guy neighborhood. Motherfuck!

"Alma, you all right?" I call out, trying not to be too loud in case those guys circle back.

"Yeah. You?"

"I didn't mean to hit that guy," I say, rushing toward her.

"Hey! What's going on? Who's shooting?"

I turn back to see Bobby Carlisle running around the corner with his Kalashnikov raised. The big guy is barefoot, wearing only a T-shirt and pajama pants.

"Some intruders tried to rob us," I say. "I got one in the arm by accident. It ricocheted—the bullet ricocheted off the firewood they were trying to steal."

"Shit. Which way'd they go?"

"Past the park, then east on Dittmar."

Greta darts out her front door with a hatchet in her hand. "What happened? Everyone all right?"

"We're good," Alma says.

"I shot a thief," I say, "by accident."

"Well, that oughta screw him up for a while. Shit, Keno. You did good! I'm goin' back to bed." Greta ducks into her house, slamming the door.

Alma rushes up, and I latch on to her. I feel her surging with adrenaline—I am, too, but she's shaking. I tell Bobby how my shot went wrong and about the dead chickens in the street. The neighbors know about the rabbit-thief's warning, and now we've definitely seen these guys. Have they been sneaking around here all these months? Shit!

"They had camo jackets, Bobby, and they ran toward the neighborhood where that group of armed guys live."

"Yeah, but lots of guys have camo jackets, and didn't you say that neighborhood is three miles away? They could be part of that group of goons, but they could just be random thieves. They could be going anywhere."

"But I've seen two other sets of camo guys outside that neighborhood. I think that place is their camp, their headquarters, and they go out looting and wreaking havoc from there. They may be killing people. I heard one say he killed a preacher."

"One of these guys who were just here?"

"No, but…"

Maybe we've scared them off? No, probably not. Shit, I shot a guy and didn't kill him. Is he gonna retaliate? They must not have guns, or they would've fired them. But if they're part of the camo guys, then they have plenty of guns.

Bobby lowers his rifle. He's jumping around to get warm. "Damn it," he says. "We need to have a meeting about this. We're sitting ducks over here."

"They must've come in from one end of the neighborhood while we were patrolling the opposite end."

"Geez. I better get home. I'm freezing." Bobby starts to trot off, then turns around. "So they came from my street?"

"They did."

"Those chickens must be Sandra's and Mark's. I'll take 'em home and give them back in the morning." He scoops up the dead chickens and hurries away.

Alma's still shaking, worrying me to death.

"Can I please take you home? This shock isn't good for you or the baby."

"I'm not leaving you out here alone."

I pull Alma to me. "But what if one of those guys grabbed you? How could I have saved you?"

"I would've shot his head off before I let him touch me."

I back away so I can see her eyes and plead with her. "Baby, I know you're fierce, and you have better aim than I do. I don't want to smother you, but will you please let me pamper you while you're building a baby? If you're out here, I spend all my time worrying about you."

"You worry about me all the time anyway."

I sigh. "Not as much, though. I'll wake someone up to help me the rest of the night... Bobby's already awake. I'll get him."

"It's not that long until dawn, is it?" She huffs like she's angry. "Let's just finish this."

I hug Alma to me, but she's stiff. "I'd die if anything happened to you."

"I know," she says. "I know."

CHAPTER 22

At home, we eat oatmeal, not saying much. Alma heads upstairs, and I tell Uncle Eddie and Phil what happened.

"We need to have a meeting about these guys," Eddie says.

"We need more than a meeting. I feel like an idiot for botching the whole thing."

Uncle Eddie looks at me like I'm some cute little boy. "Kiddo, you did your best. Don't beat yourself up."

"Whether I beat myself up or not, there's no telling what will happen now that I've pissed these guys off."

NOW, ALMA AND I ARE in bed, and she's angry again, except she's sitting up and talking, giving me hope.

"I hate that being pregnant keeps me from doing things I need to do."

Is that why she's been so distant? It seems like more than that.

"I don't know what that feels like, but I'm sure it sucks." I stroke her arm lightly, testing to see if she's open to some closeness.

"It does suck!" She pulls away to wrap both arms around herself. "I have to pee all the time, I can't carry heavy stuff, I'm always tired—"

"If you're tired, shouldn't you sleep more?"

"There's too much to do to sleep more."

"Well, patrolling all night—"

"Don't start," she says.

"Alma, I hated how scared I was for you out there."

"Well, you know what I hated? That I couldn't protect you. I wanted to shoot those guys, but I had to hide."

"Aww…" I reach for her, and she tips sideways into my arms. "Is this what's been bothering you lately?"

I feel her muscles tense up. "Bothering me? What do you mean?"

"Ever since we went pecan-hunting…" I hesitate, biting the inside of my cheek. "It seems like you're half-mad all the time, like you're far away."

"Does it?" Her voice gets quiet. "I didn't mean to…"

"Is something bothering you besides being pregnant? Does it have anything to do with that guy Ray?"

"Ray?" She pushes away from me, sitting all erect. Shit, she was softening up, and now…

"Alma?"

"Don't make me tell you. Please."

"I won't make you do anything. But you'd be helping me out if you told me, to keep me from imagining things."

She meets my eyes, and then she lets out an explosive sigh and looks past me. She's grimacing as though she's wrestling with a pain inside her.

"It's too hard to talk about." Her eyes are pleading with me, and I watch her and wait. "He abused me, okay?"

"Ray did? Oh, baby." I move to hug her, but she stiff-arms me.

"I never told anyone. Well, I told Tasha a tiny bit." There's a low moan behind her voice. "When our mom and dad didn't come home after the solar thing, I thought we might starve. We had food for a couple of weeks, but then nothing. My brothers were so skinny, especially Pedro. He would just sit there, like he didn't have any energy at all."

"Jesus. I didn't know it got that bad."

"Then freaking Ray came along. This old guy, right? He lived in another neighborhood, but he pushed a wheelbarrow full of water jugs down our street one day. We didn't have water, either, so I asked if I could buy some. Well, he looked me up and down and said, 'Maybe so.'"

I shoot to my feet. "Alma?" I'm terrified of what she'll say next.

"I'm ashamed, okay? Sit down."

I'm watching Alma sink into her shame, and I need to throttle this puke Ray. But I sit down for her sake.

"I made him think I liked him and that maybe someday I'd give him... you know... sex."

My fists are clenched. I'm quivering with rage.

"I got him to bring food and water every couple of days, and I'd make out with him."

She made out with him? I might have to barf.

"But I never let him do more, okay?" She's placating me now, and I'm ashamed I made her feel the need to. "I said it was against my religion to have sex outside marriage. I made him come and go through my bedroom window after Chris and Pedro went to sleep. We'd sit on the loveseat and make out, then I'd make him go home."

I'm breathing loud, nodding. I pull her head against me and stroke her hair.

"But Pedro—" She pulls back and turns her face away. "He saw us."

"Oh no!"

"I guess we woke him up, so he ran into my room. And when he saw that sleaze looming over me, kissing me all creepy-like, Pedro screamed. Then Ray yelled, 'Get out, you little shit!' Pedro ran to his room and wouldn't come out for two days. I tried to talk to him, but he covered his ears. When he finally came out, he wouldn't talk anymore."

"Shit, Alma. That's terrible. Poor Pedro." I pull her to me again.

"It's a good thing you guys came when you did," Alma murmurs into my chest. She's trembling all over. "It was getting harder and harder to get him to leave. He said I owed him, on account of all the food he gave me."

I want to beat Ray senseless. Preying on a hungry teenage girl, especially this girl, my girl.

I rack my brain, searching for words that aren't full of rage. "You know it's not your fault, right? Anyone smart would've done what you did. You saved your brothers… and yourself."

"It feels like it was my fault."

"I'm sorry it feels that way." I try to study her face, but she's staring away. Jesus, all us broken people. How will we survive this shit?

I knew she had a lot of pain, but this is worse than I thought. I want to take that pain out of Alma if it's the last thing I do in this world.

I LIE AWAKE AFTER ALMA falls asleep, having a conversation with her in my head—things I can't say to her yet, or ever—but I want to know what she thinks.

I mean, Ray's a camo guy. So, what does that make the camo guys? A pack of pedophiles and thieves? Are they murderers? Okay, Alma was seventeen when Ray abused her, so maybe he's not technically a pedophile, but it was wrong and he knew it, and it's so fricking abusive. He's scarred her for life. She has an astounding ability to deal with it, but I just want to hurt him.

He wanted her back, too, didn't he? He was all flirty at first, but when she didn't do what he wanted, he got threatening, and he gave both of us that steely-eyed once-over. He did walk away without causing a bunch of shit, but my gun was more ready to fire than his was, and he doesn't fool me. He could come back for Alma anytime. I don't want to let her out of my sight.

Alma probably won't want it, but I'd like someone with a gun to be near her every minute of every day.

WHEN I OPEN MY EYES in mid-afternoon, Alma's watching me sleep. She kisses me until I'm good and awake. I'm still raw over what that fuck Ray did to her. I don't know how she's lived with it. I want to do something for her, to make her happier.

"Hey, Alma. What if we move Chris and Pedro in with us?"

"They don't want to move in. I asked them again the other day."

Shit. Now I've caused her more pain. "I'm sorry. Why don't we go ahead and tell the family about the baby, so you can have more support?"

"But they're your family, not mine. What if we tell them and they don't care?"

"If they want me in their family, they have to take you into their hearts. You're part of me, the best part of me."

This gets a smile out of Alma, like maybe she's relaxing after sharing her secret. I hope it's a relief to her that she doesn't have to hold those toxic memories inside anymore.

We kiss for a while, and then we start getting dressed. Alma says, "I'll decide in the next couple of days how to tell them."

"You're the one who's pregnant. You can decide everything about it."

I'm trying to be upbeat for Alma's sake, but I'm stifling my urge to go after Ray, and shooting that guy is also eating at me. I should've killed him or not shot him in the first place. Grazing him just pissed him off, and I'm crazy-worried about what he'll do now. Why did I have to fire a warning shot so close to him?

I pull on my boots. The top stitching's coming loose from the soles. I've still got some sneakers, but they're worn-out inside and won't last much longer either. I don't know how we're gonna get more shoes. Lots of people have big holes in their shoes, like Milo, for instance.

"Damn it," Alma says. "My pants are too tight." She's trying to zip her jeans, but I don't think it's gonna happen.

"That's another reason to tell, before you start showing up in cold weather wearing tent dresses."

"Oh, you!" Alma digs out a pair of stretchy pants and wrestles with them until they're up where they belong. Then she pulls on her hoodie, so I pull on mine. Mine needs elbow patches, but Alma's looks pretty good. She doesn't wear out her clothes and shoes as fast as I do. She's all dainty but also strong. I mean, her thighs! Man, I love her thighs.

We go down the street to the composting toilet and take turns in there, and then we come back home and wash our hands.

It's eerie and empty in the house. Alma stares around, like she's looking for Nana. You get used to relying on people like Nana and Tasha, and when they're gone, it fucking sucks.

No one's making dinner. No one brought in water or chopped firewood, either. Where are they? I hope they're not sulking in their separate corners. Moping around and letting the darkness take us over the way it's always trying to do—that shit will end us.

Yep, we've got to tell them about the baby to give them a reason to get up in the morning and work so hard. Because the way we have to live with so much danger and people dying—it's depressing as fuck.

I start a fire in the patio grill, and then I get Alma gallons and gallons of water from the rain barrels, which takes a while, since the barrels are low again. I chop a pile of firewood, and then I follow Alma inside, where she's got potatoes spread across the counter.

I offer to help her cook, but she says I'll be in her way. And I would be, like a broken cog in her food factory.

I stand behind Alma, rubbing her belly, snuggling into her backside. She stops washing potatoes and leans into me. No one else is around, so I run my hands over her full breasts.

We could do this all the time if we had our own place. Someday, we should move into an empty house, but not now. Alma needs more people watching over her than just me.

"Need anything else before I go look at the wheat?"

"No, go on. Thank you for helping me." Alma even thanks me for doing chores that help me, too. She seems to be coming back to herself. But I imagine the trauma of Ray will always be with her and it could flare up again anytime. I need to be strong for her when that happens.

CHAPTER 23

I hurry down to the park. The sun's getting low in the west, and I want to see that wheat. It's warmer today, and the redbud trees are turning pink, like they do in Austin when it's almost March.

North of the swings and the slimy swimming pool, the park's all plowed with skinny rows and furrows, and they're covered with green wheat—a few acres of it. Wow, it's pretty!

I'm nervous being alone in the park, and I forgot to bring a gun, like a dumbass. But I can't help but walk through some furrows, brushing the tops of wheat stalks with my hand. It makes me feel energized that Alma and the baby will have what they need—new wheat before the bulk flour runs out.

Most of us never grew anything until the solar pulse forced us to. We were city folks and pretty lazy, spending all our time on computers and smartphones, watching TV. If we'd worked as hard then as we do now, back when we had so much food and power and cars, we could've saved the world.

I go back to the edge of the park and look off toward the tree line, then up and down the street where I shot the guy. There's a splatter of blood on the pavement. I hate that I feel like an idiot for going to a park unarmed, for being afraid to check crops close to the boundary. But I'm creeped out, flashing on the guy I shot, flashing on Ray's slimy face, and I need to get out of here.

I'm jogging home when I see Eddie and Phil out front of the Zizzos' house. Mom, Mazie, and Milo are with them. Phil's got his rifle, and he heads on down the street, doing patrol.

I stop when I get to the others, half out of breath. "Where have y'all been? Supper should be ready soon."

"I've got a surprise. Look in here." Mazie points to a box by her feet.

"Ooh, a surprise? Is it a good one?"

"Of course," Mazie says, like we never have bad surprises around here. "Aren't you gonna look?" Mazie stares at me like she can't believe I didn't look last week.

"What do you have in this box?" I stoop down and pull back the box flaps. And I'm looking at rabbits. Two cute white fluffy rabbits. Oh no. We eat cute fluffy rabbits when we can get them. Mazie won't eat them and gets half-mad at the rest of us about it. I'm worried about Mazie having rabbits that she already loves and what their fate will be.

"Wow. Rabbits."

"They're breeding rabbits," Mazie says. "Aunt Erin and Uncle Eddie said I can have them, and they can have babies that I'll take care of. But I have to let you guys eat the babies when they grow up, and I don't like that."

"That's the deal we made, though, Mazie," Mom says. "Remember?"

"Oh, I remember. I think it sucks."

"It does suck," I say. "But it's good you're helping breed rabbits so folks can eat them. You know we need them, Tater Tot."

"Still sucks."

"Yep. Still sucks." I hug Mazie and then lift her into the air above my head. Mazie squeals with delight. "You're a brave little girl, and I love you."

"Keno! I'm not little. I'm eight now."

"You're right. You're a brave tall girl, then."

"I am," Mazie says.

I look away, trying not to laugh while I set my brave tall cousin on the ground.

"I've got a surprise, too," Milo says.

"Eww! Uncle Eddie, please bring my rabbits home," Mazie says. "I don't wanna see Milo's stupid sucky surprise."

"Sure, Mazie, let's go." Eddie winks at me and picks up the box of rabbits. He and Mazie head down the sidewalk toward home.

"Come over here," Milo says, tugging on the arm of my hoodie.

"Hey, this hoodie's got enough holes already. Don't make more."

Mom and I follow Milo to the Zizzos' front porch. There, inside a box, is a dead rabbit with its head gone and its fur and skin peeled off. I kind of want to barf, but my mouth starts watering at the same time. Then Milo sticks his hand in the box and moves the rabbit to uncover another dead one in the same condition.

"Two rabbits? They're so big. That is crazy-good!"

"The Zizzos have gobs of rabbits right now," Mom says. "They said it's time to get rid of a bunch so they can breed more. We can probably get a couple more next week."

"Are other neighbors getting rabbits? I don't want to take more than our share."

"Every family got one or two, depending how big the family is."

"Did Jack get one?" I ask.

"Probably. We've been over here all day, cleaning hutches while Harvey and Kathy butchered rabbits out back."

"That's gruesome," I say. "Glad I didn't have to do it."

"I wanna learn how," Milo says.

"Do you?" Mom draws back from Milo and stares at him, a little flabbergasted.

"Someone's got to." Milo shrugs.

Milo's volunteering to do something gross? I don't want to make a big deal out of it. That could embarrass him out of doing it.

I just say, "Cool. Why don't y'all take the rabbits home to Alma and help her cook them? I'll go see if Jack got any and if he wants to eat with us."

Jack brought us deer meat once, back at the beginning of this new screwy life, before the deer around us were killed off. No way I'm leaving him in the dark about rabbit meat. I freaking love Jack, and I miss him.

I hurry to his house. Wood smoke's coming from his backyard, so I run around there. He's standing and staring at the smoking grill, all spaced out.

"Hey, Jack."

He shakes himself. "Keno. What's up?" He looks at me kind of dead-eyed, like he's scared I have more bad news for him. The news I gave Jack about Nana was the worst news of his life.

"Hoping you'd come eat some rabbit with us."

"Nah. Y'all eat it. You need it."

"But we have two big fat rabbits, Jack. The whole neighborhood got rabbits. There's plenty for all of us, including you."

He still looks unsure, so I add, "We miss you. We never get to see you anymore."

"Do you? Miss me?" he asks with a crack in his voice. His eyes are a little brighter but also teary.

I don't know if I should look away or hug Jack or pat his shoulder or what. None of those seems right for how he feels.

"Mazie will want to show you her breeding rabbits."

"Mazie's gonna breed rabbits?" he asks. "But she never wants us to eat them."

"She and Mom made a deal. I don't know the whole story. Don't you want to come hear it?"

"I do. It's just—" Jack's eyes glaze over, then he turns away. I know he's thinking how eating dinner with us won't be the same without Nana, how nothing is the same without her, how there's a big hole in his life and in his heart that he doesn't know how to fill. Because nothing can replace Nana. Nothing.

He sighs. "I just built this fire. I hate to waste it."

"I get that. But aren't you kind of wasting it anyway, over here cooking for one guy, especially when we have all that food at our place? It's not like the leftovers will keep."

"You got me there." Jack turns toward me again, wiping his eyes with the palm of his hand. "Let me lock the house and we'll go."

"Good… Great." I just want us to give him some love. It's the only thing that can help you get over losing the love of your life, or your sister. Not that you ever get over it, but it helps a ton. That and time. Maybe eons.

UNCLE EDDIE'S COOKING THE RABBITS in two oblong steel pans on top of the grill when Jack and I come into our backyard.

"Hey, Jack," Eddie says. "I was going to roast these lovely rabbits on a spit, but then I thought, why waste the fat?"

"You can fix biscuits and gravy with that fat in the morning." Good, Jack's making small talk. "Should I come over and show you how to make 'em?"

"Yes!" Eddie and I say together. We all chuckle, even Jack.

"Especially the biscuits you make," I say. "I love those things."

"I know you do."

Jack keeps talking with Eddie, and I go inside.

"How you doin', Alma?"

She's stirring potatoes that she's got mashed up with the skins off and everything. She's putting salt and pepper and garlic in there. Little green flakes are all over the potatoes.

"Oh man! Mexican mashed potatoes!" I rub my skinny belly, and we laugh.

I run to the bathroom and wash up super-fast, because rabbit and mashed potatoes. I want to hurry and put them in my mouth. My stomach's growling like a thunderstorm.

When I come back, Mom and Mazie are setting the table with cloth napkins. Phil's pouring glasses of water even. This is some kind of special feast.

I escort Alma to the old laundry room and close us inside. Alma thinks I'm gonna kiss her, and I do. But I don't kiss her for long like usual. I whisper to her.

"I know you wanted to wait to decide about telling people, but I'm thinking that everyone's all happy right now, and Jack's here. We've got a feast to eat, and Mazie's excited about her rabbits. Do you want to tell them tonight, while everyone's happy?"

"Wow," Alma says, her eyes all big. "We *could* tell them, couldn't we?"

"We could. Only if you want to, though."

"I think I do." She throws her arms around my neck, and I lift her up to kiss her better and longer.

"Supper's ready, you two lovebirds!" Uncle Eddie half-hollers. Everyone's laughing in the dining room.

I set Alma down. "Just a sec!" I call out. "Quit laughing!" They laugh louder, and I'm grinning. Alma's giggling.

"Are you ready for this, Alma?" I whisper. "Are you nervous?"

"A little. But I'm mostly excited."

"That's exactly how I feel."

"Come on, you guys!" Mazie shouts.

"We're coming already."

At the table, Eddie's slicing rabbit into servings and passing them around. The only empty chairs are on each side of Milo.

"Milo, move over, will ya? I need to sit by Alma."

"Why? Didn't you already kiss her enough?" Milo grins all goofy and scoots over. I grab his head, acting like I'm gonna give him a noogie, but I barely scuff his scalp with my knuckles, more like I scuff his mop of dirty-blond hair.

"I'll never get enough kisses from Alma."

"Aww," Mom says.

Milo says "Gross!" but he's laughing.

"Someone needs another noogie."

I can't get over it. Everyone's laughing, and we didn't even tell them the news yet. This might be more excitement than I can take.

We pass around the food and fill our plates—except Mazie's plate's not that full without rabbit meat. I can't believe how much food we have, either.

Jack bows his head and closes his eyes, so I bow mine, too. "Thank you, Lord, for this feast and for the blessings of a loving family."

"Amen," I say, and so do the other grown-ups. Mazie and Milo don't seem to know they're supposed to say that.

We dig in, and the food is so great. My mouth and stomach are in Heaven, and the rest of me is there, too. Alma next to me—what could be better? Then I get sad for a second, thinking how Nana's not here to enjoy this with us, but I sort of feel like she is here—up in Heaven, or on another plane, or however it works. I feel her. I do. Nana wants us to be happy, and this feast, it's like a tribute to her and also from her.

We all get second helpings of potatoes. I give Alma the last scraps of meat.

Everyone's finishing their food. Milo picks up his plate and licks it all over. No one tells him not to, so Mazie does it, too.

"You guys," I say, glancing around at my family, then locking on to Alma's eyes and pulling her snug up against me. She nods at me real subtle-like, which I take to mean she's ready. "Alma and I have something to tell you."

Mom gasps, like she suddenly knows. Uncle Eddie's eyes get huge, and Jack grins all big. They know. All the grown-ups do, except maybe Phil.

"What is it?" Mazie asks.

"Yeah, what?" says Milo.

"Alma, my beautiful wife, do you want to tell them, or should I?"

Alma's face is bursting with happiness—the prettiest woman in the world.

"We're gonna have a baby!" she says.

Oh, man, I might faint from this excitement.

I've never fainted before, but this has got to be what it feels like right before you go under. But I can't faint. I need to look after Alma to be sure she doesn't faint, or, if she does, so I can catch her.

I mean, the astounded looks on everyone's faces—I can't remember when I've seen so many faces look this alive.

Alma's laughing and wiping tears on her sleeves, smiling the biggest smile I've ever seen on her.

Milo starts jumping around, and Mazie joins in. Uncle Eddie shouts, "Woohoo!" He hugs Jack and then kisses Phil. Mom gulps and turns her back to us. She's shaking all over, and she runs over to hug us. She wipes my face with my napkin. That's when I notice that I'm crying like crazy, too.

Jack hugs us so tight we almost knock our skulls together. "Congratulations! You kids make me proud."

"I wish we could find out if it's a girl or a boy," Mom says. She's trying to sound happy, but I see the worry in her eyes.

"My mother," Alma says, "she could tell by the way women carry their babies, all compact up inside them or poking out a lot. I don't remember which way meant girl and which meant boy. I'm not even sure if my mom was right."

Mom strokes Alma's shoulder. "I've heard women say that, but I don't know which way means what, either. Or, like you said, if it works."

Uncle Eddie hugs us so hard he's about to crush us with his muscles. We somehow live through it, and then Phil hugs us, too, but more like a regular hug.

Mazie climbs into Alma's lap. "There's a baby in your belly now?"

"There is," Alma says.

"Right up here under my butt?"

Alma giggles. Milo startles us, guffawing in his deep, crackly voice. All of us laugh but try not to be too crazy about it. But Mazie's laughing, too. She's so happy she doesn't seem to care if we're laughing at her, like she's the family comedian and is in on the joke.

Alma kisses Mazie's cheek and sets her on the ground. Mazie scampers off, twirling around the room. My tears finally stop. I'm just happy now. I can't stop smiling, don't even want to. Though I am a little worried about Mom.

Mom stoops down, clutching Alma's hand and then mine with a killer-tight grip. "I'm gonna be a grandma." She squeals a little when she says "grandma." "I'm going to take care of you, Alma, and keep you healthy. It will be so great to have a new baby in our home."

Jack says, "I'll take care of both of you."

Then Eddie says, "You know I will."

Mazie says, "So will I. I love babies!"

Even Milo says, "Me, too." Pretty sure I never heard him say he'd take care of anybody, although he does do it—kind of a lot, if I think about it.

Beautiful Alma is making my whole family almost as happy as she makes me. She's giving us a reason to live—the best gift ever.

AFTER JACK GOES HOME WITH a smile on his face and everyone else has settled down and gone to bed, I come downstairs to get some water and find Mom crying on the couch with her head in her hands.

"Mom? You all right?"

I've startled her, and she jerks her head up, all the previous happiness drained from her face. "I'm fine." She tries to smile, but it's feeble. "It's just… you know… Tasha."

I step close to Mom. "I'm worried, Mom. But I don't want Alma to see it."

"Of course." She makes a shooing motion at me. "Talk to me about your worries instead of Alma. But for now, go to bed. I'll be fine. Sometimes I just have to cry."

CHAPTER 24

I figure we'd better go tell Grandpa and them over at the Mint this morning, before they find out about the baby from someone besides us. They'd be mad about that, along with all the other shit they're mad about.

Neighbors go in and out of the Mint's garage nowadays, but Jeri and Grandpa stay away. They still hate sharing food and water and tools. They wouldn't have a thing to eat without our neighborhood co-op. They should've figured this out by now.

But they don't want to figure it out. Then they'd have to be grateful and put themselves on the same level as the rest of us. I swear that's the way they think about it. Like being grateful would make them smaller, which is the opposite of what being grateful does.

Grandpa and Aunt Jeri have blinders on. That's what Nana would've said. Also, they don't give a fuck.

Alma and I are getting dressed when Mazie hollers from downstairs. "Come eat, everybody! Uncle Eddie and Jack made biscuits and gravy!"

"Wow," I say. "I wonder if Mazie realizes the gravy's made with rabbit fat."

Alma stops to look at me. "Think we should tell her?"

I push my dark hair back along the top of my head. It's so greasy and itchy. I really gotta wash it somehow. I lean down in front of the mirror and start brushing. That will help some, and also scratch my itchy scalp.

"If this was the world we grew up in, where vegetarians had plenty of food choices, other ways to get fat in their diets without eating meat, then of course I'd tell Mazie."

"Yeah?" Alma's watching me while she buckles her belt. It looks tight on her. So cool.

"But—" I turn to face Alma. "—I want Mazie to eat it. She freaking needs it, like we all do."

"Keno, I love the way you think about your family and what they each need."

"How's the baby today, my other baby?"

"Good. I can't feel it moving yet. I don't know when that's supposed to happen."

"Now we can ask people the million questions we have. It'll be fun to have something nice to talk about for a change."

"Keno, come eat!" Mazie hollers. "I already ate a bunch. If you don't hurry, it'll be gone."

"We're coming, Mazie!"

Alma and I crack up. Mazie already ate the gravy, so we were all worried for nothing.

"Can we tell Pedro and Chris about the baby before we go see Aunt Jeri and Grandpa?" Alma asks.

"Sure. And Doris. I know you'll want to tell her and Silas, since they took y'all in."

We hurry down to eat. We're not gonna miss out on biscuits and gravy. But, as I kind of expected, Eddie has two piled plates set aside for us, and Jack's guarding them like a hawk. Milo's eying them. We bite into delicious smothered biscuits, and we're swooning.

***

"GUESS WHAT, YOU GUYS?" ALMA'S beaming at her brothers. "I'm gonna have a baby!"

Chris's mouth falls open and morphs into a big smile. "Wow. So awesome!"

Pedro smiles with his mouth, but not with his eyes. He looks a little bewildered. These guys aren't like my loud-mouth family. But then, Pedro's mouth puckers up, his whole face puckers up, and he starts sobbing.

"Aww, what's the matter, Pedro? Come here." Alma grabs her littlest brother in a mighty hug. She looks concerned. Pedro doesn't speak; he just clings to Alma.

"Pedro, it's okay," Chris says. "Alma's still gonna love us. Right, Alma?"

"You guys are the best brothers in the world. Of course, I'll always love you." Alma's puzzled over this. She pulls Pedro away to look him in the eye. "What's wrong, boo?"

Pedro doesn't respond. I step into another room, hoping he'll feel more comfortable talking to Alma if I'm not there.

"Pedro, please tell me what's wrong. Are you worried about me or the baby?"

"No," he croaks out. "I'm happy."

"That's good. So why are you crying?"

"I want Mama and Papa to see the baby." Oh, man.

"I do, too, Pedro." There's a crack in Alma's voice. "I do, too."

Chris runs over and hugs Alma and Pedro while the three of them cry. I give them a minute, and then I join the hug.

At last, Alma says, "If Mama and Papa are in Heaven, they will see the baby. And if they're alive, then maybe they'll see us in person someday."

"They're alive," Pedro says.

"Sure they are," says Chris. Alma and I nod.

Doris says prayers and hallelujahs and fusses over Alma so much I don't think we'll ever get to leave, but it's fun to see Doris so happy.

Pedro gets cheered up, saying, "I hope it's a boy."

"I want a girl," Chris says. "She'll be pretty like Alma."

Finally, we back out the front door, grinning, and then we walk toward the Mint. The sun seems way too bright for wintertime. I've noticed this a lot lately. I don't trust the sun anymore.

"Well, that was… Wow," I say.

"Yeah, pretty wow. At least Pedro got cheered up at the end of it."

"That Doris is a cheering machine. You're gonna have more mothers fussing over you than you'll know what to do with."

Alma chuckles, but her lips get trembly.

Shit. I've hurt her. I'm not making any more jokes about fussy extra moms to Alma.

I wrap my arm around her waist, which is next to my hipbones. I want to protect her and the baby with these long arms God gave me, if God is even where I got these long-ass arms. My mom and dad don't have long arms. Probably came from some ape ancestor, like an orangutan. That's kind of freaky to think about.

GRANDPA AND AUNT JERI DON'T seem that excited about the baby. I mean, they smile and say congratulations like a robot would, or a trained parrot. They're in some kind of funk over here, so we don't want to linger.

"I think I'll take a nap," Grandpa says, like he doesn't give a shit that he's fixing to be a great-grandfather. I think he does give a shit, but he doesn't want me to know that, for some reason.

At least Aunt Jeri's not being bitchy. Maybe she's settling down.

• • •

A FEW NIGHTS LATER, I'M falling asleep when I suddenly wonder if our doors are locked. I run downstairs to check.

Back door's fine, but the front door only has the knob locked, so I flip the deadbolt.

Shit, someone's across the street, facing our house, just standing there. A patroller waiting on his partner? No, Milo and Eddie are patrolling. I slide closer to the window and pull the thin curtain back an inch, and I see Ray.

Fucking Ray? He knows where we live?

Surging with rage, I yank open the door, and Ray jerks, like he's startled. I fly across the street. He plants his feet and sticks his arms out as I launch myself at him, grabbing him by his jacket collar. He knocks me under the arms, trying to break my grip. Shit, I'm not even armed.

"The fuck you doin' here? Get out and don't come back!" I'm shaking him. He's heavy, and he's grinning at me. I rear back to punch that grin off his face, and he grabs me by the throat. Fuck! He's gonna crush my windpipe.

"Hey! Let him go!" Uncle Eddie's running at us from halfway to the park, cocking his rifle. "Get the fuck out of here!"

Ray lets go of my throat and steps back. "I'm goin'," he says.

I'm gasping and sputtering, but I shove him in the chest and knock him backward. Ray slaps the shit out of my head, sending me sideways. I'm reeling, and he yanks my arm. Pain shoots up it through my shoulder as he jerks me around to face him.

"Listen up, prissy boy!" he snarls in my face. "If I didn't love Alma, you'd be dead."

If he didn't love Alma? I'm gonna kill him!

Eddie runs up on us, firing his rifle in the air. "*Go! Now!*"

Ray takes off, darting across the street and through Jack's field, heading toward Dittmar Road.

"Shoot him, Eddie!"

"He's not armed!"

I yank the rifle out of Eddie's hands. "Hey!" he shouts. He didn't expect me to do that.

I'm barefoot, running on hard pavement, then across uneven ground full of brambles, and I'm trying to get a bead on Ray. It's hard to sight this rifle in the dark and on the run. I just start shooting. Bursts of shots, then more running. Ray's about to go over the crest on Dittmar. I plant my feet and fire off a barrage, emptying the clip as he disappears into the trees.

"Don't come back here, motherfucker!" I yell as I double over, bracing my hand on my knee, trying to breathe.

"Don't ever grab a gun out of my hands again!" Eddie barks from behind me, and I whirl around. "Stupid, dangerous fucking thing to do!"

"I need to kill that guy."

"Why? What was that he said about Alma?"

We haven't told anyone what Ray did to Alma. She doesn't want everyone knowing she was abused. "He was looking for her."

Eddie winces, like maybe he's picking up on the threat. I hand him his rifle, and we walk toward home.

"Where's Milo? I thought y'all were patrolling together."

"I let him take a break to hang out with Susie Zizzo."

Milo's had his eye on red-headed Susie for a while. The

kid deserves a break. But Eddie was patrolling alone and let Ray get in.

"You should've got me to help you until Milo came back."

"Probably should have."

Milo's in front of our house with his rifle up when he sees us approaching.

"What's going on?" he asks. "Who were you shooting at?"

"Camo guy creep," I say. "He got away."

"Same guy as before?"

"Nope. A new one. This place is all the rage for camo guys to menace. Didn't you hear?"

Eddie clicks on his flashlight. "Let me look at your throat."

I don't want him to look, but I throw my head back so he can squint at my skinny neck and run his fingers across it.

"That's going to bruise," Eddie says. "Go to bed, kid. Milo and I have got this."

Yeah, right.

Ray, that scum-sucking prick. The fuck does he know about love? He wants to screw Alma is what he means. I could choke the life out of him and never think twice about it.

He must've broken into Alma's house—that's how he found us. She left our address there for her parents.

Devious, molesting pile of pig shit. How can I keep Alma safe from him?

CHAPTER 25

I meet Milo and Uncle Eddie at the door when they come in from patrol in the morning. I should ask them how things went the rest of the night, but I didn't sleep for shit, my throat's bruised, my arm's wrenched, and I'm too worked up.

"We need to go spy on those camo guys, like now! I have to know what they're doing."

"Whoa. Settle down!" Uncle Eddie stops in his tracks, scrutinizing me, his rifle still in his hands.

"Settle down? I'm not some kid making too much noise. This is serious, Eddie. That puke Ray is a camo guy, and he was watching our house. Our house! And Rick says the National Guard in Waco's gone rogue and they're killing people for food. How do we know these camo guys aren't doing the same thing?"

"Can I eat breakfast while we talk?"

"Yeah, sorry. I made oatmeal. Alma's sleeping in."

"You made oatmeal?" Milo smirks at me. "Didn't think you knew how."

"Hilarious."

I slap oatmeal into bowls for them. It's kinda lumpy, but who cares? Eddie dumps salsa on his oatmeal before he sits down. I guess he's saving what's left of the sugar for Alma and the kids.

"So, seriously," I say, leaning toward Eddie across the table. "We have to do something about these guys. They're everywhere."

"Keno, the neighborhood is secure. Relax."

"How is it secure? We're not a gated community with walls. There are like six streets people can just walk in on. They can come from the park, the train tracks—"

"We have patrollers, and we caught Ray."

"But, Eddie, the guys I shot at came in from one end of the neighborhood while Alma and I patrolled the other end. People can come in through the backyards on our edges. Someone camped out in our park. This place is like a freaking sieve, it's so leaky."

Eddie leans back, letting his spoon sink into his oatmeal. "What do you expect me to do about any of it?"

I sit back, too. "I'm not trying to put it on you. But I think we should spy on them. How can I protect Alma and the baby from people who are obviously up to something if I don't know what they're up to?"

"Spying is a bad idea. You'll get caught. It's better to keep to ourselves and lie low."

"Eddie, that's not working."

"You went there once. I don't want you going again, okay? You're worried about being a dad. I get that. But—"

I jump to my feet. "Don't placate me, Eddie. You're in denial. You want to think we're safe, but you don't know that. And I have to know."

Eddie locks eyes with me. "Go cool off. I'm exhausted and you're ruining my appetite."

"So, I'm just a pain in your ass then? Not worth listening to?" I slump forward, shaking my head.

Eddie raises up, bracing his muscular arms on the table. "Keno, there's nothing else we can do! Patrolling is all we've got!"

Mom scurries down the stairs. "What's going on? You woke me up."

"Ask Eddie." I stomp out the back door.

I plop into a chair on the patio, squeezing my head between my hands. Eddie's acting like some comfortable old middle-class guy who doesn't notice the world burning around him as long as he's got what he needs.

I get that he's trying to protect us by keeping us at home. But that won't work anymore. I wish I could get him to see that. He's in charge of security, and he's my elder. I'm supposed to do what he says, but if he doesn't snap out of it, I'll have to stop.

Eddie's in love—that's what it is. He's missing the urgency here, the anxiety. Finding Phil was like a godsend to him. Being in his forties when he finally finds real love, Eddie's head is on another plane.

Shit, I shouldn't have to apologize for this, but I'd better. I go back in the house.

"I'm not done talking about this, but I'm sorry for yelling at you." I don't look directly at anyone. "Alma's supposed to patrol, but I don't think she should. She was too tired to make breakfast. So, I'm taking her shift and mine, and I'll be home for dinner. Alma might be mad when she wakes up. She wants to keep doing everything she's always done, but I—"

"I'll take care of her," Mom says. "I went through it, too. When you're a hard worker like Alma is, being pregnant can mess with your head."

I sigh and kiss Mom on the cheek. "Eddie, can I take your rifle? You reloaded it, right?"

"Sure," Eddie says. "Not my rifle anyway. Listen, those guys you're so worried about? You have to remember they're not lucky like we are. They don't have someone like Nana to lead them, someone who had a stockpile of food."

"I know that. That's exactly why they worry me. If you don't have a leader with morals and brains, you get chaos."

•••

I'M NOT IN THE MOOD for family chit-chat tonight. I've been patrolling in the hot sun all day and working myself into a state.

After dinner, I take the radio to the patio. I need to know more about the militia in Waco, and I haven't listened to Rick for days.

Tonight, I come in on what sounds like the start of his broadcast.

...comin' to you from the boonies of Central Texas...

"Alma? Rick's on," I holler. "Might want to come hear this." Milo, Mom, and Alma hurry out the back door.

Sorry I missed some broadcasts, folks. Been layin' low, watchin' from my roof for that rogue National Guard— that gang of murderin' thugs is more like it. Mikey Boggs saw a couple dozen of 'em in the parkin' lot at Clifton High. I ain't sayin' how close that is to me.

I already decided if they come for me, I'm fightin' back. Losin' my farm would be the death of me anyhow. Might as well take some assholes out with me.

What's all that racket? Hold on.

Alma sinks into a chair with her hands over her mouth. We're all staring at the radio like it's a TV or some shit, and we wait and wait.

Christ on a cracker! The Guard's at the Jackson place a half-mile away. From my roof, I saw a buncha guys along the main road. And now I'm watchin' shootin' and flash-bangs through my window. Looks like they got tear gas, too.

I shouldn't be broadcastin' and callin' attention to myself, but I came on to warn y'all to build yourselves some walls fast. Gather your weapons, because this is war now, and the little people are losin'.

I gotta say goodbye to my mom and dad over in Belton, if they're still alive. And to my sister Georgia in Temple and her kids. Y'all are the best family any guy ever had. I'm sorry for all the things I done wrong in my life. I shoulda moved to a bigger town when y'all did. But I like it out here in nature; more room to roam. I like the quiet.

Ain't no quiet anymore. I'm gonna stick this mic out the back door to see if y'all can hear the gunfire. The Jackson family ain't got a prayer. All those kids… Oh man. Sorry, I can't help cryin'. I love those kids, and I really ain't ready to die.

Rick stops talking, but we hear him choking back sobs and moving his mic, and then we hear a door open and what sounds like a war movie in the distance. Alma's about to tear a hole in my arm with her fingernails.

I gotta get outta here. Bye, y'all. Just gotta hide this radio— shit, they're in my garden.

Rick hushes for minutes. My heart's thrashing so hard. Then there's a huge cracking sound, like a door breaking, and men shouting garbled words.

"Y'all just busted into my house on live radio. Ain't that somethin'?"

I picture Rick grinning like a maniac.

"Shut the fuck up!"
"No! Don't!"

Gunshots ring out.

Milo leaps to his feet, screaming, *"Nooo!"*

The mic lets out a piercing squeal that splits the night, then goes silent.

We're all crying. Milo's hysterical.

"We're fucked!" I jump to my feet and kick the first thing in my path—a clay pot that sails above the patio and hits the roof post, shattering into sharp shards and tiny slivers, sending a cloud of red dust and green shoots of lemongrass into the air, and cracking the face of the lizard god.

ALMA'S GONE TO BED, BUT the look on her face after I broke her mother's pot won't leave me—a mix of sadness and horror and more than a little anger. Of all the things on this patio, why did I have to kick the one thing that was so important to Alma?

I'm out here with only candles for light, trying to glue the pot back together, like a 3-D jigsaw puzzle. It's mostly all here, but the glue has oozed out and hardened on the outside of the pot, making the whole thing a godawful mess, especially where I wedged in thin little scraps.

I'm skeeved out at myself for kicking the pot, I'm distraught about Rick getting killed, and I'm half-superstitious that I've pissed off Quetzalcoatl and he'll come for revenge. But worse, I've hurt Alma, and that's unforgivable.

Mom comes outside and stoops down to inspect the pot. "You did a good job, Keno."

"No, I didn't. Look at those globs of glue. It'll never be the same."

Mom pats my shoulder with her lips pinched together. She knows I'm right.

I wipe the pot down and set it on the patio table, and then I put more dirt in it and replant what looks salvageable of the lemongrass. I add a little water. The pot is as put-together as I'm capable of getting it, and I don't like the rock-hard stare in Quetzalcoatl's eyes.

CHAPTER 26

When I wake up the next day, Alma's not in bed. I lie here trying to forget the murder we witnessed, but I can't. We've been listening to Rick since the sun zapped us. He was our only outside news, and he was our friend.

His murder's not gonna leave my head and neither is Ray and his stalking, so I get up and bring them with me. The house is airy like the doors are open, and I smell eggs cooking. I bound downstairs, famished, but outside to the south, the sky is gray like gunmetal.

From the middle of the yard, I watch that sky grow darker by the minute. Strong winds are blowing up from the south-southeast, from the Gulf of Mexico. This is storm weather, big storm weather. For a minute, I get excited from the storm energy and the idea of a good rain, but that sky looks threatening as fuck.

I wolf down breakfast and head to the street to find Jack. We watch the storm barreling our way. Deep thunderheads cover the southeastern sky. They're starting to fill the whole sky while they go from gray to slate blue with a few spots that I swear to God are black.

"Jack, what about our crops? Can we protect them before the storm starts?"

"I don't see how." Jack seems scared, and that scares the crap out of me.

We get these crazy storms some years, killer storms with tornadoes and hail and horrible floods. I'm not worried about rising water. We're on some of the highest ground in Austin. Half of Texas would have to fill up with water before rising floods would get to us.

But water rushing across gardens as it drains downhill and rainwater pummeling our crops and soil—that shit could wipe us out completely. We can get as much as two feet of rain in little more than a day, and it seems to happen every few years.

The wheat! Hard, fast, continuous rain could wash the wheat right out of the park. A hailstorm could end it. The park's not exactly hilly but rising and dipping ground. Low spots can turn into creeks that will carry the wheat away. Boggy ground can rot it at the roots.

Our next-door neighbor June comes through her gate and reaches us fast for an old lady.

"We better cover some of these crops quick," she says before she's quite here. "Weigh down the edges of tarps and blankets with rocks to keep them from blowing away."

"Don't we need to be sure the veggies get rain on them?" I ask.

"Oh, they'll get plenty, through the blankets, up from the soil. Some covers will blow off before it's over. I was raised on a farm in Kansas. This looks like what we called a gully-washer."

A gully-washer? Shit, that sounds ominous.

"I wouldn't worry too much about the corn," June says. "If anything can stand up to hard rain or hail, it will be the corn."

"What about the pinto beans?" Jack asks. "The Mint's yard is huge. Not sure we have enough blankets to cover it."

"Pinto beans are pretty sturdy, Jack. Gardens with no houses on the south side of them, those are the most important to protect. And if the pinto beans don't make it, we have time to grow more before the first frost. Concentrate on tender vegetables—tomatoes, peppers, squash. I've got to go take care of my garden. Charlotte's already out there."

June rushes away, and I holler out, "What about the wheat?"

"Pray," she says.

"That's not hopeful," I say to Jack.

"Nope, but it's all we've got. Start praying. You go east. I'll go west. Tell neighbors what June said. We need to move fast."

"Got it." I run into our house first and tell the family. Alma has fear in her eyes, but I see her fierce bravery, too. I get Uncle Eddie to take care of our garden, and Mom volunteers to help Alma with the herbs. I take Milo with me. Phil comes to our front door as we're rushing out, and I send him to the next street over, Mint Lane.

The wind's picking up and blowing leaves around. I see lightning not far southeast. Part of me starts to panic, but my brain kicks into some kind of emergency mode, calming me and clearing my mind.

"Milo, go to Silas's first, then head down the block on that side of the street. Do you know what to say?"

"Well, yeah?" He looks at me like he can't believe I asked him that. I blink, and he's already halfway to Silas's front door.

I take off east past June and Charlotte's to the Zizzos', but they've already been covering their garden. They send their kids with me to help Mr. Bellows—he's old, and he's got most of the peppers behind his north-facing house. Then I run to every house on this side of the street.

Pretty soon, every neighbor is in their yard, throwing sheets, tarps, and blankets over as many crops as they can, finding rocks and other stuff to hold down the makeshift crop covers. I help push potato barrels and food pots into garages. Neighbors are running around like a stirred-up nest of ants.

I send Max and Danny to do the heavy work for June and Charlotte. I race from neighbor to neighbor again, asking if they need help. Milo's across the street, looking like he's doing the same.

Rain starts falling, not fast at first but getting faster. And then I think, Jack! The tomatoes! I holler for Milo to come with me, and we run two long blocks to Jack's house, huffing and puffing with our clothes getting wet. We find Jack alone in his backyard, wrestling with a blanket he's trying to throw over the tomatoes. He's way more out of breath than we are. The rain's getting louder as it strikes pavement and rooftops.

"Sit down, Jack!" I holler. "Milo and I have got this!"

"I'm fine!" Jack yells, like he's pissed. "Grab the other end of this blanket. Milo, bring us piles of rocks from the edge of the yard."

Now the rain's gushing in torrents onto our heads and bodies and blankets and crops. The wind keeps whipping this blanket and also turning up the edges of another that Jack already threw down. I remember I'm supposed to be praying, like I've got time for that.

Milo brings us loads of rocks that Jack and I place on blanket edges and push into the mud.

"Milo, put more rocks on the edges of that other blanket. Jack, got any more blankets?" We've only covered half the tomatoes and not that well.

"On the patio," Jack says, raising up and breathing hard. It takes us a while. We're sopping wet with the rain pounding so hard it hurts. Rivulets of water drip off our brows and noses and out of our hair, but we finally get the tomatoes as well-covered as seems possible.

"Let's go to our house and get dry," I say. "If we move the grill up against the house, maybe we can still cook even in the pouring rain."

When we get to our house, I say, "Go on in. I need to check the wheat."

Rain is drubbing me. It's washing fast through the streets now. I don't see any people outside except Silas and Bobby rushing to their separate houses, soaking wet stragglers in the pounding rain. Lightning's almost on top of me; thunder keeps startling me.

I run like I'm on fire down to the park and the wheat field. Before I'm quite there, I already see wheat drooping from the pounding it's taking. I tell myself that plants sometimes sag from rain and they'll perk up when it stops. But this idea's not cheering me up. This wheat looks fucked. Some of it is leaning almost to the ground. Furrows are filled with rushing water, undermining the wheat at its roots.

Mother of God.

I drop to my knees on the wet ground, and I pray my heart out, even though I'm not sure I believe in God. I pray the only prayer I know, shouting it out so I can hear myself above the roar and crack of the storm: "Jesus, please save us! Jesus, please save us!" over and over again.

Then down come big hard rocks of icy hail.

I race home like a streak, plowing through rushing street water and ruining my already-ruined shoes, covering my head with my hands to protect it from hail. My hands are getting pelted and it hurts. Clusters of icy hail are everywhere.

In my mind, I see starvation ahead and this neighborhood a wasteland. I try to cast out these visions, but they keep assaulting me, like a flashing montage in a bad movie. Yet, this is water—clean, drinkable water. There has to be something good about it. Or maybe not.

I'm huffing from running but shout with relief when the hail stops. Pretty sure we've already lost the wheat, and I want to scream in rage about that. Maybe we won't lose much more than wheat, though that doesn't seem likely.

At last, I reach our front door, where rainwater is gushing off the roof and going right past the gutters, turning our front stoop into the bottom end of Niagara Falls. I jump into the water and burst through the door.

Alma grabs me in a hug before I realize she's there. I hug her hard, then let go.

"I'm getting you wet."

"It's okay. I was worried about you when the hail started."

"Sorry I worried you. Have you been waiting by the door for me?"

"Kinda."

"Aww, baby. Let's find you a chair."

"'Kay," she says, wiping at her eyes.

"I should get that rocking chair back from Grandpa for you and the baby."

"Yeah, good luck with that."

I help her sit on the couch then stoop in front of her, stroking her arms. Eddie, Phil, Jack, and Milo are clustered in the dining room, looking toward me with eyes full of worry. I want to sit by Alma so I can comfort her while I face the rest of them.

"I'm all wet and muddy. I should go change," I say.

Alma tugs me toward her. "The couch is leather. I can wipe it down. I want you here."

"I'll wipe it." I snuggle up next to Alma on the couch and look each of the men in the eye. "I'm not happy with the way the wheat looks."

"How does it look?" Jack asks. Whoa, he's wearing Grandpa's clothes. I hope Grandpa never sees that.

"Like it's getting pounded to death and washing away."

"Goddamn it!" Eddie says.

"Seems like God already damned it."

It's dark as a dungeon in here, a dungeon with only a scrap of gray light coming through a tiny opening above us. I don't see any candles lit. I figure they're conserving candles, since we can see a little from the dim daylight pushing past the rain and through the windows.

Alma curls up beside me, clutching my wet sleeve and trying not to cry. But she's quivering, like visibly. I need to give her some hope. Lightning keeps flashing. Thunder's booming and echoing, like we're inside a bowling alley that's as big as the sky.

"I wonder, when the rain stops, if we could grab a bunch of people and run to the park to replant the wheat. I mean, some of it's already down."

"We should totally try it," Alma says, tugging on my shirt.

"Sounds a little crazy," Jack says.

"Yeah, but Jack," says Uncle Eddie, "what have we got to lose? We can at least try it."

"I'll go," Phil says. "I'll round up others to go, too."

"I'm totally going!" Milo's all enthusiastic.

"I'll go," says Alma.

"Baby, don't you think it would be too hard for you?"

"Being without wheat and flour would be harder."

I shake my head. Not having wheat or flour will make life damned bleak. But I see visions of Alma stooping to work in a hunch for hours. Early labor, lost baby, lost Alma. No. No. No!

I turn her chin toward me. "Alma, you can't."

Her face crumples as she searches my eyes. "But I want to." The muscles in her face ripple with emotion. She looks to the other men in the room. "Can't I?"

They shake their heads at her sadly. Eddie says, "Honey, it would be dangerous for you."

"Damn it!" She flops against the back of the couch, and a loud sigh escapes her. I wrap my arms around her and press my lips into her forehead, holding her tight.

Through the back window, I see someone in a yellow raincoat rushing through our yard in the drenching rain. It's Mom. She stops under the patio roof to shake herself off, then hurries inside. She's barefoot.

"Mom, where's your shoes?"

"I didn't want to ruin them in the rain. I only got a couple of stickers." She hops around on the doormat with her raincoat dripping, brushing off the bottoms of her feet. "I'm cooking for us on the Mint's grill because it's dry. Just came to see what's going on with the crops."

"Mom, you rock."

"I've been known to rock a time or two." She chuckles a bit.

Eddie tells Mom about the wheat and my cockeyed idea to save it.

"Wow." Mom looks worried. "Sounds like a desperate attempt to save what may already be gone."

"That pretty much sums up our whole lives, doesn't it?" I'm hurt, but part of me knows she's right. Not that I want her to be. "Shit. I guess it's a stupid idea."

"Not stupid," she says. "It might've worked if the rain would stop, but I don't think it's stopping anytime soon."

"Doesn't seem like it." I'm flooded with anxiety about Alma with no wheat. Her face seems frozen in shock. I don't know how to help her. We shouldn't've had this conversation in front of her.

Jack breaks the desperate silence. "We need a plan for patrol tonight. I'm too old to tromp around in the rain for hours."

"Nobody should be patrolling in this deluge," Mom says.

"We'd be too absorbed protecting ourselves to notice dangers," Eddie says.

"But, if someone's going to attack us—" I'm getting panicky. "—the rain would give them cover."

"Why don't we go talk to other neighbors about it?" Phil asks.

"Good idea," I say. "Let me go change."

Mom says, "I better go watch those beans and get some potatoes going." She rushes into the downpour, yellow raincoat, bare feet, and all.

The lightning and thunder are rolling northwest, with longer intervals between them. Milo and I have to dig a while, but we find a raincoat upstairs. It's an expensive-looking man's trench coat with wide shoulders. I give it to Milo—temporarily, I tell him—since his shoulders are bigger than mine. But I don't want him wearing this coat every day and ruining the damn thing.

When we get to the bottom of the stairs, Eddie pulls me aside. Alma is at the dining table, watching the rain through the bay windows. Eddie backs me into a corner where she can't see us.

"Listen. Why don't you stay home with Alma? She's being brave, but you might be missing how scary being pregnant really is for her. She's barely an adult, she doesn't have her parents, and it's a damned apocalypse with no doctors. We've got nurses but no medicine, no medical equipment."

"And no wheat." I'm kicking myself for not realizing how scared Alma must be. She's so good at acting brave.

Eddie keeps going. "She spends lots of time alone, waiting for you. That's got to be hard on her. You don't see how worried she is when you're not here. I know from my sisters that pregnant women have a lot going on with hormones and emotions. Alma doesn't act out her emotions, but she lost her best friend, another pregnant teenager, in these same circumstances."

"God, you're right."

"I don't see why I can't supervise the farming until the baby's born so you can concentrate on Alma. You can work in gardens in the yards around us, where you'll be close to her all day. She could go into early labor, and you'll need to be close if that happens."

I gulp so hard I almost choke on my tongue.

"Your priorities have to change."

"You're right. Thanks for pointing it out." There's too much to learn in this world.

Uncle Eddie gives me a hug.

The lightning and thunder have moved on, but it's still raining like crazy. Doesn't seem like the rain has cooled this thick, drippy air one bit. You could practically take a bath in it.

"Let's go," Jack says. "Get this over with before dark."

"Is it nighttime already?" Eddie asks.

"Full dark's probably an hour away," says Jack. "We were out there covering crops for hours." Shit, I guess we were.

Eddie turns to the other guys. "Keno's staying home to help Alma. Four guys are plenty for this."

They file out the door. Milo looks so grown-up in that trench coat with his sandy hair in a ponytail, the shadow of a beard. I feel sorta proud of him.

I stand there for a minute, partly listening to the gushing water out front, partly scraping up courage to face the facts that Eddie put to me. This is a serious life we're living, and I've got to be more in tune with the needs of my brave pregnant wife. It scares me, but I'm determined to do the right thing.

"Alma." I reel around to face her across the room and clap my hands together. "How'd you like for me to wash your hair for you?"

Alma's face is like a beacon of light inside this dark house.

"Wow. Really?"

"Really, baby. We should hurry before the daylight's completely gone. I'm getting towels, soap, and shampoo out of this bathroom."

"I'll get a pitcher. We can stick it into the rain from under the patio roof."

"What do you think if we hide on the side of the house and take showers in the rain?"

"Ooh, I love that. But I'm keeping my underwear on."

"Ha. If you have to. Guess I'll keep mine on, too, then."

Alma and I carry bathing stuff to the patio. We dart our eyes around to be sure no one's looking, but nobody's out in this rain. We laugh and peel off our clothes except for underwear. I grab the soap and shampoo, and with me gripping both Alma's arms, we dash into the rain and around the side of the house.

"I'm so holding on to you to be sure you don't slip," I say. I nuzzle her dripping neck when we reach the most secluded spot—away from the windows next door.

There's a bush between us and the street to give us cover. This grass is sloshy and soggy with patches of mud. It's a drainage swale to take water from the yards to the storm drains in the street.

Beautiful Alma and I take a shower in the rainstorm. I lather up her hair then mine, and we stick our heads under the eaves to let gushes of rainwater rinse out the shampoo.

We soap up our bodies, even inside our ridiculous underwear. It's so wet it's see-through. Everything we've got is on display. We rinse off and linger in the falling roof water. We're laughing, and for these few moments, we're not thinking about drowned wheat.

If God or Nature is going to drown us in a gully-washing storm after depriving us of water for a year and a half, then fuck it, because we're so taking showers in the crop-killing rain.

CHAPTER 27

Alma can't keep her eyes open after dinner and goes straight to bed. She's so droopy-eyed and deflated that I go with her to be sure she gets there all right.

As soon as I come back down, the guys gather around to tell me their new plan. Jack says he and Bobby are each standing guard on their own front porches. They live on opposite ends of the neighborhood, so that might work.

"We're going to Phil's," Uncle Eddie says. "We're taking turns standing sentry on Phil's front porch overnight. You and Milo might want to do the same here."

"How come?"

"When we were out talking to neighbors," Phil says, "I kept hearing footsteps in the grass behind me. I told myself it had to be rain. But then, I swear to God, I heard someone running through wet grass and around the side of a house. It was dark by then, and I couldn't find anyone, but there's no way that noise was rain."

"Shit. Where?"

"Over on Mint Lane, down toward Bobby and Melba's."

"Then I'm definitely standing sentry."

"I'll get the rifles and load them," Milo says. He's suddenly a man before my eyes. He's the only one among us who's killed someone before.

"Bad night to not have a patrol," I say.

"Yep," says Eddie, "but we're better off with more people watching from out of the rain."

We guys pat each other on our backs. Jack, Phil, and Uncle Eddie leave the house, all of them with guns drawn. Milo goes upstairs, and I carry firewood to the garage, hoping it will dry out by tomorrow, until Milo comes back wearing the trench coat, a rifle in each hand.

"Want to take turns?" I ask. "Like in shifts?"

"We could," he says as he hands me a rifle. "But I kinda think we should watch one from the front and one from the patio, so someone has an eye on the Mint."

I gulp. "You're right." I feel like Milo is my big brother or dad or something. "I'll take the patio. I'll check on you in the night to be sure you're awake, to help me stay awake, too."

"'Kay." Milo ducks out the door with his rifle.

I CAN'T SEE MUCH ON this patio except rain, silhouettes of things, and dim candlelight from our kitchen table, plus more candlelight upstairs at the Mint. It's probably not midnight yet. It could be—I've been out here a while. I'm pretty antsy, and it screws up my perception of time.

The rain's so noisy, it could be disguising anything. I keep thinking I hear sounds made by people—breathing, whispering, squishy footsteps in the grass—but I'm hoping to hell it's just rain. It's probably not an animal. They've all been killed off, except for feral cats. It could be a cat, or a rat, or a few of them. If someone's out here skulking around, they could be crouched behind the hedge or cedar fence, and I wouldn't be able to see them from here.

Alma was sound asleep when I checked on her before I came out here. I was glad—I didn't want to tell her what Phil heard and that we're all standing guard because of it.

I put on a rain parka and walk the edges of the backyard. I'm afraid to look over the fences and hedge, but I make myself do it. I don't see anyone or anything that shouldn't be there. From the street-side fence, I see a glint of metal above Jack's doorstep. His rifle, I imagine. I hope he doesn't get sick from being out in the damp.

Since I'm up, I better check on Milo. I start to cut across the yard to the front gate, but Milo might shoot me if I approach him from the yard on a dark, stormy night. I shake myself off on the patio, keep my rifle with me, and walk through the house. I don't want to scare Milo, so I stamp my feet and tap quietly on the door before I open it.

"Hey," Milo says. He's tucked under the eaves inside the nook to the left of the door. He looks cramped in there, but he has to stay that far back to keep away from this damned waterfall.

"You okay out here?"

"Fine. Good," my cousin says. He might as well be my brother.

"Want me to bring you a chair?"

Milo slides his eyes toward the waterfall. "Can't really sit on one."

"Guess not. I can bring you some tea."

"Nah. I'm good." His voice is gravelly, it's so deep. Stuffed up, too, from standing next to a freaking waterfall.

"I'm proud of you, Milo. You've really stepped up lately."

He shrugs, looking down with a faint smile. He's probably blushing, but it's too dark to tell. All right. No use embarrassing him. I want to ask if he's scared, but of course he is.

"Hey, if it's still raining at daybreak, you should take a shower on the side of the house like me and Alma did. I haven't been this clean in forever."

Milo grins. "Maybe I will. Probably should get back to watchin' now, though."

"Probably should, Mr. Adult." I have the urge to rough up Milo's hair or play-punch him, but I can't get to his shoulder in that nook, and he might shoot me if I fuck with his hair. "See ya in a couple of hours. Having trouble staying awake yet?"

"Nope. Not really." A man of few words, my Milo. One of Nana's phrases.

I go sit in a patio chair, propping the rifle across myself and keeping my hand near the trigger guard. My worry about crop destruction, asshole intruders, Rick getting murdered, that stalking prick Ray—it all has me too agitated to think straight.

The Mint's back door jerks open. I hop to my feet as Grandpa steps outside.

"Keno! Bring your guns and patrollers and get over here! Now!"

Fuck. I sprint into the rain with my rifle, yelling, "Jack! Milo! Eddie! Come quick!"

"Hurry up!" Grandpa barks, and he steps into the Mint.

"What's going on? Grandpa, where you going?"

"Get in here. Hurry!" He calls from inside. I stomp across the Mint's patio and yank open the back door. Grandpa's standing in the doorway from the house to the garage. "Out here!"

I run past him into the garage to find the big roll-up door wide open with rain pouring inside.

"What—?"

Grandpa steps into the garage with a lantern, and I see it. The gasoline! All ten of the full gas jugs plus the two garden wagons that we stored over here are gone. Jesus Christ!

"Shit, Grandpa. Why was the door unlocked?"

"Don't know. Ask your damn friends!"

Milo, then Eddie, then Jack skids to a stop in front of the open garage.

"They got the gas. They're pulling it in our wagons. They'll be slow. Let's catch them!"

"Hank, when did this happen?" Jack shouts above the rain.

"Heard them rolling wagons in the garage and called y'all."

Milo, Eddie, and I take off, instinctively heading toward the park. If they went any other direction, I would've seen them—probably Jack would've, too.

They must be close. We've got to be running twice as fast as they can run pulling wagons. But the rain's still pouring like a motherfucker, and we can't see more than a few meters in front of us. We run all the way to the park and don't find a goddamn thing.

We spread out, with Eddie and Milo running through the park to the woods and me running north two blocks then east down Dittmar until I meet up with Eddie and Milo, catching their breaths at the far edge of the park woods.

"Fuck! Did they hide somewhere? Did we pass them? How are we gonna replant the washed-out crops?" I plop down on my butt in the middle of the empty street in the blinding rain. "I told you, Eddie! We have to do something about those guys!"

"Okay! We have to do something, but there's nothing we can do right now."

"We should go after them," Milo blurts out. "Let's go!"

"Hell no!" Eddie cries. "There's only three of us! And I'm responsible for you, so *no!*"

I jump up. "But we've got the cover of the storm. We can't just sit here and let them take everything we need to survive!"

"I'm not letting you run off half-cocked. We'll make a plan in the morning."

"You're wrong, Eddie. So fucking wrong."

"Cut it out. Go home and guard your house!" Eddie runs toward home.

Milo and I shake our heads at each other, and we follow our uncle through the soaking rain, my anger building and building.

"After this, I'm done listening to him," I tell Milo.

"Me too," he says.

The sky's a tiny bit lighter by the time we reach home and stop in front of the waterfall.

"Guess I'll take my shower now," Milo says.

"I'd rather be chasing those guys, but since our uncle won't let us, you might as well get clean. I'll stand guard out here."

He runs inside for soap and shampoo.

I squeeze into Milo's sentry nook with my rifle pointed at the eaves. Goddamn thieves are gonna be the death of us.

Before long, Milo's splashing on the side of the house. Right after he stops, Doris Barnes comes out across the street with Pedro and Chris to wash laundry in buckets they've left in their driveway. I watch them, trying to get my mind off what just happened.

Alma startles me when she opens the front door.

"Milo said you were out here standing guard," she says.

It's light enough now for me to quit, and the rain, at last, is slowing down. I shuffle inside, fall onto the couch, pull Alma into my lap, and hug her with all the energy I have left.

"I just want to hug you," I say, "then I'm gonna make you breakfast. I saw some dry firewood at the Mint."

"Aw, Keno. Really?" Alma snuggles into me, and I breathe in her scent to wake me up and keep me alive.

Eddie doesn't show up to make a plan. Fine. I'll just have to make one myself.

CHAPTER 28

I never could've guessed how much rain we got from the storm, but Jack and Mr. Bellows figure it was eighteen to twenty inches. Freaking unreal. The pace and force of it did the damage. That was too real.

The crops were pretty well pummeled. It's hard to look at them—flattened out, washed away, all broken to crap. Neighbors gather with my family, and we walk from one yard to the next, surveying the destruction. We cry over the wheat; we stay slack-jawed all day. The work we have ahead of us is mind-breaking. Makes it hard to even get started.

Alma doesn't go with us to check the crops. She says it's too much heartbreak for her, and I'm glad she's not seeing this. It's bad enough for her to see the crops in our own yard.

We've lost about half the squash, peppers, cucumbers, and tomatoes. The peas, green beans, and melons were practically drowned. Lentils and pinto beans don't look too bad. Potatoes and other root veggies are growing in the barrels that once held our bulk food, and we stuffed them into garages, so they're all right. At least Nana left us with a big stock and variety of seeds.

We have to wait until August to plant oats, but they grow fast. We can't plant more wheat until late fall, so we'll have to try quinoa for now. But our flour will run out before the quinoa's ready, and quinoa won't be nearly as useful. It's gonna take days before we can even walk in the boggy sludge of our former wheat field, and more days to stack dead wheat to dry for mulch and to plant quinoa by hand. Still, as long as it doesn't freeze early this year, we should have time for the quinoa to mature, if the summer heat doesn't kill it. Too many ifs, but it's all we've got.

What worries me most is the soil. It was so shallow to begin with, only a few feet deep above the limestone bedrock. And with the way we plowed front yards into furrows for the corn, it's like we built canals to carry our soil away.

Eddie's organizing tweeners and teens who are smaller than Milo to crawl into storm drains and scoop out sludgy soil goo before it hardens like concrete, which would make flooding worse in the next big rain. Because there will be a next big rain. There always is one in Austin, if you wait long enough.

We'll add the drain crud to the compost piles, where we'll try to work in more nutrients so we can build the lost garden soil back up. One piece of luck is that this year's corn crop was pretty well-established, so I think it will survive. But if we don't do something big to make that soil better, next year, there won't be much yield in our mini cornfields.

I'm seriously wondering if farming our subdivision has any prayer of working over the long haul.

Plus, all the while I'm counting up crop losses, I'm boiling about the assholes who stole our gasoline. It's so malicious. Yeah, we might be able to get more gas, but for all they knew, they were leaving us to die. Without gas, we're hundreds of years behind with farming technology. We don't even have horses or plows.

With all this work to do, how will I ever get away from here to spy on the camo guys?

***

WHILE WE WERE OUT COVERING crops during the storm, Grandpa pumped a couple hundred gallons of water from the cistern into jugs and buckets so that the cistern had room to catch more rain. Wish we'd thought to keep it more pumped out, or that we'd used more of the water—we could've caught thousands more gallons if the cistern hadn't been so full.

Once in a while, the old man does something right. I just wish to God he'd used his damned machete to chase off those gas-stealing fuckwads.

After a couple of days, we open the cistern for people to take thirty gallons per person for laundry and cleaning. It's a thing we'll only do once in a while, when the cistern gets topped off.

So much laundry and so many sheets and blankets are getting washed that we're running out of places to hang them. Even our second and third sets of sheets are clean, when most of us haven't seen clean sheets since the world fell apart.

All the fences are covered with drying sheets and blankets, defining our boundaries, billowing in the breezes, slightly stained by the cedar fences, but making it look like a party around here.

A farewell party for the crops.

CHAPTER 29

Today, I'm trying to focus on what's in front of me, but how can I? Crops that look like Godzilla stomped on them, assholes stealing our gas, other assholes I had to shoot, still another asshole who traumatized Alma, Rick getting murdered by the fucking National Guard that was supposed to protect him.

God has got some serious answering to do with me, if he ever comes out of his hidey-hole.

All this bullshit is making me hard and cynical and angry, so fucking angry. I never thought I could feel so much rage.

It's like I'm on a Spin-Out carnival ride that's whirling so fast, and I'm plastered to the sides of the big-assed spinning wheel by the centrifugal force, only I'm not strapped in. I'm just spinning and spinning, faster and faster, and I'm in danger of rocketing off the planet, never to return.

Christ! Somebody, please come save us over here!

For days, I've been doing what Eddie suggested: working in gardens close to home; checking on Alma every couple of hours. Near dusk, I come in the house after cleaning up the pepper garden in Mr. Bellows's yard. It's a huge job, and I've done nothing but rip out dead plants by their roots in the broiling sun the whole damned day. Nana's outdoor thermometer says it's ninety-five degrees in the shade. Shit, it's only March! It's gonna be like working inside a skillet by April.

I'm sunburned all over, hungry as hell and thirsty, and I ache down to my pinkie fingers and toes. I'm stinky and sticky with sweat, and I'm in a freaking bad mood about it. But I kind of don't give a fuck.

Alma can see the mood I'm in the minute I come in the back door. I guess it radiates off me so everyone can see it, but especially her. The only reason I care about my screwed-up attitude is Alma. And the baby. They shouldn't have to put up with me when I'm like this.

"What's up, Keno?" Alma asks from across the kitchen counter. She's wearing her scrutinizing face, the one she uses to read my bad moods with painful accuracy.

"I'm hungry and thirsty as fuck."

She twists her mouth sideways. She's none too pleased with me, and I don't blame her. I'm none too pleased with myself.

"Where's everybody?" I ask.

"Milo's hanging with Danny, Mazie's with her mom, your mom's having dinner with the Zizzos, and Jack's patrolling. Don't know where Eddie and Phil are."

I go up to Alma in the kitchen, wrap my dirty arms around her, and kiss her hard. Even in a bad mood, I can't keep my hands off of her, with her belly all round now and smooth. I get horny just looking at her. I want to screw her right here, hard and long and deep, but mostly hard.

This bad mood of mine makes me want sex even more and in a fiercer way. But it would be disrespectful—unacceptable— to go after Alma the way I want to. And I'm frustrated as fuck about it. My dick is hard and throbbing in my pants.

"Better go wash up," I say, so I can break away to go jerk off in the upstairs bathroom. Because I have to right now is all. I'm gonna come in my pants if I don't.

Alma squints at me. She's wondering what's wrong with me. But I can't tell her what's in my head, not with the mood I'm in. That would be disrespectful, too.

So, I run upstairs, lock myself in the bathroom, yank off my pants, and get to work.

I hate the world and everything in it except Alma and the baby, and even them—with the crushing responsibility of it on top of all the other shit—even they piss me off sometimes. It's not their fault. I know this. But still, I'm in a flaming rage.

I hear Uncle Eddie come in through the front door. He's talking all loud to Alma, saying I-don't-know-what. I'm not stopping what I'm doing for him or anyone else.

"Keno?" Eddie hollers.

Shit! I try to ignore him. I'm venting my rage, and this is the only relief I've got.

"Keno, come down here. You're gonna like what I have to show you."

Eddie just won't shut up. Can't a man jerk his dick in peace in this hellhole? Or a man who's supposed to be a man but doesn't fucking feel like one?

"Keno? Supper's ready," Alma calls out.

"Okay! I'm all filthy and trying to get clean with no water up here!"

Oh, I'm filthy all right, coming and coming in my hand.

I wash up as fast as I can, staring into the mirror in the fading light, trying to straighten my face and slow my breath so it won't be obvious what I've been up to. Why should I care if it's obvious? Men jerk off. So what?

I rush out of the bathroom, throw on a less filthy T-shirt, and run down the stairs only touching every other step. I'm suddenly all energized, and people are waiting on me, like I need that pressure on me, too.

"Look what I've got!" Uncle Eddie says the second I show my face. He's grinning his head off. He's got two big-assed bottles, one in each hand, and he's waving them around. I have to get all the way up to him before I can read the labels in the candlelight.

"Black Label Scotch? Where the hell did you get that?"

Eddie can't stop grinning, and I'm grinning with him. Maybe this is exactly what I need.

"Me and Phil found it in the Mint cellar in a cabinet. I brought these bottles home for us."

"Let's get drunk and break shit." I laugh. This is a goofy saying in Texas, but Alma's glaring a hole straight through me, and I don't care.

We sit down. Eddie sets the big bottles of crazy-expensive scotch on the dining table. The squared edges of the bottles reflect the candlelight like prisms, throwing sparkles of light around the room.

Alma scowls at the bottles, and she scowls at me. She dishes herself a plate from the kitchen. She doesn't set the food on the table the way she usually does, she's that mad. My gut clenches about this, but part of me thinks, fine.

What's she so mad about anyway? Can't a man get pissed off when things keep pissing him off? Can't he ignore his wife and jerk off—just fucking once—when he's practically killed himself working in the hot sun day after day so his family will have something to eat?

"Let's get some food," I say to Uncle Eddie, "so we can get busy drinkin'."

Alma drops her fork, and it clangs against her plate.

"What?"

She folds her arms and glowers at me, her brown eyes reflecting the gleam of the candlelit scotch bottles, her pupils like laser beams.

"Well? What?"

"You're gonna get drunk tonight? Seriously?" Tears well in Alma's eyes, angry and hurt tears, tears that just hang there, making the candlelight all wavery in the liquid of her eyes. "I thought you'd want to be with me."

"Yes, Alma. I'm going to get drunk. So what?" I glare back at her, hating myself for it, but I'm so pissed I can't stop. "I suppose you think it would be bad of me to get drunk because I haven't worked hard enough to deserve a break? Like I don't have enough heartache to make me want to drown myself in this fucking scotch?"

"Keno, cut it out!" Eddie's shaking his head at me. "Why would you talk to Alma like that?"

Now I'm breathing all fast, glaring at Uncle Eddie with his back to the windows.

And behind him, the sky outside explodes with color, its reflections swirling around the room. Alma screams.

"The fuck?" Eddie shouts, and we're all on our feet with our faces plastered to the back-door window while the sky twists and changes like a neon kaleidoscope of red and blue and yellow and green. Undulating bands of light, like the northern lights we had, but every color of the rainbow.

"Another solar pulse!" I turn the doorknob. "I'm going to—"

"Don't!" Alma latches on to me, and I squeeze her hand, but fear and the need for truth have me peeling away to run upstairs for the wind-up radio.

"Hey, you can see it better up here in the big arched window," I call downstairs.

"What are you doing?" Eddie asks as he and Alma make their way up.

"Auroras are supposed to make radio waves. I want to see if I can hear them on the radio." I rush with the radio to the big front window and open it. "Holy shit! It's crackling and sighing out there."

"Oh my God. I hear it!" Alma says. Eddie looks dumbstruck.

I crank up the radio and turn it on, but there's no sound coming out of it, only the sounds of the light show outside. I twist the dials in a panic, switching from AM to FM and all seven shortwave bands, but there's no static like usual, no cracking and popping or any sound at all.

"Maybe I can't hear it over the outside sound?" I take the radio into the bathroom and close the door. But there's no buzz, no crackle, not even a vibration in my hands.

"God damn it!" I yell, and I rush back into the game room with Eddie and Alma. "It's fried!"

"Maybe it'll work again when the lights go away," Eddie says.

"Don't think so." I step to the window and start detaching the screen.

"What are you doing?"

"Checking the solar panels."

"Keno, you can't go out there." Alma looks scared to death.

"Yeah, I can. We were outside for the other two. We were a half-mile from home for the second one." I look at Alma in her fear and I try to smile, but I don't have it in me. "It's electromagnetism, not lightning. Be back in a minute."

With ultra-intense multicolored light shooting across the sky above me, I climb out the window and clamber over the roof crest to the solar panels that point south and southwest, facing the backyard. Part of me is fascinated by the light show, but the strobing and flashing are making me dizzy. I'm thirty feet off the ground, and this ain't no Fourth of July.

Before I reach the panels, I smell it. Burned electronics, like our TV smelled after lightning fried it when I was a kid. Scorched wiring and circuitry.

No, no, no! This can't be right!

I scramble across the roof from solar panel to solar panel until I'm in the middle of all three dozen of them, where the burnt smell is so overpowering I gag on it. Still not wanting to believe it, I fall to my knees. There's nothing inside the panels to burn out, so I trace the wiring to the east edge of the roof. Red light pulses in the sky, but not bright enough for me to see much. Then a yellow stream of light followed by lime green. And I see it—the inverter on the exterior wall below me is black with soot.

"God damn it!"

It's all fried. All my hopes for freezers are dead like the cock-sucking wheat. It's all I can do to contain myself as I slide down the front roof to go back inside.

I reach the big window, and Eddie and Alma move aside to let me come through. "The solar's fried to a crisp," I say before my feet hit the floor.

"Oh no!" Alma cries.

I tromp past Alma to the bathroom and the radio. "Radio's fried, too. It's all fried!" I slam the radio into the stone counter, and the radio shatters to pieces.

"Goddamn it, Keno. We coulda fixed that." Eddie's at the bathroom door in half a second, blocking my exit with his arms braced against both doorjambs.

I wave my arms like some kind of angry preacher. "You can't fix it. We're being bombarded with electromagnetic waves, and these must be stronger than the one that fried the grid, because that pulse didn't fry the solar panels or small things like fucking radios!"

Eddie's eyes are huge and full of alarm. "Okay. But you still have to quit acting like a horse's ass."

"Now you sound like Grandpa. Let me out of here."

"Not happening."

I lower my head, ready to charge into him. "Get out of my way!"

"I'm not letting you out until you calm down."

"I am not a goddamned kid, Eddie. You can't put me in time-out anymore. Get out of my fucking way or I'll knock you down."

My eyes and Eddie's are locked in some kind of death stare. We're huffing at each other like buffaloes.

"Stop acting like macho assholes. Both of you!" Alma's eyes are sad now, full of anger. And pain, lots of pain.

"Arrgghh!" I sweep my hand across the counter, and radio parts fly everywhere.

"Stop it, Keno. Just fucking stop!" She runs to our room and slams the door.

I stand frozen, scowling at the mess I've made of the radio and the bathroom and my life. The damage I've done just pisses me off more. This rage I've been building is spewing out of me, and I can't hold it back anymore.

Eddie gapes at me and steps aside. I fly out the bathroom door and down the stairs.

"Alma, I'm sorry," Eddie says, as though he's talking through our bedroom door. "I don't know what's wrong with my snot of a nephew, but I'm going to get to the bottom of it. He's been about to blow for days."

What did I ever do? Fucking nothing but work my ass off to take care of all the broken people in this insane place.

In four long steps, I'm out the back door, slamming the shit out of it. The glass in the door rattles so hard I almost break it, too. Fuck! I pace in circles in the yard to the manic pulse of the lights above me, rage roiling in my gut and my brain. I could kill someone—if I knew who to kill to make this shit stop.

I want to stomp off into the night and keep stomping my way out of the neighborhood, out of this state and country that used to be a country but isn't anymore. Row a boat to freaking France or Spain or Africa, where maybe they still have power and civilization. Maybe they do, but who even knows?

But I can't leave. I'm stuck here. And wherever I go, my rage and grief will go with me like a blood-sucking leech.

Eddie jerks open the back door.

"Shit, kid!" He's carrying a candle in a clear glass bowl that he sets on the table. He's wearing a contorted grin, like he finds me funny, like this is some joke.

"Uncle Eddie, if I were you, I wouldn't come near me. No telling what I might do."

"Yep. A bit out of control, aren't ya?"

I huff at him, curling out my nostrils, clenching and un-clenching my fists.

"I'll get us some glasses if you think you can keep from breaking them."

"Whatever."

"Then I'll pour myself a glass, and I'll sit and watch you pace. See if you can avoid drinking a bunch of scotch and talking to me about whatever the fuck is going on in your head."

"God damn it. I don't know how to stop feeling this way!"

"Okay, that's a start. I'll be back in a minute, and we'll keep going with that."

"What the shit is wrong with me?"

"I don't know, kiddo, but hold that thought. And you'd better be here when I get back or I'll hunt you down and throttle your ass."

Uncle Eddie vanishes as colored lights pulse overhead. I flop to the ground on my butt, lean into the fence, and pound my thighs with my fists. That just makes me madder. I grab fistfuls of my hair and tug it hard, painfully hard, yanking at the roots. Hell, I don't need to waste water on my hair. I'll yank it out by the handful. Maybe I can bleed this rage out of me, since nothing else works. I could bleed out right here, like Tasha did.

And it's this image forever stuck in my head of Tasha bleeding to death, her face so pale, her so scared and crying, "Don't let me die!"—this is the movie in my mind that makes me scream out with all the force inside me.

"God, you piece of shit asshole! Why in your own name are you doing this cruel shit to us? What the fuck is wrong with you?"

Now I can't stop. I yell some crap about God having his head up his ass. I'm screeching and squalling, and my pain's blasting out into the night. I've got my chin in the air, screaming at the sky, holding the ache in my gut.

Fast footsteps outside the fence. Two sets of them.

"Keno? What's wrong?" It's Jack.

"Did something bad happen to you, kid?" It's Bobby.

Yeah, Bobby, like everything!

Uncle Eddie bursts out the back door.

"Thanks, guys. I've got this. Come on, Keno. Let's sit on the porch, see if I can keep you from drawing a bigger crowd." Eddie yanks my rigid body to its feet.

"Sure you don't need some help?" Jack asks.

"Is he drunk?" Bobby asks.

"No, but he's fixing to be," my uncle says. "Sorry, guys. Thanks." Eddie half-drags me to the patio. I want to jerk away from him, but he's stronger than a goddamned gorilla. He plops my ass into a chair.

From the corner of my eye, I see Jack and Bobby still watching me, colored light flashing on their faces. Jack is frowning hard.

"Bobby, Jack," Eddie says, "I found some scotch. If you guys come back with a glass, I'll give you some."

Jack says, "Patrolling," and nothing else.

"Right. Well, if you come back at dawn, chances are, we'll be here."

"Y'all drunks be careful over here," says Bobby.

"Might want to go inside," Jack says. "Especially if more yelling's going to be involved."

"Duly noted," says my uncle. He stoops down to face me. "Keno, buddy, is more yelling going to be involved?"

"Fuck if I know." I'm still holding my gut, trying to breathe right, letting my hair hang in my face to hide the look of it. "Y'all better go patrol. Something bad could be happening while you're over here shooting the shit."

"Yeah, I think we'll do that." The disappointment in Jack's tone cuts me to the quick.

CHAPTER 30

Uncle Eddie looks me over while I slump in the chair and avoid his gaze. He's got glasses on the table, but I'm waiting for the goddamn scotch.

"Don't move, and if you're a good boy, I'll get that scotch now."

"If you want a good boy to drink with, you've got the wrong guy."

"I'm looking for my good Keno. You know, the heroic one? What happened to him?"

"Off in the ozone somewhere. If you're not gonna get the scotch, I've got pacing and shit to do."

"Sit tight." Eddie steps in the house and grabs a bottle off the table. He comes back, pours two drinks, and thrusts a glass toward me. "Take a big swig, kiddo, then start talking."

I want to slap the glass out of his hand. "If you're gonna interrogate me or some shit, I'm already done with this."

"Drink it and shut up then. Why should I give a flip?"

"Some bedside manner you've got." I grab the glass and choke down the biggest swallow I can take.

"Keno, you know you need to talk, so get on with it."

"So, you're some kind of therapist now?"

"That's right. This is Eddie Crenshaw's scotch therapy session, and you are on the clock. I'm more expensive per minute than a rich-assed lawyer." He pulls a chair in front of me and scoots up until our knees are almost touching.

Eddie watches me and takes a slug. I see that my glass is almost empty, so I chug the rest.

"Do much drinking before, Keno?"

"Not much, but I've been drunk a few times."

"Okay, good to know." He leans forward and refills my glass. "Make that last longer than a minute."

"Got a timer?"

"So, are you gonna tell me what's going on in that brilliant, screwed-up brain of yours?"

Crickets chirp in the silence that follows, like they came on cue or some shit.

"What did you do, sleep with someone else?"

"What kind of question is that? You know I love Alma."

"Not acting much like it, are ya?"

"Apparently not. Is my minute up yet? Because I'm finishing this drink now." I gulp down the drink and thrust out the glass for a refill.

"This one has to last two minutes," he says while he pours. "After that, it's ten."

"Fair enough." I take another slug.

Uncle Eddie leans back in his chair. "When you were yelling just now, did I hear you yelling at God?"

"Good ears you've got on you. I called God a piece of shit asshole, I believe."

"That's what you think God is?"

"Right now, I do. Don't know what I'll think tomorrow."

"I thought you were a guy who liked God. What made you change your mind?"

I'm in the middle of killing that glass of scotch when he says this, and I almost choke. "You really have to ask me that?"

"I'm asking, aren't I?"

"Shit, Eddie. Take a look around, why don't you? If you can see past your nose in this dark-ass place. Oh, wait—if you're not blinded by the swirling, colored strobe lights from the sun that just burned up every civilized thing we had left."

That knocks Eddie back a few beats. Takes him a minute to say, "Seems like you're in a dark place."

"Never said I wasn't. I think the two minutes are up."

"I don't want you puking. You need to slow down."

"As soon as I quit feeling like this, I will."

"Feeling like what, exactly? You still haven't told me shit. Are you going to be like this all night, or are you going to talk about your bullshit?"

"I don't know what to say about my bullshit. I just want to get drunk so my bullshit will go away for one fucking minute."

"It's that bad then, your bullshit?"

"Pretty bad, I'd say."

Eddie squeezes my knee. "Keno, honey, you're killing me here."

"Seems to be what I keep doing tonight: hurting people I love." I suck down my whole glass of scotch and hand it to Eddie. He fills it, looking in my eyes like a plea. "I hate hurting people I love, but mostly, what I hate, what I really truly hate—"

My hand starts shaking with the scotch glass in it. I feel another eruption coming, an eruption like Mount Vesuvius.

Eddie sees my hand. "Better drink that before you drop it and waste it," he says. So, I slug it, and then he sets the glass on the table. He grips both my hands, looking so deep into me that I can hardly look back. He murmurs, "Tell me. What do you really truly hate?"

"God."

"God and?"

The eruption comes, this time as a torrent of tears.

"Me! I fucking hate me!"

I have stunned myself.

My eyes are glued to Uncle Eddie's, and his are so sad.

I'm shaking like a shutter in a hurricane, and my face is slippery wet. An upsurge in my core drives me to my feet. A loud, scary moan comes out of my mouth, rushing up from deep in my gut, deeper even. I stumble into the yard and the streaming light.

Eddie grabs my shoulder from behind and wheels me around. He clutches me to him so hard that air shoots from my lungs into his face. He jams his fingers into my hair and pulls my face against his shoulder. I squirm around, trying to escape, trying to get more air so I can moan and scream again, and he squeezes the crap out of me until I collapse into him, letting him hold me.

"Shh, baby. Shh," he says.

"But I—"

"Shh. Just cry, honey. Cry until you can't anymore."

And so I do. Loud-ass wailing cries, with whimpers and breath-catching in between. Then moans—loud and quiet and squeaky moans that hurt me, scraping across my insides, shooting across my throat like a rasp, exploding from my mouth one after another after another.

It's like I have an anguish generator inside me, pain and rage and heartache I've been holding inside since the sun zapped us, some since Tasha bled to death, newer pain about Nana being gone. Moans over my dad leaving us when I was two then moving to Cali when I was twelve. Cries of rage about Ray. Wails over that poor guy Rick, his life cut short when all he was trying to do was generate some light in this dark world.

Moans and wails about me hurting Alma, that she might stop loving me, and why should she love me? Alma, who would never deserve to be hurt by anyone, but especially by me. I'm supposed to take care of her and cherish her forever. Then sobs over my paralyzing fear of the birth and how the baby and even Alma could die, and there being no doctors or medicine to save them, and my crippling dread of accidents that could hurt them, or assholes with guns running loose in the world who could show up any minute to shoot us all dead.

Eddie's shaking with me. His heart pounds hard and fast next to mine. He's got a grip on me that could crush me, but it's a little too gentle for that. Like he's holding me together against forces working to rip me to shreds. I freaking love Uncle Eddie, and I have hurt him. Still, he's trying so goddamn hard to help me.

"I'm right here holding you, Keno, and you're safe, so just cry."

I wrench myself away from him. "No one is fucking safe! I don't even care if I'm safe. What about Alma and the baby?"

"Things will get better."

"You don't know that! People are getting killed by the National Guard. They're supposed to protect us, but they killed Rick. And we have asshole criminals watching our house and robbing us of our only way to replant. Even God is out to get us with that rainstorm. And now the sun's gone ballistic again. There's no reason to think things will get better. They get worse every day! This is the life we're stuck with for what might as well be forever."

"Okay. Let's say you're right. What does this have to do with you hating yourself?"

"I'm supposed to make things better! But every time I try, I fuck it up."

"Who told you that you have to make things better?"

"Nana did." I point at my chest. "I did." I look at the lights shooting across the sky. "I promised Nana on the day she died that I would get us some power, but now I can't keep that promise. I also promised to take care of everyone, and I can't do that, either."

There's no candlelight in our bedroom window. Alma must be so scared and lonely, feeling all her pain. And instead of helping her like I need to and want to, I've wounded her more. She's been hurt too much by life, and I made her think I would never hurt her, like I fucking tricked her, since I ended up hurting her, too.

Something rustles behind me. I freeze inside and whirl around. There's a shape looming in the side yard.

"Who's there?" I shout, wishing I had my damn gun.

"It's me," says Mom. "I heard you crying and ran over here from the Zizzos' place."

"Aww, Mom." I can't say more. The moans and wails are gushing out of me again. Mom rushes to me and hugs me from the front while Eddie hugs me from behind.

"Can I sit you down?" Eddie asks. "I need another drink."

"No shit," I mutter with half a sad chuckle, wiping my hands across my face.

"You've got something to drink? As in liquor?" asks Mom, who's crying with me but also excited at the thought of booze.

"Hey," I say, "the skylights are fading away."

"Yep. That should be good, right?" Eddie says.

"They've already done their damage, so…"

Mom and Eddie lead me to the glider, closer to the guttering candle in its bowl. Mom sits beside me, wrapping me in a hug and rocking me in the glider while I cry and stutter for air, quivering in my mother's arms like a two-year-old.

"I'll get you a glass, Erin," Uncle Eddie says.

Mom snuggles her face against my hanging head and strokes my shoulders. "Is that scotch I see? Real live actual scotch?"

"Fucking A." Eddie disappears inside.

The scotch bottle on the table might hold the answers to the universe, the way the candle glows through the amber liquid and throws a golden haze over the world, and Uncle Eddie looks like a wavery spirit made of light when he comes back outside with Mom's glass.

CHAPTER 31

"Keno?"

Someone's poking me. I can sleep through this, no problem.

"Keno!"

I jerk my head up. A sledgehammer pounds me in the forehead and knocks me back to the pillow. Or, shit, maybe not. A vise is squeezing the crap out of my head.

"Are you still drunk, Keno? Alma said you would be. She's super-pissed at you."

Who's talking? And why's my head in this vise? I can't open my eyes. I mean, I try to, but the sun knocks my eyelids closed. I'm not awake anyhow.

"You must still be drunk. That was some stupid shit to do."

Is that Mazie saying I did stupid shit?

I might have to puke. If I raise my head again, I will definitely puke. Like I can even figure out how to raise my head.

"Keno, Alma needs to cook out here. She said she wants you out of her face. You better do what Alma says. She's about ready to kill you."

Someone should kill me to put me out of this misery. Alma's smart, so she would know that. If she comes out here yelling at me, I will deserve it, but I'm sure I'll puke on her and she'll divorce me. Then I'll just be a fucked-up guy covered in puke and plastered to this—where am I? The patio? How did I get down here? I'm sandwiched between a sleeping bag and a sheet. Aww… someone made me a bed.

"Mazie, where did this pillow come from?"

"I put it there. I've been watching you. I kinda thought you were dead, and I freaked out."

"Oh, Mazie," I whine. I've scared her, and she doesn't need that shit. I try to lift my head again, but the pain. Holy shit! "I'm sorry. That was real bad of me to scare you like that."

I watch Mazie sit back on her knees. "It was super bad. Me and Alma might not forgive you."

"You better move away from me, Tater Tot. I'm gonna puke any minute."

"Gross!" Mazie scoots backward so fast I can't follow her with my unfocused, half-open eye. "You better puke in the yard. If you puke on the patio, Alma will kill you for sure."

"Yep, I better. Here goes!"

I jerk myself up and lunge for the patio edge farthest from Mazie and the grill, my stomach heaving, the world swirling, squeezing my lips together to hold this horrible-tasting shit in my mouth a second or two longer.

I don't think I'm gonna make it to the grass. But the vomit kind of propels me past the patio edge, where I hurl out massive gushes of it. Golden liquid vomit; bean vomit; watery vomit.

I stop for a second and try to catch my breath, but it comes again. And again. This is crazy! It's got to be impossible to have this much puke come out of me. It's like I have a fat hose up my ass, pumping puke into me so I can vomit it out. I hurt so much I wouldn't even know if I had a fat hose up my ass.

Finally, I stop a little longer, holding my stomach and groaning. I sink to my knees, wiping my mouth with the back of my hand, surveying the vast spray of puke before me.

"Holy shit, Keno!" Mazie squeaks from behind me, making my head ring. "You puked a ton! This is even more than Milo puked when he had the flu before the sun zapped us."

Now Mazie talks like me and Milo do? "Holy shit" and "puking a ton," and "the sun zapping us"? Man, me and Milo have got to be better influences on her. Some good influence I am, because I'm puking again.

Charlotte steps out on her back porch next door and looks down at me, here on my knees across the fence.

"Keno, I'm not surprised by this."

"Well, I am! 'Scuse me a sec." I point at my mouth. I've got to *puke* again. "I think I'm gonna pass out."

"Hang on, honey. Mazie, give this to Keno for me." Charlotte comes down her steps and hands something to Mazie across the fence.

"What is it?" Mazie asks.

"A bottle of mint tea and some Tylenol. Slug it down, Keno, and get to bed."

Shit, I've been a menace to those nice ladies and my whole family, and now I'm crying.

"June—I mean Charlotte. I'm sorry. Alma's fixing to kill me."

"Yes, I believe you have some apologizing to do."

"If she ever speaks to me again, can I bring her over to visit you guys, for, you know—an exam?"

"Honey, we examined Alma yesterday."

"You did?" I flop to the ground over that. I don't even care if I get more vomit on me. "No wonder she's so mad at me. I didn't give her a chance to tell me."

Oh shit! I shoot up to my knees again.

"Is Alma all right?"

"She's fine, honey. We listened to the baby's heartbeat. Alma was excited to have you listen, too."

Tears spurt out of my eyes. "Oh man. I've been a world-class shithead."

"Apologize. A little groveling won't hurt you. She'll forgive you. Give her time."

"I'm going to grovel the rest of my life over missing a chance to listen to the baby. That's the absolute worst."

"Not good, but not the absolute worst. Go to bed. Mazie and I will throw some soil over your mess." She's so polite, she doesn't even say the word "vomit."

"Thank you, Charlotte." I climb unsteadily to my feet. "Mazie, I hope you don't stay mad at me too long."

"I'm not mad anymore. You're too funny to be mad at."

"Ha!" I laugh, but I wish I hadn't. "I'll try to entertain you more often."

"Not by getting drunk, though."

"You got that right."

I don't know where Alma is, but I'm sure she doesn't want to see me. Somehow, I manage to stumble up the stairs, toss my pukey clothes in the empty bathtub, throw a quilt over a futon in the game room, and crash in my boxer shorts.

IT'S DARK WHEN I WAKE up. God, I've wasted the whole day. I hear Mazie and Milo downstairs, hooting about some game. I need to find Alma, but what will I do if she won't forgive me?

I go to our room, but she's not there. I find some clothes and linger in the bathroom, brushing my teeth with only a dab of toothpaste and a worn-out brush, trying to slow my breath. I notice Mom reading in Eddie's room as I pass. I slink down the stairs and peek into the living room. Just Milo and Mazie. No Alma. There's no light or noise coming from the kitchen or dining room, either. It's dark as hell on the patio. Shit, did she leave me?

My heart's pounding all out of sync. I'm fearful down to the marrow in my bones. When Milo and Mazie see me, they stop yapping and stare at me. I stare back.

"Where's—?"

"Patio," Milo says.

"In the dark?"

"Uh… yeah."

I stop with my hand on the back doorknob, breathing deep. But nothing I do will slow my heart. I need to get this over with.

I yank open the door, and Alma startles. She's curled up in a ball on a lawn chair with her feet in the seat, surrounded by pots of herbs. I can't see her face, but I feel her dark mood.

"Oh. It's you," she says.

I sit down across from her, but not close. We breathe for a while. There's no use trying to protect myself from this. It's gonna hurt, whatever I do.

"Alma, I'm so freaking sorry."

She huffs at me, and tears shoot out of my eyes.

"Is there…? Do you…? What can I do to make this up to you?"

She doesn't answer. She buries her head under her arms.

"I love you so much," I say. "I never should've treated you like that."

"Hush," she says. "I'm thinking."

"Sorry." I lean back in the chair with my hands over my face, trying not to cry out loud. I count to twenty, and still, she's quiet. I shift in my seat.

Alma uncovers her face and sets her feet on the ground. "I've been arguing with you in my head all night and all day. For twenty-five damn hours, I've been arguing with you. But you weren't there. You checked out."

"I woulda talked to you this afternoon, but I thought you wanted me out of your face."

"That's not the point!"

"Okay, then what—?"

"Shut up and listen to me. Do you know how lonely it is to argue for a whole day with someone who's not there? Don't answer that. It's really, really freaking lonely…" She stares at me. "Well, aren't you going to say anything?"

"You told me not—"

"I wanted to run away, but there's nowhere to go. I wanted to hit you and kick you. I wanted to divorce you."

"God, Alma, please don't do that. I would deserve it, but please don't."

"I've already had this argument with you while you were passed out. I pictured this conversation, you know? I knew you wouldn't want me to leave. And when I thought about you begging me to stay, I knew I'd want to. So, the question is, what am I going to do about you and the way you put so much pressure on yourself until it makes you act crazy? Because you can't do that shit again. You can't!"

My crying won't stay silent anymore. "I don't want to do that shit again. I don't know how it ended up happening."

"I do. You had a ton of trauma and didn't deal with it. You take everything that goes wrong like it's a personal insult to you. You think you should be Super Keno and take charge of everything, fix everything, be responsible for everyone. You hold yourself to a standard that even God couldn't meet. It's an ego trip is what it is."

"An ego trip? I never meant—"

"I know you didn't, but that's the result. How could you possibly think you could handle all this shit by yourself?"

I sigh and press my hands into my face. "I never thought of it that way. I can't step outside of myself and look back in."

"Which is exactly why you can't do it all by yourself."

Alma steps over and sits on the footrest in front of me. She puts her hand on my knee, and I grab hold of it like a lifeline.

"Baby, you try so hard to be a hero. And you try so hard to be a man. But you're also only eighteen. You're a sweet, vulnerable boy who's lost his sister and his grandmother. You have to work so hard to keep us alive. Your father's been absent for years. Your mom's traumatized. Your aunt and grandpa are nutso. You're taking care of your cousins and me and all the neighbors, too, in the middle of threat after threat after threat. You can't fix everything, baby. You need to forgive yourself for that."

"But if I don't fix it, who will?"

She shakes her head, sighing. "I'm not saying don't try to fix things. I'm saying you have to accept that it's not in your power to fix all of it, and you have to quit getting so pissed off if you fail."

"I don't know how to do that."

"I'll help you, because you know what?"

"What?"

"I'm sick of being mad at you." She grabs hold of my face and kisses me deep, with lots of tongue. Then she scoots into my lap until she's pressing her round belly and breasts into me, and I'm melting inside.

"Alma, you're some kind of amazing saint."

"I won't be a saint if you ever do that shit again."

"If I ever do that shit again, I'll shoot myself."

"I'll be super-pissed at you if you shoot yourself."

"Guess I better not, then."

"Damn straight." Alma kisses me again, real slow now, on the lips but not with her tongue. She leans back again, and her face is serious. "Next time you start feeling that way, you're going to tell me so I can help you."

"Thank you. Thank you so much."

"It's a deal. How's your hangover?"

"Better, mostly."

"Good. So, here's what's going to happen."

"I'm listening. I still can't believe you're talking to me, so I'm really listening."

"Sweet. So, we're going to take deep breaths, we're going to kiss one more time, then we're going to eat dinner together like civilized people—except the food is cold."

"That's okay."

"Then you're gonna make love to me."

"Oh, man. I didn't know if you'd ever—"

"Don't call me 'man.' I'm your pregnant wife, and you're my man who put this baby inside me. We're going to move on as adults who're about to be parents for the rest of our lives. And we're going to take care of each other and our baby—our other children, if we have them. And we're going to be bursting with love. We'll go through whatever hard shit life throws at us—but together. Okay, Keno? Are you ready for this?"

"Even in this apocalypse, we're going to do this?"

"I'm not letting an apocalypse or anything else take our choices away from us. Screw the apocalypse!"

"Ha! I'm not gonna let this apocalypse take me away from you anymore, even in my head."

"Good." Alma beams at me.

"Please don't ever leave me."

"I won't."

My mind's racing and my tears are drying up. Suddenly, I feel more like a man than I've ever felt before. I have a woman in my lap who loves me and who I'm so very grateful is here. And we have a baby coming, a son or a daughter we're going to protect and raise right. Instead of feeling giddy-happy like I usually do about Alma, I feel a spark of contentment in the core of me, like a strong man might feel, a man with love and convictions inside him.

"Alma, you are a beautiful woman inside and out. I'm ready for a life with you forever."

I take Alma's face between my hands, and I kiss her like I'm actually a man.

CHAPTER 32

I'm so grateful that Alma's forgiving me and I'm trying to keep my spirits up, but it's rough. I'm glad I blew that toxic emotion out of me, too, but I'm still raw inside. And now I've got the sun to worry about again, and what it could do to us next. If it sends a geomagnetic storm that's big enough, it could suck the atmosphere clear off the planet.

And really, those rogue northern lights must be caused by something changing with the sun. What it could be, I don't know, but the magnetic poles can't shift so fast and so far. The problem almost has to come from the sun itself.

It's just one trauma after another, everywhere we turn.

Alma, though—wow. Forgiveness is a wonder drug.

Tonight, we're going to listen to the baby's heartbeat. I'm hyped about that. And some evening this week, we'll visit June and Charlotte together and they'll tell us about the birth and what my role in helping Alma should be. We think it's about four months away, but we don't know the due date because we're not sure when she got pregnant.

June and Charlotte will be in charge of the birth, medical-wise, but since they're old and birthing babies takes strength, they want Alma to pick two younger, stronger women to help and get trained. She wants my mom and Doris.

Alma's so excited about this, which helps melt my fear for her. Not all of it, though. Not sure I want all my fear to go away. I might not be alert enough to protect Alma and the baby as fiercely as I need to.

Last night, Harvey and Mark were on patrol when a bunch of teenagers ran into the neighborhood, racing down the street and grabbing corn off the stalks. Harvey and Mark had to fire a shotgun to get the assholes to leave. So much shit keeps happening that I can't keep track. It builds more fear inside me every time, fear I'm determined to keep a handle on.

It's probably like this all over the country—that's what blows my mind. If the founders of the United States weren't already dead, they'd be having heart attacks over the way our country turned out.

I could have a heart attack over it, but I'm going to do my damnedest to stop brooding and be strong like Nana—maybe think up some brilliant shit of my own.

TONIGHT, ALMA GOES TO OUR room while I talk to Eddie to be sure we're cool. Eddie says I'm just having growing pains about becoming a man.

At first, I think he's being dismissive of me, until he says, "Buddy, you put a lot of pressure on yourself to know what you're doing as an adult, but here's a little secret about adults." He leans up close to my face. "None of us know what we're doing."

"Ha! You could've saved me a ton of heartache by telling me that sooner."

"It never occurred to me that you didn't already know it. You never hesitate to tell us when we're wrong."

I hug Uncle Eddie for five minutes straight, or that's what it seems like.

***

"HEY BABY, I SAY QUIETLY to Alma when I rush into our bedroom, trying to slow down. "Or, hi to both my babies. How are the two of you doin'?"

Alma's sitting in bed with a candle lit and some almost-clean sheets, another miracle I keep marveling over. She's got Nana's stethoscope and a big smile waiting for me.

"Me and our baby are good. He or she has been kicking me in the ribs today."

"Kicking you? Does it hurt?"

"It surprises me, but I pretty much love it. Sit down here on the bed."

"Sure." I slide off my shoes and sit, giving Alma a questioning look. She scooches up her T-shirt to just below her breasts. Her round belly sets off sparks inside me.

"Let's explore," she says.

Alma places my hand on the top right part of her belly, beneath her pulled-up shirt. I lean forward to see our hands better.

"Feel my ribs right here?" she asks.

"Yeah? You've got cute ribs."

"Silly. Scoot your hand back a couple inches. The baby kicked a second ago. Press down a little and keep your hand there. See if he or she will kick again."

I wait, watching my hand, wondering if this is going to happen now or—

"There! Do you feel it?"

A tiny force bumps beneath my hand, pushing the skin up on Alma's belly and sending a thrill clear through me.

"I did. I do. I feel it!" Tears squirt into my eyes and swirl around. I have to blink to see. I keep my hand in place, and the baby kicks Alma under my hand a couple more times.

"Hi, baby." I am swamped with awe. We keep sitting this way, astonished at what we've created. Finally, the baby stops kicking or stretching or whatever babies do up in those wombs. Alma kisses me real soft and gentle. My heart swells.

"Want to listen to the heartbeat now?"

I gulp. "May I?"

Alma giggles. "Yes, you may. Let me find it first." She plugs the stethoscope into her ears, leaning back on one arm while she probes around her belly with the round end of the instrument. She stops a bit, listens, and then slides the scope over and listens some more. A smile starts in her eyes and fills her face. "Here it is. I'll hold this end in place, and you put the earpieces in your ears."

I have no words for the wonder of this.

I'm taking the plugs from Alma's ears when she says, "Aw, Keno, your hands are shaking. You don't need to be nervous. It's fun, like meeting your baby for the first time."

And this is supposed to make me less nervous?

"Cool," I say, but my hands keep trembling as I stretch the ear thingie.

"Take deep breaths," Alma says. "I'll do them with you. It's like practice for the birthing."

"Oh, practice," I barely say. Looking into Alma's eyes and breathing deep with her—this is helping.

"Ready?" Alma asks.

I stick the plugs into my ears while Alma's giggling, which is super-loud. "Shh," I say with a little smile.

Now tears are streaming down my face, because I do hear it.

"It sounds watery, like 'ga-blum, ga-blum, ga-blum.'"

Alma starts talking. I have to release one of my ears from this device to understand her.

"That's because the baby's in water—or not water, you know, amniotic fluid."

One of my ears is still listening to this heartbeat. "I don't know enough about this. I've got to read all your books."

"Don't worry, baby. You'll learn what you need to know from me and your mom. You have your work cut out for you, keeping us fed and protected."

"I do, but I want to help you, too."

"You will. I'm not worried." Alma doesn't seem worried at all. She has faith. I want so bad to have faith in life, like she does.

"Okay, teach me, please." I listen to the baby's heart a while longer, sniffing back tears, until the intensity and beauty overwhelm me. I have to take out the ear plugs. "Amazing. You and the baby are amazing."

Alma leans over and pets my face. "So are you. The Amazing Keno, my man."

"Ha!" I'm not amazing at all, but I'm totally amazed.

Alma blows out the candle, and we snuggle together under the covers with our clothes on. We don't make love. We don't need to. We're about to burst with baby love.

But as I'm falling asleep and coming down from my baby high, I'm suddenly swamped with the daunting responsibility of this new life we've made. Fear surges inside me like I've never felt before. Not fear for myself, but for Alma and our child.

PART III

CHAPTER 33

I wake up before dawn, glued to Alma, bonded to her body and soul. But it's this bond that makes it clear I have to tear myself away. If I'm really a man now, I have to do what needs to be done.

While everyone's still asleep in the house, I go to the garage and fill my rucksack with binoculars, a knife, ammo clips, bottles of water, and leftover biscuits. I load a rifle, and I stash it all behind a tool chest in the garage. I'm not telling Alma what I'm planning until the last minute. I don't want her talking me out of it.

Outside, I chop firewood like a piston in an engine, piling up enough wood to last a week. At breakfast, I ask Alma if we could please have dinner early today. She looks a little puzzled but says, "Sure. Why not?"

I tote our water rations from the cistern to the house, I take a wagon to the pond for more water, and I retrieve our monthly share of pinto beans and lentils from Silas's garage. I have a talk with Mom about the food stock, and she rushes off to negotiate with others to save what's left of the flour and cooking oil for pregnant women, nursing mothers, and kids. We'll all be short on veggies until we grow some more.

Then I gather a crew to pick corn so we can make cornmeal and corn flour to sustain us while we wait on the quinoa. By afternoon, I'm running from garden to garden to check the crops and the crews. I help a while in each garden that needs it with hoeing, staking, picking, planting. I bring cabbage, carrots, and yellow squash home to Alma—even snag a few new tomatoes.

"Salad!" Alma says, and I make the salad for her in my own messy way.

We have our early dinner, and I try to sound encouraging about the crops. I help Milo get going washing dishes. The others are talking in the living room.

"Listen, Milo, if anything ever happens to me, you're gonna take care of Alma, right? You won't give her trouble? You'll just help her all you can?"

Milo narrows his eyes at me. "Sure, I will. Why are you—?"

"Just promise me, okay?"

He gulps. "I promise." I hug him, and he frowns at me as I walk away.

"Alma, Milo's got the kitchen. Let's go to bed."

"But it's not dark yet."

I snuggle into her neck, murmuring, "It doesn't have to be dark to go to bed, does it?"

"Ooh," she purrs. "Let's go."

PINK AND YELLOW LIGHT FROM the sunset shines through the windows on Alma, giving her skin a golden glow, making her black hair sparkle. She looks like a goddess—a pregnant goddess who loves me. My heart glows, pounds, races at the sight of her. I slowly unwrap her from inside her clothes, happy with every piece of skin I uncover, as though it's new and I've never seen its full beauty before.

She lays me on my back and peels off my clothes. She puts my hand inside her. "Feel me tingling in there?" she whispers. "I'm tingling for you." I watch her black-brown eyes grow bigger and brighter the more I stroke her inside.

Oh, God! We tangle ourselves into each other, making love so sweet, so intense, I didn't know it was possible. I swear, we're one glowing organism, like we're surrounded in a white halo of light and no one else exists except Alma and me.

We linger latched together, catching our breaths.

"Keno, that was beautiful," she says, and I tense up.

"You're beautiful." I cup her face in my hands. "I have to do something you're not gonna like."

She shoots upright and whimpers, "What?"

I sit up and stroke her arms, peering into her eyes.

"I gotta go spy on those guys with the camo and AKs. I have to know how all these guys like Ray and the guy I shot are connected, see if they're building a militia."

"But… that's too dangerous."

"After what happened to Rick, we can't have militias anywhere near us."

"What are you gonna do? Kill them?" I feel her blood racing fast through the quivers in her arms.

"Not by myself I'm not."

"You're going by yourself? You can't!" Fat tears pop into her eyes.

"I have to. No other guy around here can move as fast as I can except Milo, and I'm not taking him."

She wipes my hands off her arms and backs away from me.

"How can you do this after last night, after meeting our baby?"

"That's exactly why I'm doing it—to protect the baby and to protect you. It's my job!" I reach for her, but she bats my hands away.

I jump up and scoop dirty clothes off the floor, throwing them into the laundry basket.

"What are you doing?"

"I don't want to leave a mess for you."

"You're acting like you're gonna die."

I slump down to sit on the edge of the bed. "I'm procrastinating is what I'm doing. It's already dark. I'm waiting for you to give me your blessing."

She sighs and drapes herself across my back, her breasts and belly pressing into me. "Please, can't I talk you out of this?"

"I have to protect you even if you hate me for it."

"You're scaring me." She pushes away.

"I'm scared to go, but I'm more scared of being attacked."

"Don't talk to me!" She flops down with her back to me and slaps a pillow over her head.

I shoot up from bed, throw on the darkest clothes I've got, and pull on a black stocking cap.

"Alma, please! I'm doing this because I love you," I beg one last time, but she's not talking. I reach over to touch her, but she jerks away.

"Fine! I'll see ya when I see ya," I snap, and I'm out the door.

I stop in the bathroom to smear some of Tasha's mascara on my face, raking the brush across my cheeks and spreading globs of black goo with my fingertips. In the mirror, I look like a badass. I'm pissed off and hurt, and I'm rushing with dread and adrenaline, but I have to do this. That's all there is to it.

When I come out of the bathroom, Alma's standing behind our bedroom door, watching me. "You better come home to me," she says.

In two long steps, I've got her in my arms.

***

I CAME ON THIS PARTICULAR night because there's no moon, but now I'm regretting that bright idea. I keep stumbling on debris as I trot down the street. But it's worse in the roadside grass, where things are hidden that can cut you or trip you. I stop when I reach the construction site. The scrap lumber and a lot of the wiring is gone now. I hunker in the building shell and take a slug of water, checking the rifle, chambering a round. It's eerie and lonely as fuck out here. I don't smell tires burning this time. Don't know if that means a thing.

If these camo guys band together to raid neighborhoods like a barbarian horde, we haven't got a prayer.

I slink through the trees at the rear of the building shell then lope behind fences, coming out to the cross street between the two burned houses. I watch for a while with the binoculars, then hang them across my chest and take off in a crouch, hurrying past the schoolyard, moving from one bush or tree or fence to another. Two corners down, I duck behind the bridge posts at the creek, and I use the binoculars again.

Two raggedy guys in camo with rifles braced in front of them, tromping back and forth across the next intersection. I wait and watch but don't see anyone else. They're too militant to be neighborhood guards, with their flak jackets, automatic rifles, and bandoliers of ammo and the stiff-legged way they march. How many houses are they guarding? Are there more guards in other places?

Staying low, I retreat one block and head to the next parallel street. I creep up until I see three more guys at another intersection. How many people live back there? Are there families and kids, or is it just men?

I sneak through front yards on residential streets, trying to skirt the guarded area from a block or two away, going in a circle to find their perimeter. So far, their area seems to be two blocks wide and three deep, with guards at every outside intersection, one with a small fire burning, but I haven't made it to the back end yet.

Behind some of the guards, I see piles of burned tire pieces and columns of cars sitting on rims. Why did they burn tires? Such a polluting waste. Looks like they burned them all up. Why do they burn anything at their guard posts when it's so hot? For intimidation? And who are they trying to scare—folks on the outside or inside?

Beyond the boundaries, most houses seem abandoned and looted, but I have no way to know if any of these houses are occupied. I'm quiet as a cat, flinching at every noise I make or hear. I don't hear much: guards mumbling to each other, a possum scurrying into a storm drain.

Finally, I reach the back side, four blocks in, but I go two blocks past. The blocks inside the perimeter are short with big yards, and the streets are twisty, but there's got to be sixty or more houses in there, though some are burned. Shit. It's too dark to tell if they're farming or what else they might be doing. I need a higher perch to see into the middle and into backyards.

I retreat half a block and scramble up a big live oak tree, careful not to rustle the leaves and small branches. I lie on a fat limb and look through the binoculars.

It's a damn garbage dump in there. I smell the stench from up here. Loads of beer and liquor bottles, soda cans, piles of garbage—some in bags but most of it in a loose pile that's full of crumpled food bags, boxes, tin cans, and rotting crud.

Then, there's something in a big heap over on the north edge—bones. God, are they human? I refocus the binoculars and study the bones. Animal carcasses—mostly small, like squirrels and rabbits, probably some dogs, but a few that are larger—maybe goats or deer?

What are these guys? A bunch of feral animals? They're looters and thugs. They must burn tires because it makes them seem badass. They don't care about wasting resources or ruining the air. All the broken store windows around here—liquor and convenience stores, the Mexican market—these guys! Probably robbed gun stores, too, for their camo and AKs.

A house on their south edge has less junk around it than the others. Up on the rooftop, a Confederate flag—the freaking Stars and Bars. A bunch of racists? Shit. I zoom in on this house. Two guys go inside and come out with rifles and boxes of ammo. Within a few minutes, three more guys do the same. Soon after, a couple of guys take rifles inside and come out empty-handed. This must be their arsenal.

I wonder how much ammo and guns they have in there. Could be a little, could be tons. The house is pretty big. Damn it. How can we compete with that? There's no reason for them to have all that firepower unless they intend to use it.

I think of militias as having a military level of organization, a command structure. They wouldn't live in a trash heap, would they? These guys look more like rednecks or bikers. Are they gun zealots randomly looting, or do they have a grand plan to rob South Austin blind? Maybe they're white nationalists, like those Proud Boys.

Then I see Ray, and my stomach turns. He's standing with a group of guys to the side of the arsenal house, making gestures in the air with a pistol in his hand, like he's having an argument. There's a fire near him, so I can see his greasy hair. Definitely the hard-ass leader of the looters. Fucking pedo creep. I ought to shoot him right now.

I aim at him, my hands and rifle twitching. I'm gulping for breath. *Think, Keno, think.* Goddammit, if I shoot him, I'll never make it out of here alive. But I want to—man, I want to. I keep him in my sights, taking dozens of breaths before I finally lower the gun. *I'll get you later, Ray.*

Jesus. I've been up in this tree quite a while. I don't know how long I've got until daylight. I climb down, thinking I'll go the long way around looter territory and hightail it home.

From two blocks past the guarded neighborhood, I hustle, staying low, toward where I think Dittmar is, but this road curves west, coming out half a block from two guards. I step slowly backward.

"Hands up, motherfucker!"

I duck down and freeze.

"What've we got here?" another guy yells, and I run, darting behind cars, leaping over hedges. The rattle of military gear comes from a block behind me. Rifles cock. Fuck, they're gonna kill me.

I vault over a cedar fence into a backyard. By the time they reach the fence top with all their gear, I'm jumping another fence, then another, tramping through an ashy fire pit, tripping on junk metal. I grab a fat piece of iron rebar and a short-handled spade.

"We've got a live one!" someone screams. "All hands on deck!"

I swing the rebar at a guy rushing toward me when I come through a gate. He goes down just in time for me to slam the spade into the knee of another guy. He's screeching curses, and I keep running in a blind panic, zigzagging, looking for cover, apologizing to Alma, crying for my mom.

Sounds like a gang running behind me, but I don't look back. I might be outrunning them.

A rifle shot zings against the pavement near my feet, and I jump sideways over a hedge as more bullets whiz past. I scrape a hunk of skin off my forearm as I hit rocks on the ground and roll across a yard. I vault another set of fences until I'm on another street. My arm's throbbing like crazy, but I'm running for my life.

I finally reach Dittmar and plunge into a thicket of trees lush with undergrowth. I know this spot. There's a narrow run of raggedy woods along here, but I bet these guys know it better. A dog barks behind me. Fuck. They have dogs?

From the cover of the woods, they seem farther away, but their sounds are probably muffled by trees and weeds. I adjust the rifle so it's in front of me, click off the safety, and run east through this skinny stretch of woods.

Shit, I can't go home. They'll follow me there. And it's gonna be daylight any minute. I've got to find a place to hide and wait until nightfall to make my way home.

The guys on my tail sound like they're in a smaller stretch of woods behind me, but it won't take them long to get here. I see a break in the trees up ahead. Congress Avenue. I veer north where the woods get wider, reach Congress, and dart across where they shouldn't be able to see me from Dittmar. I dive into a patch of trees behind a subdivision.

Mom's old house is a couple of miles north of here, but just to my south is a bigger tract of woods, lots of acres with big healthy trees. Which way should I go? I can't hear those guys, but I can't hear anything above my loud breath. With daylight approaching, I need cover now. I launch myself toward the big woods.

I duck behind the second row of trees, shaking like a leaf, trying to breathe over the pain in my bloody arm. I turn and watch the outlet at Dittmar. No night vision with these binoculars, but faintly, I see four guys run up to Congress, huffing and puffing. I thought there were more guys than that. What happened to the rest of them?

The four guys stop. Two of them aim rifles around. The other two double over, catching their breath. They're older and chunkier than I am, weighted down with military gear. That's the only reason they haven't caught me yet.

The guys bunch up at the intersection. Looks like they're arguing. One steps out onto Congress and waves for the others to follow. They shake their heads and turn around. He throws his arms in the air, yelling at his friends, but they keep going. Finally, he follows them back down Dittmar. I watch until I can't see them anymore, scanning and scanning for another group that could be hiding somewhere.

At last, I trot painfully through these woods to the far back corner. If they come for me, there's a warehouse past the woods. Maybe I could find cover there. I survey it with the binoculars. Looks like a basement stairwell on its back side, and also some outbuildings.

With a route of retreat in mind, I settle in a clump of bushes under the tall trees, keeping my rifle at the ready as dawn arrives. My arm hurts like a motherfucker. Blood's dripping off it, leaving a trail for the assholes to follow. I yank a bandana out of my pocket and wrap it around the place where a chunk of skin is missing.

Daylight lasts thirteen, fourteen hours this time of year. I feel Alma crying in my bones. My whole family will be crying by the time I get home, if I ever get there.

What have I done? I've stirred a hornet's nest full of heavily armed asshole thugs. Not a militia, which might be bigger and more disciplined for a fight, but these guys, who are like a pack of wild dogs. The yards I ran through were full of scrap metal and garbage—no gardens, no kid toys, no farming tools except that spade. No flowers, no laundry hanging to dry, no storage tanks of water, which tells me no women and kids, unless they're fighters, too.

Ray and these other creeps must've been surviving on looting and hunting, but the animals are getting killed off, and there's almost nothing left to loot. They've got to be hungry and thirsty.

The creeps I shot at on patrol at home were stealing from families. I wonder if they're organized about this. They could have plans to invade neighborhoods as a gang, and they would be lethal as fuck if they did.

Wait, what am I thinking? They already know where we live. Ray was there, right? And the asshole I shot. Still, I don't want them chasing me home, so I'd better stay here.

CHAPTER 34

Mosquitoes eat me for breakfast and lunch while I wait in these woods in the simmering heat. Any minute, I'm going to run screaming out of here before they suck me bloodless. Gnats already drank my eyeballs dry. Some even worm their way under my eyelids when I close them.

I doze off for a while. A rabbit rustles leaves close by, and I think about killing it. I could eat the whole thing, but a fire would give me away and I'm not hungry enough for raw rabbit. I make the three biscuits I brought last for hours. Stale and dry as sand, but they keep my stomach from growling. I should've brought beans.

I need to pee. But when I push off the ground with my hands to stand up, holy shit, my arm almost collapses. Goddamn, it hurts. I plop down and remove the bandana from my wound. The skin around it is bright red and hot to the touch. Oh man.

I planned to wait until dark to go home, but I better go now so I can stop this infection from getting worse. I'll have to go a mile south and sneak through the back sides of the stores and strip malls on Slaughter Lane to stay far enough away from these assholes.

IT'S AN HOUR OR SO until dusk, and Alma's on the patio cooking when I come through the back gate. I hurry across the yard, and she blows air in my face as I reach to hug her. She swats me with a potholder, surprising the shit out of me.

"Where the hell were you? Do you know how worried I've been? How worried your whole family is?"

"Shit, Alma, I'm sorry. I almost got shot!" I peel off my rucksack and drop it to the ground.

"God, I knew it. I told you not to go!" She surveys me up and down. "There's blood all over your arm. What did you do to it?"

"I scraped a chunk off it. I think it's getting infected. I was hoping you'd fix it up."

"Fix it yourself! I'm not your mother!" She darts inside and slams the door.

"Damn it, Alma! I did this for you. Why don't you get that?"

Boiling inside, hunger and exhaustion pressing down on me, I drop into a chair and eject the chambered round from my rifle, then eject the clip.

"Shit!" I hurl the clip across the yard, wrapping my arms around my head despite the pain, jiggling my legs, agitated as fuck.

"'Bout time you came back!" Uncle Eddie hollers from across the street-side fence. He's got his rifle. Going out to patrol, I guess. "I want to hear all about it, but…" He pats the rifle barrel. "You better apologize to Alma."

"I tried already."

He gives me a crooked smile. "Better try again. Take a breath and go do it."

I let out a deep sigh. "All right." I go through the back door and stop just inside to let my eyes adjust to the dim indoor light, scanning around for Alma. There she is, in the kitchen.

"I'm sorry, Alma. Please, can you forgive me?"

Mazie lets out a screech from the backyard. I didn't see her out there. I whirl around and rush outside as Mazie screams, "Let him go! You're hurting him!"

What is that? Something's so wrong, I don't understand what I'm seeing.

It's the whiskery asshole I shot and his bald, tatted sidekick. Whiskers has his arm hooked around Uncle Eddie's neck. They're on the sidewalk by the Mint's fence. Tat Man's pointing a pistol at Eddie's head, and Mazie's screaming.

Alma bolts out the door and pulls Mazie into the house just as Whiskers sees me and grins the scariest grin I've ever seen.

I need my rifle, but I threw away the clip like a fuckwad. Gulping for breath, I step forward and throw my hands in the air. Time stops still; my focus kicks into hyperdrive.

"Been waiting for you," Whiskers growls.

Eddie's eyes are bugging out of his head, but they soften when he looks at me.

"So, I'm here now," I say. "Take me!"

Eddie shakes his head side to side so subtly it's hard to see.

Milo's in the shadows on the corner across the street, aiming a rifle this way. I slide my eyes away from him, hoping these guys didn't notice my surprise.

"Let him go. You want me? Here I am." I step closer.

"No, no, no. That's not how this works," Whiskers says with an evil sneer.

"Eddie, can you breathe?" I keep inching forward.

"Yup," Eddie says, but he sounds breathless to me.

"When I saw your skinny ass with that black gunk on your face," the whiskery fuck says, "I knew you were the one who shot me."

"Didn't think you saw me then."

"Saw enough to figure it out." He taps his head. "Used my brains. Figured you came to our place to get some—what do you call it? Retro…? Retro-Bution! So, what did you steal?"

"Got a lump on my head where you hit me with that rebar," Tat Man says, rubbing the back of his head. "Nasty little fuck."

"I didn't steal. I wanted to know who you were. Maybe make some kind of trade deal."

I step forward again. I'm at the back gate, which is partway open, and I step through.

"Stay the fuck back!" The tatted asshole presses his gun against Eddie's temple. "We don't need to make no deal. The way I see it, everything you've got is ours now."

Whiskers raises his voice like he's got a megaphone. "Don't get any ideas that these other folks can overpower us. I know what you're thinking. There's more of you than us. But if we don't come back, our friends will be here to wipe you the fuck out."

Milo squats behind a hedge with his rifle. I don't want these guys to see him, so I keep them talking. I've got to save Eddie. His face is beet red.

"Loosen your grip on my uncle's neck, and we'll talk. We can give you food."

Slowly, I step into the street, still with my hands up, and these guys turn to face me. They're backed up against the Mint's fence. I'm trying to get them in the right position for Milo to shoot Tat Man. Whiskers has a pistol in a holster at his hip. When Milo shoots, I'm gonna grab that gun.

"We want meat, and ammo, and water," Tat Face says. He doesn't have tats on his face, but he's got them everywhere else. "Got any Oxy?"

"No."

"Come on. All these old fucks around here? Someone's got Oxy."

"If they had it, they used it up long ago."

Uncle Eddie is gasping for breath and turning purple. Time is fast and also slow, like we're in a time warp.

"Loosen your grip on his neck! Please! Maybe I can find you some liquor."

"Now you're getting the idea." Whiskers lets go of Eddie's neck for a split second, then regrips him—not loose enough, but the purple is leaving Eddie's face.

"I need me a woman," Tat Face says. "I want that pregnant Mexican girl."

"No, man!" Whiskers barks to his partner. "She's Ray's girl."

Ray's girl? *Ray's girl?* Vomit shoots into my mouth, and I choke it back down. Milo raises his eyes and rifle above the hedge. Then, from the corner of my eye, I see a streak of movement across the fence behind these fucks. Metal glints, reflecting the sunset. Before I can turn—

Thwack! Down comes Grandpa's machete on Whiskers's head, splitting his skull and face down the middle, brains and blood shooting everywhere. I lurch toward Tat Man, who's screaming bloody murder while Eddie is wrestling himself free from the lock of Whiskers's dead arms.

Tat Man swings to aim his pistol at me. Eddie lunges to tackle him, and Tat Man swivels to fire a shot straight into Eddie's forehead.

"*Nooo!*"

Eddie's eyes roll back in his head, the light inside them instantly gone.

Milo shoots Tat Man's brains out, but it's too late. They all fall to the ground in pools of brains and blood and gore.

And Uncle Eddie is deader than dead.

"Grandpa, what the fuck did you do?" I vault the fence and yank the bloody machete to get it out of his hands. He tries to hang on to it, but I'm insane and I knock him to the ground, snatching the machete and waving it in his face. I want to chop him to pieces.

"I was saving my son," he yells at me, huffing for breath.

"You got him killed! Might as well have shot him yourself!" I'm in a blind rage, and all I can see is that hole in Eddie's head. "I should kill you for this!"

Suddenly, I'm surrounded by men backing me away from Grandpa, wrenching my grip free of the machete, yanking me across the Mint's yard and through the hedge, slamming me down on a patio chair at home and not letting go of me.

Because I'm shrieking and screaming like a lunatic, "*God damn it! God damn it! He's dead! He's fucking dead!*"

Aunt Jeri and Mom rush toward Grandpa from different directions.

"*Do something for Eddie. Maybe he's not dead!*"

Jack says, "Keno, he's—"

"*Shut up! Shut the fuck up!*" I close my eyes and am assaulted by flying brains and gushing blood. My eyes shoot open, but I'm still seeing it, like I'm on a poison drug trip. I slap at my head, but the brains and blood won't fucking go away. And the hole, the dark empty hole.

People surround me, but I don't know who. My heart's exploding. I'm sweating buckets but also freezing. Milo's over there screaming, fenced in by other people. Mazie's shrieking like a banshee, and Uncle Tom scoops her up and runs her into the Mint. Phil's on the sidewalk above Eddie, kicking the shit out of the fence until the slats break free.

"*Oh God, Eddie. I'm so sorry! Godddd!*"

I shoulda killed those guys when I had the chance. If I hadn't fucked up my shot... If I hadn't invaded their neighborhood and pissed them off... If I'd melted Grandpa's machete into a puddle of molten steel... I should have stopped him!

Men crowd around, firing questions at me, but I'm somewhere else, lost in replays of splattering brains, gleaming machetes, and that fucking hole in Eddie's head. Alma latches on to me from behind, shaking like crazy, sobbing into my ear. I pull her around and into my lap, but I can't feel her. I can't feel my hurt arm. I can't feel anything at all.

"Snipers," I mutter, and people turn to look—mostly men from our patrol team. "Snipers!" I shout, scooting Alma off my lap and rising to my feet. "I want a sniper on a roof on every corner of our neighborhood. Everyone else, go inside. We'll have a meeting as soon as the sun's all the way up. Eat breakfast first."

The men draw into a circle, sorting out who's gonna be a sniper on what roof at what times. Jack says he can't climb up to a roof, so he'll take care of Eddie. Old Mr. Bellows offers to help him, and so do Kathy Zizzo and Doris Barnes.

Alma tugs on my arm, saying, "Baby, you need to eat."

"Not now," I say.

"Then let me fix your arm."

"Not now, please!"

Alma stares, and I run to Milo. My arm is numb, my brain is numb, and my heart has left town.

I pull Milo to his feet, wrap my arm around him, and lead him to his dad at the Mint's back door. I go out the gate to Eddie, but as soon as I step onto the sidewalk, I whirl away to puke into the storm drain.

CHAPTER 35

I'm in a nightmare, praying to wake up, while I scrape the brains of my pretty uncle off the sidewalk with a shovel and dump them into a bucket. Phil's watching me in some sort of dead-eyed trance, curled up whimpering against the fence he broke.

There's no moon again tonight, which seems fitting. At least I can't see what I'm cleaning up as vividly as I see it exploding in my mind. There are no northern lights, either, like the heavens have gone black to mourn my uncle.

I hoist Eddie's lifeless body with his sculpted muscles over my shoulder and lay him in a garden wagon with his legs draped over the end. Kathy Zizzo spreads a cloth over his face. There's not much behind that face anymore.

I think, *He needs a pillow,* and I squelch the knifing pain in my chest.

Jack, Mr. Bellows, Kathy, and Doris lift Eddie's dead killers into wheelbarrows. They're going to bury them in the poisoned soil by the train tracks after daylight, when it's safer. Can't waste patches of good soil to bury murderers.

We can't have a funeral for Eddie tomorrow. We've got to prepare for an assault. Max comes up and asks how he can help.

"Get two more shovels and a lantern," I say, "and meet me at the little hill where we buried Tasha and Nana."

"Sure. Whatever you need." Max races away.

I start pulling Eddie's pitiful funeral wagon down the street. "Come on, Phil, let's bury our boy."

"God!" Phil cries out, punching the fence at his back, but he stands up and drags along behind me, stone-faced. Someone should play bagpipes or a violin, some sad-as-fuck funeral dirge, but we can't make noise in case we're being watched. So, we go silently around the corner and down our street, toward the little hill that's become our family cemetery.

Silas Barnes is standing on our roof with his rifle braced in front of him, running his eyes along our perimeter. Bobby Carlisle's lying on his stomach on a roof at the next corner, his rifle propped on the roof crest. He takes off his hat and holds it over his heart. I have to choke back a sob.

When we reach the hillock, Phil helps me get the wagon over the curb and Max trots down the hill to push it from behind. At the hilltop, I pace the ground. There's not much room left up here to bury anyone. I use the shovel to draw a rectangle in the dirt.

"It'll have to be here."

It takes us hours before we have a deep enough grave in the hard, rocky ground. I stay in the hole while Max and Phil hand Eddie down to me. I give my favorite uncle the last hug I can ever give him, but he doesn't hug me back.

Cringing from the chill of his body, I lay Eddie down and arrange him as best I can.

Doves are cooing while we fill the grave with dirt and smooth the top into a mound. The sky's getting cloudy and blocking out starlight.

Phil sinks to his knees, holding his gut and sobbing. I put my hand on his shoulder and squeeze it, but I can't cry. I'm some kind of robot, too full of sadness and pain and anger to feel it anymore. And my mind is a dark, whirring blur, trying to land on an idea to save us.

When Phil shows no signs of slowing down on his crying, I clear my throat.

"Phil, I need to get back. These guys are gonna come after us any minute. Do you want Max to stay with you? Or I could send someone else."

"No, go on," Phil chokes out, latching on to my pant leg. "Make a plan to kill every last one of those fuckers. When I come back, hand me a gun and point me in the right direction. I'll do whatever it takes."

I lean down to hug Phil, who sobs harder. "Eddie was the love of my life," he says.

"I know, man. He felt the same way about you."

Phil flops to his back on the ground and covers his face, and we leave him there. I would say it's the saddest thing I ever saw, but it's just one in a mountain of them.

Max and I go down to the street, and my mind suddenly hits on a way out.

"Wait here," I say to Max, and I run back up the hillock to Phil. "Come on, man. Let's get some gasoline."

"Gasoline? Now?"

"I'm pointing you in the right direction, Phil. Let's go."

BY THE TIME WE GET back to our garage, we've still got a couple of hours until daylight. We load up the tank pump and other tools plus all the empty gas cans into the four wagons we have left. I get four rifles out of the house, and we head to the Mint.

Once there, I unlock the garage and get Max and Phil started loading more empty gas cans, and then I slip into the house and tiptoe to the room that Milo sleeps in when he stays with his parents. He's awake when I open his door.

"Let's go get some gas," I whisper, and Milo's already throwing on his shoes.

We go straight to the convenience store on Menchaca where we got the gas before, and the tank seems to be at the same level we left it at months ago. I'll bet other more noticeable gas stations are more cleaned out, but this little one's been overlooked.

By the time we fill all our cans except the three diesel ones, there's not much gas left in this underground tank. We fill the diesel jugs for Jack's tiller.

It's almost daylight when we get back to our garage, and we store the gas and wagons inside.

"What's your plan?" Phil asks me, his eyes puffy and bloodshot, his face strained as fuck.

"You need to sleep."

"Can't do that," he says, and I blow out a loud sigh.

"Then go relieve Bobby as a sniper on the Patrowskis' roof, and get some rest in the afternoon, even if you don't sleep. All of you, meet me back here at dusk. Milo and Max, go eat breakfast. As soon as you get a chance, go to the dump and gather up about three dozen beer bottles. Be sure they're not cracked. See you at the meeting."

"I'm not goin' to any meeting," Milo says angrily.

"Relieve Silas on our roof then."

"But, Keno, what's your plan?" Phil asks.

"I'm hoping we don't have to use it. I'll tell you about it if we do."

"Plan B, then?"

"More like Plan X."

**

ALMA'S STARTING A FIRE IN the grill with one candle lit and only a little smudge of light on the eastern horizon. She rushes to hug me. I hold her in my arms, but I'm about as loving as a pile of nails.

She backs away and studies me. "You're covered in I-don't-know-what, and you smell like death. And gasoline. Go clean up so you can eat."

"Who cares if I'm dirty and stink like a cesspool? Eddie was murdered, and we're gonna be attacked. Do you expect me to be all civilized and sit down to a lovely breakfast?"

She glares at me, shaking her head. "Just go!" She points into the house.

"Shit, I'm going," I mutter, and I stomp across the threshold.

But Alma gasps. "Jesus, Keno. The cut on your arm is filthy and bright red. Get up there and get it clean. I'll come up and bandage it for you in a bit."

I look at Alma with her big pregnant belly and our baby inside her. She's pissed at me, and I don't blame her. She's got to be in pain, too, from grief and carrying the baby around. I haven't comforted her or helped her. She might as well have an automaton for a husband.

"Sorry. I'll bring the bandaging supplies down so you don't have to climb the stairs."

She blinks at me, taking a breath. "Thank you."

But upstairs, I can barely undress. I'm so tired and my arm is so sore. I wonder if we have any coffee hidden somewhere.

My body is filthy, and my mind's a thin scab over a gash of horror. Who needs to be clean for a goddamned war? But I think of Nana telling us we need to have dignity no matter what, and I use a whole gallon of water to wash up.

CHAPTER 36

"Let me put goldenrod on that cut and bandage you up," Alma says when I come downstairs. I wish I could feel more grateful for her help. The pain from her rubbing herb paste on my arm is intense, but it's helping me feel less numb.

"Your mom says Grandpa strained his back with the machete," Alma says.

"Good. Wish it had killed him," I say.

"You shouldn't talk like that."

"Don't try to get me to be nice right now. How about that?"

"I know you're grieving, but don't be a shit."

I hang my head and spike my hair with my fingers. "Sorry."

Mom comes downstairs with her hair poking out everywhere. She stands several feet away from me, quivering. Except for her red eyes and nose, there's no color in her face.

"Aww, Mom." I start to get up and go to her, but she thrusts out her hand like a stop sign.

"I came to tell you I love you and I'm going to see Eddie before the meeting."

"Do you need someone to go with you?"

"No! I want to go alone."

Suddenly, I understand why Mom couldn't let me touch her after she found out that Tasha was dead and why she doesn't want my sympathy now. Something inside each of us is wielding our grief like a shield. Or a cudgel.

Mom's turning around to leave when I say, "I brought those guys here. It's my fault that Eddie's dead, isn't it?"

She flips her face toward me with a tight grimace. "I don't know, Keno. I don't know anything anymore."

So, it is my fault is what she means.

Jack knocks on the back door and comes on in, and I go to the table to talk to him.

"I warmed up last night's dinner for you," Alma says, and she slides a plate of beans and veggies in front of me.

"Thank you."

"How're you holding up, kid?" Jack pats my shoulder.

"Don't ask." Part of me wants to cry and let Jack comfort me, but it's not even something I could do. Too numb on the outside, too explosive on the inside, one spark away from impaling everyone nearby with shrapnel when I blow. "Think there's any chance those assholes were bluffing and their friends won't actually come for us?"

"There's a chance, but a slim one. We have to play the odds and be ready."

"But how can we even be ready? How do we protect the old people and kids? What about Alma? And Sandra—I heard she's pregnant, too."

"Is there room for them all in the Mint cellar?" Jack asks.

"It'll be tight, but they can squeeze in if they have to."

"Then, at the meeting, we'll get people to set up the cellar so they can stay there for days, if it comes to that."

"I can't believe we have to do this, but okay," I say. "The bigger problem is: how do we win a fight? I saw as many guys awake over there as the total number of shooters we've got. Even if only half those guys were sleeping, they're still double our size. They have way more guns and gear than we do, plus they're not weighed down with helpless people to protect."

"They don't have women and kids, old people?"

"Didn't seem like it. Garbage everywhere, no gardens, no laundry drying, no water tanks. Hard to imagine a woman with kids living that way."

"She would if it's the only choice she's got," Jack says.

SOON, SILAS, DORIS, PEDRO, AND Chris show up at our back door. I wonder if Chris knows how to handle a gun. He's thirteen. But how can I put Alma's brother in harm's way? I'd better leave that decision to her.

Within minutes, most of the neighbors are crowded onto our patio. All the men and some women are armed to the teeth—at least armed as much as they can be. We don't have automatic rifles for every trained shooter, and we don't have enough pistols and shotguns to arm everyone else. This is not something we've planned for. I'd be surprised if we have enough ammo to hold out for a single day.

Since I've got a rifle in a wagon in the garage, I pull the pistol from my hip pocket, check it over, and give it to Alma.

I explain to the gathered neighbors what I saw in asshole territory. Then Jack tells them his idea of hiding vulnerable folks in the Mint's cellar.

"I'll go get started on that," Mom says, the strain on her face adding years to her age. "Someone will have to handle Jeri and Dad, and that's my job." She's as agitated as Milo and I are. When you're grieving and angry, meetings are like getting your fingernails ripped out.

"I'll go with you," Kathy Zizzo says.

"So will I," says Bobby's wife Melba. Her baby's wound up in a cloth across her front.

People start debating what to do. Jack and Bobby go back and forth about military tactics, like distractions and flanking and breaking sieges. I try to follow it, but it all seems absurd.

"We're not a trained army. We're not even an untrained one. We have to do something else."

"Who put you in charge, Simms?" Bobby asks. "You're a kid."

Someone else says "Yeah!" but I can't see who.

"He's Bea's grandson," Jack says. "She groomed him to be a leader. His uncle was our leader, but he's gone."

Tears hit my eyes over Eddie being gone.

Bobby swats a mosquito on his arm, and blood splats out. "So, y'all have your own family fiefdom now, where leadership is passed down in the family? What are we—your serfs?" People grumble, like maybe they agree with him.

"No, wait!" I hold up a hand. "I don't want to be the leader, okay? I'm just starting the discussion. I have ideas, but I want to know what everyone thinks. We decide as a group."

Bobby makes half a snort sound. "I'll go along for now because it's an emergency, but things need to change around here. I'm not putting up with this forever."

"Sure. Lots of things need to change, but we'll figure it out together... After this."

Bobby barely nods, so I go on.

"Seems like we need someone posted past the park with some kind of signal to let us know when the assholes are coming, so we can take our positions."

"Good. I can organize that," Jack says.

"We need more people to help us fight. Maybe more people would make them think twice about attacking us."

"Who would that be?" Silas asks. "We don't know anyone else."

"There's that guy who stole the rabbit. He and his neighbors were trying to help each other, or that's the impression I got."

"He said they weren't doing so well," Harvey pipes up. "We'd have to feed them, and no telling what else they'd need. We're in no position to do that."

"But it could make the difference in whether or not we survive."

From the way neighbors stare at me, I can tell this idea won't fly.

"Yeah. We don't have time to organize that anyhow." I pause, racking my brain. We have no idea what we're doing, but I can't say that. "That's all my ideas right now. What do y'all think?"

"We set up fortified positions in our yards and houses, on our roofs," Jack says, "and we pick them off one at a time."

"Too many of us will end up dead. It won't work." I whirl away from the group and take off pacing around the yard. "There has to be a better way."

With his rifle at the ready, Milo watches me from our roof, then seems to remember he's supposed to be watching for danger and turns his back to us. Phil glances at me from the roof on the next corner and goes back to scanning the perimeter.

Neighbors murmur among themselves, spreading out into the yard, and I keep pacing. My mind's like a high-speed train that's fixing to fly off the rails. I need a better idea than the only one I've got, but it won't come to me. Everything I think of gets us killed. Even though people say they don't want me to lead, they also seem to want me to figure things out. The responsibility for all these lives is on me, and it's terrifying.

"We could send a delegation to make peace with them," Doris says, and Silas frowns at his wife.

"Doris," he says, "what would we have to give them to make peace with them? We'd have to be their slaves for life."

"You don't know that, Silas." Doris crosses her arms, looking more obstinate than I've ever seen her. "They might be just as scared as we are. They might welcome the chance."

"They might," I say, stopping my pacing to focus on Doris and Silas. "But, even if they say they want peace, how do we know they'll keep it? They're thieves and looters. At least two of them were murderers. Not exactly trustworthy." I go back to walking the yard.

"Blah, blah, yadda, yadda, yadda." People keep debating, but that's what it sounds like to me. A bunch of useless gobbledygook. I stop and survey the sky, which seems normal today, as though it's taking a break from its campaign of fuckery against us.

There's only one answer to this. I turn to squarely face my neighbors and raise my arms in a plea. They gape at me. They're waiting, but I can't tell them.

Because, as far as I'm concerned, we have to go on the attack.

In my racing mind, I hear Uncle Eddie arguing with me. "You have no justification to do this, Keno." But that's the argument he would've made before they murdered him.

The other people in the camo neighborhood didn't kill Eddie. We don't know that they're killers. But they have that rebel flag, like white nationalists would. How many of us will die if we wait for them to attack us? I can't ask the parents and old people in front of me to risk themselves that way. I have to fall back to Plan X.

I take a deep breath. "Let's get ready to be attacked while we try to think of other options. I don't have one for you. Wish I did."

Bobby goes down to stand watch on Dittmar past the park, taking Jack's airhorn with him. Max goes a few blocks into the empty neighborhood behind us with a referee's whistle to do the same.

The rest of us make a plan to defend ourselves—picking out initial spots to fight from as well as fallback positions and divvying up the jobs to be done. Those bastards could attack any time, but probably not until nightfall. It could even be days, if we're lucky.

Fuck luck. It's all up to us.

CHAPTER 37

People scramble around, boarding up windows at the Mint and our house, plus the ones on the side street where Jack's house is. We're thinking they'll be coming from the east or south, so these houses are for falling back. Other folks are pushing cars into place and stacking wood and buckets and whatever barriers they can find along the park-end of the neighborhood, creating positions for our shooters to hide behind. I run around, helping, but I also have my own agenda.

In the late afternoon, I see Milo's friend Danny and take him aside. "I need your help with a secret mission, but it's dangerous as fuck. Want to help?"

"Shit, yeah. What do I do?" He brushes hair from his face and squares his muscly shoulders. He's a trooper of a kid, but his enthusiasm for danger is a little worrisome.

"First, sneak your darkest clothes out of your house and dirty up those white sneakers so they don't shine in the dark. Then meet me at our garage in ten minutes."

In about five minutes, Danny meets me where I have the garage door open only a couple of feet. He ducks inside, carrying a wad of clothes, his sneakers covered in dirt.

"Good man. Go ahead and put those clothes on."

"So, what's the mission?"

"I'll tell you when you need to know. Right now, while the neighborhood's all chaotic, I need you to sneak two of these wagons out of here. Milo and Phil are on sniper watch on this side and they're with us, so go out north to Dittmar and wait in some trees or bushes across the street. It may take a while, but I'll send others when they can sneak out."

Max peeks beneath the door. "I've got your beer bottles, but the wheelbarrow won't fit under this door."

"Hang on." Shit, someone's gonna see him. I raise the door another foot, and he shoves a wheelbarrow full of beer bottles into the garage.

"What's the plan?" Max asks.

"Top secret. I'll explain when we're on our way." I stand back to look him over. His face is full of determination, but he's gangly and uncoordinated. I hope he can handle himself in a fight. "Your clothes look pretty dark. Turn your T-shirt inside-out so that logo won't show." He gulps and pulls off his shirt. "Who replaced you on watch?"

"Harvey," Max says.

"That's a good job for Harvey. Do you know who's relieving Bobby?"

"Silas was gonna do it, but Bobby said he wanted to stay. He wants to be in the front of the fight."

"That's good. He's our best fighter. So, Max, you go with Danny—he knows what to do. First, help me get the tools out of this wagon and put the bottles into it. Let me get you some motor oil." I grab three bottles of oil off the shelves.

"What for?"

"No time to explain. I gotta find us a couple more people. When Phil and Milo come down from sniper watch at dark, we'll meet y'all over there. Here, take these funnels, and while you wait for us, pour motor oil into each bottle about a quarter way up, but only as many bottles as you can keep upright in the wagon. Here's some rags to pad the bottles so they don't rattle against each other." I hand him a pile of Grandpa's red rags.

"Shit, Keno, what are you up to?" Max gapes at me, and so does Danny behind him.

"You don't have to go, man. Seriously. We could get killed."

Max licks his lips and rakes a hand backward through his hair, running his eyes over the wagon carts and their cargo. He nods sharply. "I'm going. I just hope you know what you're doing."

"So do I. It's the best idea I've got."

"Well, I don't have any ideas, so let's do this."

"Okay, time to go." I give Max and Danny quick hugs and duck out the door. "Coast is clear. Hustle!" And out they come with two garden carts full of gasoline and another full of bottles, rags, and oil.

I whistle softly to Milo, who crouches and looks down at me from the roof. "Let them pass," I say, and he nods.

Danny and Max trot west toward the railroad tracks, pulling three wagons behind them. I watch them until they turn right on a dirt trail, and then I run to Greta's house. Of course, she's not home, so I go in search of her while I also make sure that Silas is going to replace Milo on the roof at dark and Mark is going to replace Phil. Shit, I have to get this other wagon of gas out of here while Milo and Phil are still on watch.

Finally, I find Greta boarding up the front window at Jack's house. She's tough-minded and athletic, and she's usually game for whatever needs to be done. I hold a board while she hammers in the last few nails, and then I talk to her quietly.

"I need your help on a secret mission. It's fucking dangerous."

She puts her hands on her hips and searches my face. "Everything's fucking dangerous. What do you need me to do?"

"Come with me."

"What's all this gas?" Greta asks the instant we duck into the garage.

"We need to get it out of the neighborhood, like now."

"Keno, what in the world are you doing?"

"I'm not letting these cocksuckers attack our neighborhood and kill kids and parents and old people."

Greta narrows her eyes at me. "So, you're gonna burn them out? That's sick."

"We're gonna burn down their arsenal."

"Shit." She runs her hand from her forehead, over her cheeks, down to her chin. "Okay, let's do it."

"Thank you. Take this wagon, go west to the trail, then go down to Dittmar. Danny and Max are waiting. They should be hiding in some trees. Milo, Phil, and I will be there right after dark."

"Okay. Super Greta at your service." She gives me a dorky grin, and I have to laugh, but only for a second.

"Wait. Almost forgot." I go to a shelf, pull off a plastic tub, and stuff it into Greta's wagon. "When you get over there to wait for us, pour the gas off the rags that are soaking in this tub, but put the lid back on it."

"Whatever you say, boss."

I duck out the door—check to be sure no one's looking. "Go!"

And Super Greta hurries from the garage, trotting fast and shooting furtive glances everywhere as she hightails it out of the neighborhood, pulling her wagon into the pink and purple sunset.

***

I'M BACK IN THE GARAGE, closing and locking the door, when the door into the house suddenly opens, startling the shit out of me.

"Keno," Alma says, "what are you doing out here? Where's all the gas?"

I lead Alma to sit on a crate and crouch in front of her to tell her the general plan. She looks more horrified by the minute.

"Joaquin Simms! What about your soul?"

"How is it any better for my soul to let half our neighbors get killed in an attack when I have a chance to stop it? I can't put you and everyone else at risk like that. Better a few of us than all of us."

Alma's eyes burn with intensity as she scrutinizes my face and pushes her fingers up into my hair. "You're not the sweet boy I married anymore."

"I'm not. I'm sorry. The world won't let me stay sweet."

She pulls my forehead against hers, peering into my eyes. "This new manly Keno turns me on."

A laugh shoots out of me, despite my anxiety. "Seriously?"

"You're my fierce protector, baby. And I'm your fierce pregnant wife."

"Alma." I sigh, and she lays a powerful kiss on me, but she cuts it short.

"Get going, fierce one. Go save our asses while there's still time."

I bury my face in her breasts and run my hands over her belly, feeling the shape of the baby inside her. "I'll help you get settled in the cellar," I say.

"Nope. Your mom's already there. I'm taking June and Charlotte over there pretty soon. You better go before they show up. I made a ton of burritos and put them in plastic bags. I thought you'd need them while on guard, but you can take a bunch for your crew."

"Don't you need them in the cellar?"

"Told you I made a ton. Everyone else was doing hard labor. My job was to cook."

"Baby, you're amazing."

"Yes, I am. Now get out of here."

I almost choke on the emotion roiling inside me. "Alma, if anything happens to me—" She presses her hand to my mouth.

"Don't say it. I love you, I'm saying prayers, and I'll see you in the morning."

I help Alma to her feet and hug her like it's my last chance. She hugs me the same, then peels my arms off of her.

"Go, already!"

"Okay! I'm going!" I follow her inside with the rifles, lay them on the couch, and run upstairs to put on dark clothes. I grab Tasha's mascara out of the bathroom. When I come back down, Phil and Milo are here, and Alma's loading them up with a rucksack full of burritos and bottled water.

"Alma," I say. "I need one more favor, please. Can you distract Silas on our roof so we can sneak out of here? It'll take a few minutes for us to get out of his sight."

"Sure. I'll start crying and get him to tell me the whole plan that will make me safe."

"You're good. I love you to the moon and back."

"That's not far enough."

"Okay. I love you to the farthest galaxy and beyond."

"Same to you," she says, and she steps out the back door. "Oh, Silas!" she cries out like a sob. "I'm scared to death! How are we ever going to survive this?"

Milo, Phil, and I lock eyes, grab rifles, and dash out the front door, running like our lives are on the line, because they are.

MAX, DANNY, AND GRETA ARE having anxiety fits by the time we get there. I hand out burritos and water, and we scarf down dinner while I explain the layout of the camo-guy neighborhood and where the arsenal is. I draw a funky map in the dirt.

"We'll start a fire behind the arsenal here, then toss Molotov cocktails on the roof and out in front. But first, we start a fire on the other side of their territory as a distraction, so they'll all go over there, making it easier for us to burn the arsenal."

"Keno," Greta says, "what makes you think burning down their arsenal will be enough? They'll already be armed, and they'll run out of there with their guns, straight for us."

"We'll slow them down. We'll hobble them. We can shoot the most ferocious ones."

"I think you have to trap them in a ring of fire."

"God, Greta. That's, like, a war crime!"

"Yeah." Phil's eyes are steely. "But how else do you kill monsters?"

"We can leave them one way out. They have to drop their guns before we let them out."

"I don't know," Greta says.

"Me neither," says Phil. "Let's just kill them all and get it over with."

Damn it! I shouldn't have brought angry adults with me. These kids will listen to me, but not Greta, and definitely not Phil, who's wounded and out for revenge. But revenge is useless bullshit.

"Phil, I'm pissed off and crushed over Eddie, too, but the people in that neighborhood didn't kill him. Two guys did that. We don't know if their friends are even coming for us. We need to disarm them to make sure they don't. Scatter them to the winds."

"They'll regroup and steal more guns," Greta says.

"Maybe so. But this will buy us time."

"To do what? Lower our guard so they can sneak up and kill us?"

"Greta, Phil, we're doing this my way. If you don't like that, go home and help there. If my plan doesn't work, you can mount your own attack another day."

"Like there's gonna be another day," Phil mutters.

"Goddamn it, Phil! Stop that shit! There has to be another day. I've got a baby coming. And you know, Phil—"I lean up in his face. "—you know that Eddie wouldn't like us thinking that way. So cut it out!"

Tears flow out of Phil's eyes and down his cheeks as he glares at me.

"I'm sorry, Phil. If you need to go home, there's no shame in it."

He clenches his teeth so hard I hear them grind together. "Let's just do this."

"Help me pour gas into these bottles and stuff the gas-soaked rags into them. I already cut some wine corks in half for stoppers." I pull wine corks and more funnels out of my rucksack, and we get to work. I also hand each person partly full boxes of kitchen matches. We pad up the gas bombs with dry rags so they don't bump against each other.

"Whoever pulls this wagon has to go slow and be careful as fuck."

"I'll do it," Greta says. "Can't trust delicate work to men." Everyone stares at her. "What? I'm kidding."

I realize I don't have enough mascara to darken every face, so I pour a little puddle of water on a patch of dirt.

"Cover your faces, arms, and hands," I say, and we make muddy messes of ourselves.

We head east on Dittmar slowly, a wagon train loaded with explosive power. I stop them when we get even with the park so I can run over and tell Bobby what we're doing. Don't want him shooting us, and I want him to know how many shooters he's missing for guarding our families.

"Shit, Keno. You sure about this?"

"No, but I don't want them coming here."

"For a kid, you've got some balls on you, man. I'll give you that." I gulp, and Bobby looks straight into my eyes. "Give 'em hell!"

WE'RE A RESTLESS LITTLE CARAVAN out here in the deep dark—lots of fidgeting and sighing, our feet too noisy when they slap against the street.

"Practice being quiet as death," I murmur, shivering at my own words. "I don't wanna hear one footstep, sniffle, or sigh."

"Yes, Sergeant," Milo whispers, a sideways grin on his face. I give him the evil eye, half-humorous and half-not.

When we're almost to South First, I stop them again. "Last chance to empty your bladders, blow your noses, cough up loogies, say your prayers and mantras, whatever you gotta do. 'Cause once we cross South First, it's game on."

Greta ducks behind some bushes. "Peein' back here. Stay away."

We guys take leaks, slug water. Max and Phil blow their noses into the street.

"Huddle up," I say, and we crouch in a circle. "They have guards at every outside intersection, so we have to stay a block back from their perimeter. When we get there, we split into three teams of two. Milo and Danny, you take one wagon and go one block past the back end of their perimeter. Spread a line of gas along the curb and over anything flammable. Stop pouring and get yourselves and the gas cans several feet away. Be sure there's no gas drippage for the fire to come toward you. Greta and Max, you stay on this side and do the same with the gas. Phil and I will go to the other side. The intersections are farther apart over there, so we should be able to get close enough to douse the back side of the arsenal, plus along the street.

"I'll whistle when we're ready, and Greta, you light your fire. When the assholes run to your fire, we'll light up the arsenal. Milo, you wait to light your fire until you see mine. Then, all of you run back around to the escape hatch we're leaving in front for them to get out. Duck fast behind cover, where you can fire at them if you have to.

"We're only creating the illusion that they're hemmed in by fire. We can't get close enough to light up everything, and we don't need to. We've just got to take out the arsenal and scare them out of there unarmed."

"Who's throwing the cocktails?" Greta asks. "Up until the solar pulse, I was the best right-fielder in Austin women's softball."

"I was a high school quarterback," Phil says.

"Okay. We split them up. Greta, you toss a couple into your side so that the fire over there looks threatening enough to get them all to run to it. Save the rest in case we need them later. Phil can toss them on the roof of the arsenal and out front of it."

"Are you sure we made these suckers right?" Greta asks. "Don't want them exploding in my hand. How'd you even know how to make them?"

"Science geek," I say, and I leave it at that.

We start to go, but I say, "Let's ditch one of these wagons. We'll hide it in the bushes and stuff the cocktails in with the gas cans. Fewer things to slow us down."

We do all that quickly, then check one another's eyes. "Remember, quiet as death."

CHAPTER 38

The closer we get to camo-freak territory, the louder our wagon wheels sound on the road. I spread us out at first, but that's not good enough. We roll our wagons across overgrown lawns, where the wheels still make noise, but less than they do on asphalt. When we get to the schoolyard, we pick up the wagons and carry them, one person on each side. I just hope nobody drops one.

We reach the separation point, and I use the binoculars to scout the first camo-guy intersection a long block away. A guard all alone, but shit. It was one thing for me to slip past guards on my own, another thing entirely for six people with three carts full of lethal cargo. Plus, there's a lot of noise coming from inside the compound—sounds as though people are hurrying around. Are they prepping to attack?

We move sideways between streets that lead to intersections with guards. I motion for Greta and Max to stay put, and I lean up to Max's ear.

"Spread the gas," I say like a breath. "Listen for my whistle." He nods, and I add, "Stay safe." Max swallows hard, Greta snaps off a quick salute, and they start pouring gas on the street, bushes, and weedy lawns.

The rest of us skirt the perimeter from a block away. The activity inside the compound is making me jumpy; I can't get control of my heartbeat. What if these guys catch us before we get the upper hand? I'm keeping Phil with me; I don't trust him not to go full-on berserker and fuck it all up.

A block east of the back end of the perimeter, Milo stops and turns to me. He knows this is the spot for him and Danny to do their jobs. We set down our wagons, and I grab Milo in a mighty hug. I hate leaving him here.

Milo pushes on my shoulder to back me away, looking at me with sad but determined eyes. He nods sideways for me to go on. If anything happens to these guys, I'll die.

Phil and I lift our wagon and slink away, but I glance back to see Milo and Danny pouring lines of gas across lawns and bushes and down the street. Jesus God, this insane plan had better work.

Within a minute or two, Phil and I reach the arsenal building from a block behind it. The house between the arsenal and us is burned out. Since we're between intersections on an outward curve in the street, guards on either side of the arsenal shouldn't be able to see us. But if they hear us, we're dead.

I take two jugs of gas from the wagon, and Phil does the same. I take my rifle and chamber a round and sling it over my back. Leaving the cocktails behind, we pick our way around the burned house with two gas cans apiece, avoiding charred lumber and other burned stuff as best we can.

At the next street, directly behind the arsenal building, we set down our gas cans. Phil helps me grab partly burned lumber scraps from the yard we just passed through, and we stack them silently against the back of the arsenal. Phil douses them with gas while I grab more wood to stretch out the pile until it covers the width of the building, a few feet up the wall.

More gasoline, then we make separate trails of gas into the street. We've only emptied two of our four cans. I catch Phil's eye and shake my can, asking him what to do. His eyes land on the burned house behind us. We take our cans and back down each side of that house, tossing gas on the building and the wood scraps strewn across the yard.

We get back to the wagon and stick our gas cans inside. I whisper to Phil, "Can you throw a Molotov cocktail this far?"

"Told you, I was a quarterback."

I nod at him, and we set some cocktails in front of us.

"Ready?" I mouth.

"Yes," he says, and I let out a whistle, putting the binoculars to my eyes to stare across the expanse of asshole territory. No fire yet. Was my whistle too soft? We wait several beats for fire to erupt from Greta and Max. There's an old pickup truck with its bed full of semi-automatic rifles. God, they *are* getting ready to attack. Lots of guys are busy in there—not like it was when I spied on them two nights ago.

Phil whistles louder, and I see smoke, then flickers of yellow flame whooshing down the length of Greta's street. Within seconds, a Molotov cocktail explodes on that side. Good, Greta, good.

"Fire!" a camo guy yells, followed by all kinds of shouting. "Fuck!" "Motherfuck!" "Get the water tanks!" Oh shit. Water's not gonna work on gas. Men are yelling and running toward the fire from all over the enclave. I can't see well enough to tell if any of these guys is Ray. We have no way to know if the guards nearest to us have abandoned their posts, but it's time for us to go.

I light a cocktail and hand it to Phil. "Roof first, if you can get there," I mutter, and he rears back like a good quarterback would, hurling the bottle of gas with a spin on it so that it lands on the arsenal roof. Fire bursts out of it and spreads across the roof and down the sides of the building.

I want to yell "Touchdown!" but I light another cocktail. "Get the woodpile in back," I whisper, and he tries but falls short. Still, he hits a trail of gas in the yard, and fire streams along the line into the street, where it meets the other trail and heads back toward the woodpile.

I hand Phil another lit bottle, and this time, he puts a perfect spiral on it, slamming it into the woodpile, and the whole back side of the arsenal erupts in flame.

I'm elated for seconds, and then I hear screams, like screams of pain. Oh, God. Someone's in there. Men? Women? I can't tell.

Fire shoots up behind the rooftops on the back side of the enclave, where Milo and Danny are, and I'm suddenly horrified. We've gone too fucking far!

But Phil rears back and hurls a Hail Mary over the top of the arsenal, and fire explodes on the street inside. I didn't hand him that bottle. He's lighting them himself. He's already lit another one, and he's slamming it sidearm into the house next door to the arsenal.

I grab Phil by the arm. "Enough! Stop it!"

Fire is heading our way, catching the burned-out house aflame and coming through the yard toward us. There's screaming in the enclave. So much screaming. God damn it. God damn it.

Phil's eyes are wild and also hollow, like he's in a trance. He wrenches free of me and lights another cocktail.

"Phil! You better toss that into the burning house and stop, or I'm gonna beat you bloody!" He glares at me, then shakes himself and tosses the firebomb underhanded into the fire.

I grab the wagon handle. "Let's go!" We race to the outlet we left for people to escape and dive for cover behind some bushes.

But no one's escaping. The guys inside are running around like their brains are broken while the fires that surround them grow bigger and brighter. Men run out of houses in their underwear, like we woke them up. Except for the burning arsenal, there's a layer of housing between these guys and the fires, but shit. Some of them are standing in front of the arsenal and waving their arms like they're cursing it. Do they think it spontaneously combusted? I don't understand. And where's Ray? I need to find Ray.

Greta and Max dive behind a hedge down the street to our right, aiming their rifles into the inferno. Milo and Danny should be here by now. Where are they? Did they forget the plan? Are they burned?

Inside the enclave, guys aren't getting touched by fire, but they're clustered around two bodies on the street. I don't need the binoculars to know that these bodies are burned. The stench of charred flesh gags me.

Why aren't they running or shooting at us? What am I missing? Are they fucked up on smack?

But one of them picks up something in the street and waves it in the air. It's the brown neck of a beer bottle. He's yelling, and a whole lot of faces turn toward the escape route and us. We duck.

The flickering reflection of firelight in the night sky gets suddenly brighter, and I peek out to see a big live oak aflame next to the arsenal. Within seconds, fire is jumping from one tree to the next, running fast along interlocking branches and racing across canopies and down trunks, catching in bushes and dropping flaming limbs and embers onto rooftops and the men below.

Then a herd of maybe forty men in camouflage moves toward us in a kind of controlled slow-motion charge through the opening we left them, their rifles pointed in our direction. Why did we come over here? We could've stayed hidden. I thought I could call them out and get them to surrender. How stupid am I?

A leader is in front of the herd—I thought Ray was the leader. This other leader's making hand signals to spread the group wider. I jump up and shoot him in the head. Men scatter, firing over my head as I duck. Before I can blink, Greta and Max hurl Molotov cocktails at the men, who are breaking into chaos. A bottle bursts into flame in front of them, stopping their forward motion. Another hits a guy's rifle butt to set his clothes on fire. He's screeching so loud. Mother of God.

Phil raises up and strafes the herd with his AR-15. Some guys hit the ground and crawl like fast-moving snakes toward the flames behind them. Others jolt backward like they've been hit. Greta shoots one between the eyes. Then shots are hitting them from the side. What?

And I see Milo on a roof with a burning tree in front of it, picking off guys at a rapid rate. I raise up and start firing, too. But I have a bolt-action rifle and I'm slower. A guy turns and aims at Milo, and I hit the fucker in the shoulder. He drops his gun. But another guy shoots and hits the roof at Milo's feet. Milo scurries backward over the roof crest. Where's Danny?

I want to run to Milo and get him out of here. But we started this bloodbath, and now we have to finish it.

Are we winning? We might be winning. I'm fired up with adrenaline about this; some kind of relief's washing over me. Maybe I made a great plan.

But behind the scattered men, four more appear and race toward us, firing AKs. I'm plastered to the dirt, peeking through the bush in front of me. Those aren't men. They're boys, Milo's age and younger. Tweener kids coming at us like armed, rabid rats. How do we kill fucking kids?

They're about to burst out of the enclave right on top of us when a tall pine tree goes up like a torch and falls over them, scattering flames that pop with pine resin. Phil and I leap sideways out of the way, but those kids are caught in the flames. What are we doing? We're monsters!

A kid who looks like a younger Milo, a blond, skinny boy, stares into my eyes as flames catch his clothes, and his shrieks rise above all the others. His screams ricochet all through me, and I shoot him in the eye.

Kids are screeching and burning, and the air is riddled with the stink of charred flesh. Men are shrieking, burning trees are collapsing, burning roofs are caving in, burning bodies are running in circles and rolling on the ground. The bed of the pickup full of rifles roars with flame.

Phil is staring at burning people, frozen with some kind of gleam in his eyes. I yank the AR-15 away from him and fire at burning men and boys, trying to kill them before they have to feel themselves burn for another instant.

Greta and Max are shouting, "Woohoo!"

I whirl to face them, aiming at them without meaning to. "Shut the fuck up! You're insane!"

Milo and Danny come flying around the corner toward us, running like lightning with their wagon full of gas cans, and somewhere from the middle of the inferno, a burst of shots rings out. Danny and Milo hit the pavement as bullets ping against the street just past them.

I hand the AR-15 to Phil and shake him. "Shoot them! Shoot them all!" Phil snaps to and shoots into the flames without stopping while I run to our boys and drag them to their feet to duck behind a stone wall.

Phil changes clips and keeps shooting like a madman into the blaze, but no one's moving in there. Where's Ray? Is he dead in there? I haven't seen him. What if he's not here?

"Cut it out, Phil!" Greta yells as she reaches him. He stops firing and looks at her, empty-eyed. "They're all dead, man! Stop!" Phil gapes at her, and she pushes his rifle barrel down.

Before us, the fire's getting brighter, threatening to spread beyond the enclave and our half-circle of fire surrounding it. More trees are catching fire. They haven't been trimmed since the sun zapped us, and their branches stretch across roads, lacing themselves into the branches of other trees. I didn't think of trees when I thought of this insane plan. What's gonna stop this fire from taking out half of South Austin?

I run to Phil. "Gather up the wagons. We need to get out of here."

He looks at me with those dead eyes. "Wagons? Oh, wagons." He lopes off to retrieve them where they're scattered around.

"What about the gas cans we left over there?" Greta points toward where she started her fire.

"Forget the gas cans!"

"No, man. We need them!" She trots over and snatches a wagon handle from Phil, then rushes around the corner, saying, "Go on. I'll catch up."

"We'll wait!" I holler.

"You're dead, prissy boy!" Fuck, that's Ray.

I whisk my head to peer into the inferno. Ray's charging up the center of the compound, skirting clumps of flame, leaping over burning corpses, heading straight toward me with his AK poised to shoot.

Milo raises his rifle, but for once, I'm quicker, and I shoot Ray in the center of his chest. He's still stumbling toward us, firing a burst of shots that go sideways, and then he falls face-down into a burning tree limb, his camo jacket erupting in flames. He rolls over with his face up, holding his chest and screaming like a demon from Hell.

My rifle still up, I watch, stunned, as Ray's hair catches fire and his face starts to bubble. I gag and spin away, breathing in smoke and choking. Takes me a minute to get a grip.

I sputter out to Danny and Milo, "Gather up our rifles, and if there's extra ones you can get to without getting burned, grab them, too."

Max plops down on his butt and starts bawling.

I step to him and clutch his shoulder. "I get it, man. But let's go. We've got the rest of our lives to cry."

Milo and Danny come back with six or seven rifles between them.

"Come on. We'll meet Greta at the corner." As soon as we get there, we see her running toward us with a wagonful of gas cans.

"Go, go, go!" I point toward home and we run, dragging our wagons, with the fiery pits of Hell burning behind us and a throbbing hole in my chest where my soul used to be.

When we reach Dittmar and the extra wagon we stashed, I lurch forward to puke and puke and puke until blood comes out of my mouth.

"Fuck, Keno," Max says. "Are you bleeding inside?"

Greta puts her hands on my shoulders. "Probably popped a blood vessel in your throat. You all right?"

"Right as fucking rain." I spit out more vomit and blood. "Get me out of here." I climb to my feet and we run.

CHAPTER 39

Day is breaking by the time I can see our home compound through the binoculars. Looks like half the neighbors are waiting in the park, sitting on the monkey bars, standing atop the slide, climbing the swing set, straining their necks to stare east toward the conflagration we started—the fucking massacre we perpetrated—smoke and flames still visible to the east above the tree canopy.

"Is that them? Way down the street?" someone shouts, and I turn my back and sit down on the pavement, covering my face.

"I can't go in there!"

"Why not, man?" Danny asks.

"They're gonna treat us like heroes. We are *not* heroes!"

"Come on, Keno," Greta says. "We saved the neighborhood with your plan. Enjoy the kudos."

"Fucking kudos? You think we deserve kudos? They oughta take us to the Criminal Court in the Hague. We burned forty, maybe fifty men alive. We burned kids. Fucking kids!'"

"They were armed kids trying to kill us," Greta says.

"I don't care! We shouldn't've been in that position. We shoulda been smarter than that!"

Behind me, I hear the crowd running toward us. I look at Phil, whose dead eyes are deader than ever. I look at Max, who's been crying all the way home. I feel like both of them and more. Only Greta and Danny seem elated at our so-called victory.

Milo's got a stoic, unreadable expression on his face, and he's studying me with tired eyes. He pulls me to my feet and squeezes my arm. "I got you, man."

If I had any emotional bandwidth left, I'd collapse against Milo and cry for a month. But a crowd of neighbors is upon us, slapping our backs, hooting and hollering, grabbing us in hugs, smiling and laughing and dancing around. I make my way past them and sprint for home.

"Keno? I heard you were back," Alma says from the kitchen when she hears me slam the front door. She comes around the corner into the living room and sees me, and the rosy color in her cheeks drains away.

I shake my head at her, but no words come. I jerk my head back, lean into the door, and cry out some kind of wailing lament that sounds like a roar.

"Oh, baby. I'm so sorry," she says. "Let's get you upstairs."

I flinch when she reaches to touch me, and she draws back.

"Oh," she says, closing her eyes, taking deep breaths. She hooks her finger in mine and leads me to the upstairs bathroom, sits me on the closed toilet, and carefully peels off my clothes. I keep flinching, and she notes my every twitch.

"We'll have to burn these clothes," she says.

"They'll go up like a fucking torch."

"Yeah. Come sit in the bathtub. I'll give you a bath."

"You can't carry all that water up here."

"Don't worry. Just wait here. Close your eyes and rest."

Outside the bathroom, I hear Mom asking about me and Alma answering too quietly for me to follow. I try to do what Alma said and close my eyes, but my head is full of burning boys and pain-riddled screams.

Mom says, "I'll get you some water. Then I'll bring food."

And Alma says, "Thank you."

When Alma comes back, I'm drawn to her presence like a magnet, and I squeeze the fuck out of her hand. I'm needy enough to suck the life clear out of her, so I let go.

"Baby, you're in shock," she tells me.

"It's worse than that," I mutter, my voice breaking. "The things we did—"

"Shh... shh..." She's petting my head, and I zone out until Mom taps on the door and sets a big jug of water inside the room.

"I should pour that water for you," I say to Alma.

"Nope. I'll just lean it over the tub and let the leverage do the work."

"Leverage." I sigh.

She covers me in water, and I sink down in the tub to let my head go under. I could stay here. I don't have to kill anyone down here. But Alma is soaping me up, and her touch is the only reason I come up for air. I have no feeling in my heart, but I'm putty in her hands.

Alma gets me clean while I stare into space. She has me stand, dries me off, and dresses me. She sits me on the closed toilet again, then bandages my arm.

"Be right back." As she shuts the door, she says to someone, "Can you help me get him to bed?"

"He needs help?" Mom asks.

I need to get out of here.

I don't want Mom or anyone else to fawn over me and give me sympathy.

"Drink this," Alma says. I didn't even know she was there. I drink some kind of tea, and my mind floats away. Then faceless people lead me to bed in a bad dream I can't escape.

I need to get out of here.

***

I WAKE UP SCREAMING, AND it's dark outside. The next night? Maybe I didn't scream, because Alma's asleep, curled up beside me, her hands locked around my arm.

I screamed in my dream; I know that. I watch Alma sleep. I want to love her, but I don't feel anything except horror and exhausting dread.

I need to get out of here.

Before people wake up, before I have to see them worrying about me. Before anyone tries to thank me again for what we did.

They must've drugged me. I'm in some kind of twilight, drifting in and out of dreams.

"GOD, YOU PIECE OF SHIT asshole!"

"No one is fucking safe!"

"Ray abused me, okay?"

The sky's twisting with color. Undulating bands of light, like northern lights, every color of the rainbow.

"Hands up, motherfucker!"

And I run, darting behind cars, leaping hedges. I vault over a fence then another then another, tripping on junk metal. Zigzagging, looking for cover.

A rifle shot zings against the pavement, and I jump sideways over a hedge as more bullets whiz past. I plunge into a thicket of trees. A dog barks behind me.

"Grandpa, what did you do? You got him killed! I should kill you for this!"

"God damn it! God damn it! He's dead. He's fucking dead!"

And the hole, the empty little hole.

Fire bursts out and spreads across the arsenal roof. Phil slams another cocktail into the woodpile, and the whole arsenal erupts in flame.

Screaming. So much screaming. God damn it. God damn it. Fire's jumping from tree to tree, dropping flaming limbs onto rooftops and men. Phil strafes men with his AR-15.

A kid who looks like Milo, a blond boy. He's too much like Milo! He stares into my eyes as flames catch his clothes.

Kids screeching and burning, air stinking of charred flesh, men shrieking, burning trees collapsing, burning roofs caving in, burning bodies running in circles.

"You're dead, prissy boy!"

Ray's hair catches fire; his face starts to bubble.

Grandpa's machete hits Whiskers's head, splitting his skull and face down the middle. Tat Man screams bloody murder and fires a shot straight into Uncle Eddie's forehead.

"Noooo!"

Eddie's eyes roll back in his head, like he's trying to see where the bullet went.

SHIT! I MIGHT BE THRASHING in bed, but if I am, I'm too doped to stop. I can't wake up. I've got to wake up.

I need to get out of here.

I'M IN A DEEP HOLE *of pain, and I'm screaming and screaming with no end. I can't stop. Can't even try to. It feels like my new reality. I'll be screaming for eternity now.*

But then Nana is here with her hand on my heart. The younger, healthy Nana. She caresses my forehead with her other hand.

"Shh… shh…" she's saying. "I love you."

"Nana, he has a hole in his head!"

"I know, honey. I'm so sorry."

"Is he with you?"

"Not yet, but I hope he will be."

"Is Tasha there?"

"I can feel her, so yes."

"Nana, I need you! I need all three of you!"

She places both hands on my heart and presses down, kindling a warmth that spreads through my freezing muscles down to my fingers and toes. A bright yellow light shoots out of my chest and fills this hole I'm in.

"He's in your heart, Keno. We are all in your heart. Use your love to get you through."

"But it's my fault, Nana. I started this shit, and now Eddie's dead."

"Honey, you couldn't have known it would end this way."

"But what do I do now?"

"You know what you have to do."

"But you set this place up for us. You were brilliant to do that."

"The only certainty in life, my love, is that things always change."

"Are you saying—?"

She runs her hand down my cheek and smiles sadly.

"I'm saying you know what to do."

I STARTLE AWAKE. I'M GETTING out of here.

CHAPTER 40

Alma's on the patio when I come downstairs carrying a half-loaded hiker's backpack with a bedroll attached. The sun is rising, and Alma looks busy, like she's cooking a big breakfast.

I stop at the coat closet to get a rifle and a stash of ammo for it and for my pistol, plus stuff to clean the guns. Looks like Milo, or someone, already cleaned them all up and organized them. It's hotter than sin, but I take a light jacket just in case. I can use it for a pillow, if nothing else.

While Alma's all occupied out back, I get more stuff I need from the garage and kitchen. For food, I get a bag of oatmeal, another of dry beans, a shaker of salt. I fill some liter bottles with water and stuff them into the pack.

I close my eyes, I crack my neck, wishing I could feel, terrified of feeling. Finally, I carry my gear to the patio.

"Keno! You're up!" Alma says, watching the pan she's taking off the fire. "Did you see that the northern lights came back last night?"

Then she looks at me, at the backpack, at the rifle. "What are you—? Oh, God." She sinks into a chair, studying my face.

I set down my gear and kneel in front of her, laying my hands on her thighs.

"I have to go find us all a safe place to live, a place with walls. Because I can never, ever do what we did again."

"But those guys are dead now."

I cringe. "I know it. Believe me, I know it. But they won't be the last threats, and this place is played out. It's not defensible. The crops and soil are fucked. The solar is dead."

"We have a life here, Keno."

"I don't believe it can last."

"But the cistern... and the chickens... and—"

I hug her. I can't totally feel it, but I can't argue with her. Not now.

"Nana came to me in a dream. She told me that I know what to do."

I pull away from Alma to see her eyes grow big and round.

"And this is what you know you have to do?"

"Yes."

She searches my face, wincing. "Then you have to go."

I let out a deep sigh, releasing some of my fear, my fear of losing Alma. "Mom and Milo, Jack, all the other women, they'll take care of you. I'll be back as soon as I can get here."

"You have to eat breakfast. I'm not letting you leave without breakfast. You haven't eaten for a day and a half."

I don't want to eat breakfast, but I study her eyes and see her worry, even though emotions seem alien to me.

"I'll eat breakfast if you sit with me in the garage while I eat it. I can't face anyone else, and they'll be getting up soon."

"Baby, what happened to you?"

"You don't want to know. I don't want to put that shit in your head. It's gonna take me a lifetime to get it out of mine."

"I'm sorry, baby."

"I killed Ray."

She whisks her hand to her mouth; her eyes swim with tears. "Thank you for—"

"Please don't thank me. I can't accept thanks for such horrible shit."

"God, Keno." She runs her hands over my face, brushes hair from my eyes. "Let's put some biscuits in your pack. Then help me take breakfast to the garage."

But when I open the door into the garage, I'm slapped in the face with the stink of gasoline and char. Wagons and gas cans are strewn all over; memories assault me. I close the door.

"Let's eat here in the laundry room, our make-out place." I close us inside, then pick Alma up and sit her on the counter, keeping one hand on her while I eat with the other.

When my food is half-eaten and I can't take another bite, I move to go, but Alma spoons more food into my mouth.

I smile at her. "Nice trick, but it's time."

"I'm not having this baby without you," Alma says, and she looks determined enough to hold that baby inside no matter what kind of pressure it puts on her to get born.

"We have at least three months, don't we? I'll be back for that. No way I'd miss that."

"Better plan on two months, just in case."

She wants to cry. She will cry when I'm gone. But she's making a mighty effort to be strong.

"Tell Milo to take the crew to get more gas for the tillers. And tell Greta to go back to that neighborhood to see if any ammo's left."

"You gonna leave us all instructions, or are you gonna go?"

"This is the part where we're supposed to kiss like there's no tomorrow and tear ourselves apart."

"I can't kiss you right now," she says.

I sigh. "I can't kiss you, either, not because I don't love you, not because I don't hate to leave, but because I can't feel."

She nods like she's trying to understand, like maybe she can see it in me.

I hug Alma to my side and stroke her hair.

"Just know that whatever happens, I'm doing this out of my great love for you and our baby, and I will always love you more than my own life, until the end of the world and beyond."

"I believe you," she says with hardly any breath.

I press my face gently to her belly and our baby, then peer into her eyes one more time. I help her down from the counter, kiss my fingers, and touch them to her cheek.

Months ago, we cut the sides off the washer and dryer in here to build rain-barrel systems, so now all the insides of these non-working machines are exposed. There's no laundry in this laundry room, just junk piled on shelves. But it was a private space for Alma and me to kiss when we couldn't wait to get upstairs. And now life has wounded us so much that we can't kiss goodbye.

Alma is my heart, and I'm leaving her standing alone in her fierce beauty, inside the broken, echoey laundry room, with nothing but a promise that I'll return.

ACKNOWLEDGMENTS

My undying gratitude to the folks at Southern Fried Karma Press for their belief in my ability to write this story and for their ongoing help and encouragement. Special thanks to publisher Steve McCondichie and to editors Pinckney Benedict, Hayley Swinson, and Mandi Jourdan, each brilliant in their individual ways and all of them sweet as pie.

Thanks also to the mega-talented Olivia Hammerman for the book cover and interior design, to Jenny Kimura for the ebook interior design, and to the marketing, administrative, and audiobook team at SFK: Alison McCondichie, Lizabeth Engelmeier, and all the others behind the scenes.

For their exceptionally good help with draft after draft of everything I write, heaps of gratitude to my critique partners Laura Creedle, Aden Polydoros, and Flor Salcedo. I am blessed to have such talented writers to advise and assist me. They're also great at talking me through whatever life throws my way.

Special thanks to Marva Mouser, my biggest fan and cheerleader-in-chief. And thanks also to BookPeople, the largest independent bookstore in Texas, for hosting my book launch event for *If Darkness Takes Us,* and for being the coolest bookstore ever.

So many more excellent writers to thank—Mindy McGinnis for hosting me on her blog with *Sometimes Even Old Ladies Get Published*; Mae Clair for her book-cover quote and for blog-hosting *Living Off the Grid: My Life as Research*;

R.R. Campbell for hosting me on his Writescast podcast, *Drama, Character, Stakes and Throughlines* (winner of the 2019 Writescast Listeners Choice Award); Sarah Meckler for hosting me on the GSMC Book Review Podcast Episode 215; and Teri Polen, Denise Alicea, The Writers League of Texas, and the UCLA Extension Writers' Program Alum Success Stories for fun online interviews. Guest blog posts, interviews, podcasts, and readings are all linked on my website: https://brendamariesmith.com/.

Many thanks to the Writers Community on Twitter for tons of encouragement over the years and to Twitter friends who help me in ways great and small: Branwen O'Shea, Mary Holm, M.H. Reardon, Peggy Rothschild, Chris Bedell, Michelle Hauck, R. Demille, James Fuller, Michelle Hazen, Stephanie A. Higa, Abigail Taylor, Paul "Doc" Lafferty, and so many more. Thanks also to the folks at Goddess Fish Promotions for managing my two virtual book tours, and to all the lovely bloggers who hosted me and my books and who made me feel welcome.

Endless appreciation to all my friends, relations, and general readers who purchased, read, and reviewed the first book in this series, *If Darkness Takes Us,* and who showed up for my book events and listened to my online readings. Especially, thanks to my extended family who drove hundreds of miles to support me. There are far too many of you to list here, but I love and care about each of you, and I hope you enjoy this sequel.

Neither last nor least, thank you to my immediate family: our sons Aaron and J.D. Longnion; Ron, Jeremy, and Matt Goebel; their partners Damey, Elizabeth, Rebecca, John, Lauren; our grandchildren Miles and Sophia Longnion; and our newborn grandson, Tucker Wayne Goebel.

I can never thank my husband Doug Goebel nearly enough for all the ways he loves and takes care of me year in and year out, acts as my muse, protects me from pandemics and killer freezes, and inspires me to be a better person at every turn.

And finally, thank you to my protagonist Keno Simms, who sprang to life from the ether so fully formed in the first draft that I couldn't type fast enough to keep up with him, and who revealed layer after layer of depth the more I got to know him.

I learned about teenage boys and their transitions to manhood from our five sons and my seventeen years of raising them while they were teens. They were a handful to be sure, but they never failed to inspire me with their sincerity, heroism, and stalwart sense of justice. Plus, they were loads of fun. Seeing what fine men they have become gives me a sense of satisfaction too deep to describe.

Thank you, dear readers. Wishing all of you peace, health, and happiness in the years to come.

BRENDA MARIE SMITH lived off the grid for many years in a farming collective where her sons were delivered by midwives. She's been a community activist, managed student housing co-ops, produced concerts to raise money for causes, done massive quantities of bookkeeping, and raised a small herd of teenage boys. Brenda is attracted to stories where everyday characters transcend their limitations to find their inner heroism. She and her husband reside in a grid-connected, solar-powered home in South Austin, Texas. They have more grown kids and grandkids than they can count.

SHARE YOUR THOUGHTS

Want to help make *If the Light Escapes* a bestselling novel? Consider leaving an honest review of this book on Goodreads, on your personal author website or blog, and anywhere else readers go for recommendations. It's our priority at SFK Press to publish books for readers to enjoy, and our authors appreciate and value your feedback.

OUR SOUTHERN FRIED GUARANTEE

If you wouldn't enthusiastically recommend one of our books with a 4- or 5-star rating to a friend, then the next story is on us. We believe that much in the stories we're telling. Simply email us at pr@sfkmultimedia.com.